MW01008011

Pearly
Everlasting

ALSO BY TAMMY ARMSTRONG

FICTION
Pye-Dogs
Translations: Aistreann

POETRY
Year of the Metal Rabbit
The Scare in the Crow
Take Us Quietly
Unravel
Bogman's Music

Pearly Everlasting

A NOVEL

TAMMY ARMSTRONG

HARPER

An Imprint of HarperCollins*Publishers*

PEARLY EVERLASTING. Copyright © 2024 by Tammy Armstrong. All rights reserved. Printed in the United States of America. No part of this book may be used or reproduced in any manner whatsoever without written permission except in the case of brief quotations embodied in critical articles and reviews. For information, address HarperCollins Publishers, 195 Broadway, New York, NY 10007.

HarperCollins books may be purchased for educational, business, or sales promotional use. For information, please email the Special Markets Department at SPsales@harpercollins.com.

Originally published in Canada in 2024 by HarperAvenue, an imprint of HarperCollins Publishers Ltd.

FIRST U.S. EDITION

Library of Congress Cataloging-in-Publication Data has been applied for.

ISBN 978-0-06-339614-2

24 25 26 27 28 LBC 5 4 3 2 1

For all the bear-whisperers who keep the faith,
despite the odds. This is for you.

There either is or is not, that's the way things are. The colour of the day. The way it felt to be a child. The feeling of saltwater on your sunburnt legs. Sometimes the water is yellow, sometimes it's red. But what colour it may be in memory, depends on the day. I'm not going to tell the story of the way it happened. I'm going to tell it the way I remember it.

—CHARLES DICKENS

First

What do I remember first? Maybe sleet stuttering against the lean-cabin's two small panes of glass—sometimes from the east, sometimes from the west—or the wood fire sawing through the deep winter months, overheating and furring our room with oily pine-cone dust and the punky kindling scooped out from the rotten hearts of stumps. Or the creak of red cedars—their crowns tangled up in storms, in that overly possessive way trees have of pressing in too close. Or maybe the spat of rain on the splint-shingle roof—spruce, green, pliable—flipped bark-side-down to varnish and keep the waters out. Or maybe the coyotes, howling their serenades, harrying deer, while wide-throated owls hooted from the boughy, wind-eaten wilderness, unafraid to meet their own echoing replies.

Maybe it's a bit of all these far reaches that shaped me while I slept my first months away, deep inside a wicker basket, beneath a moose-skin throw. He was there then too—my brother, Bruno—curled up against my spine, his pale snout tucked under my chin, one of his long-clawed paws always resting against my ribs.

a howl when the wind picked up

Some might still talk about us, down in the valley. I suppose we've become another story to swap between radio shows on wintering nights. But I've been up here on Greenlaw Mountain so long now, I'm not sure I'd even recognize me and my brother, Bruno. I do know—if I believe the other stories—shortly after I was born in lumber camp 33, strange things began to happen that would suggest my life would not follow a traditional path. First, I was born with long nails—the good sort for grubbing in stumps and digging sleep-holes. Each night, Mama trimmed them while I slept and each morning she'd find them back—yellowed and sickled and stronger than the day before. This happened for the first month of my life and then my nails grew in again like any baby's should.

The second thing that happened was a tramp from the Outside, calling himself a *jeteur de sorts*, a spell thrower, came into camp hoping to predict futures and collect some coins. Though we had no money, Mama invited him into our lean-cabin and offered him a pannikin of tea.

He peered into the little wicker basket where I slept and said, "This one here, with hands like a groundhog? She'll see some things in her life." He leaned in closer to study me some more. "Sure as rain, she'll see that Jack in the Dark. Face to face."

Mama had snatched me up and held me tight. Jack in the Dark was just something the woodsmen talked about when shadows caught at the corners of their eyes—a many-pointed flicker, a howl when the wind picked up, making the woods itch. They had a saying for him too: *He's in the trees. He's in the ground. He's in the wind. He's all around.* He was a creature felt more than seen, who could leap the sling of a ridge or skim a rising river or bring strange things to your door. Touched by the devil, riding his bone horse home. He had no business with the newly born.

"Everyone knows," Mama said as she sent the tramp away, "Jack in the Dark ain't nothin' real." Before he left, she gave him a poke bag of bread for his travels because *jeteurs de sorts*, though capable of casting spells, could also repent their transgressions, if they chose to. They were, in her way of thinking, capable of being saved.

And thirdly, Papa, our camp cook, brought home a squalling, still-blind bear cub who would come to be thought of as my brother and who would dictate, through little fault of his own, the trajectory of my life. Some might say a baby and a bear cub have no business living together, but I can assure you: seeing the world through our eyes might change your mind.

Though neither Bruno nor me have exact birthdays, I know he was born when bears are born: in January, in a den beneath a fir tree, near a cracked boulder with a sparkling vein running through it. I was born in February on a pile of fir boughs, when the deep snowbanks and ice shelvings rotted in reefs of mist. A false spring, Mama called it. Not to be trusted. That singular week of thaw, all those years ago, a team of swampers, cutting brush and wind-thrown trees, in preparation for a new tote road, noticed their horses spooked when they approached the foot of a low, knuckly ridge. As they stood beside it, a faint sound carried out from inside the rock like the cries of a baby—formless and colicky. Later that day, after dinner, the men told Papa about the horses, half joking that Jack in the Dark must be sleeping down there in a tree hollow. Like the other animals, he'd gone to ground, among the eyebright and vetch, the fall before. But here he was again, scaring horses, kicking up storms of cone scale and needle—giving away the animals' wintering world drilled with sleep-holes.

Besides being camp cook, Papa was a good outdoorsman. He thought a bear might be about, as horses shied away from anything bear. Even sleeping bears. The men said no. Bears don't move much in the winter. With dinner cleared away, Papa went out to check for himself. He found a fault in the mealy snow, a hole rimed with frost, at the foot of a gaunt fir—a breathing chimney that marked where something slept deep in a den, waiting true spring's arrival. This was where the crying came from. Papa dug into the snow with his snowshoe until he found the telltale bracken marking the den's threshold. He cut a sapling with his hatchet and poked it down, down, down into a mangle of roots and a ground-fuggy hollow until it yielded to something soft. He reached in and brought it out. A single cub. A first litter. No bigger than two apples side by side. There was no sign of its mother—tracks neither in nor away. Back then, bears were hunted and used up, just as the wolves had been hunted into stories a century earlier, though men still claimed from time to time to see one running with wild dogs, living just out of sight.

Squalling, toothless, blind—Bruno came into camp swaddled in Papa's mackinaw. And from the moment Papa set him down in the basket beside me, Bruno wanted to stay close. It would have been too cruel to let such an orphaned creature die from hunger, he said. Ivy, my sister, danced around him, begging Papa to let him sleep in the hollows of her hands. And the woodsmen came in shy, hoping to stroke the crest of coarse hair along his skull with their rough knuckles.

So Mama rocked us together in her cane-backed chair, in the corner of the room where the lantern's flame caught on drafts, sending long, warped shadows along the axe-hewn walls. And in that chair she suckled us together, saying, "This here's your brother and this here's your sister."

One photo of our time together exists. It was taken by Song-catcher—whose birth name was Helen but I always called her Song-catcher—who came from the Outside to collect our lullabies and murder ballads. Songs carried from family to family on coffin boats, across highlands and outlands— kept alive, here, in the waste places and cutting grounds. The borderings of New Brunswick. She and her companion, Ebony, came from the Outside to see us because there'd been rumors passing between lumber camps, running back through the trees, of a woman who lived deep in the woods and suckled wild animals. I imagine they traveled first by train and then a cold hard pull over claggy one-haul logging roads, banks nearly six feet high with snow. I suppose the story of me and Bruno must've felt a bit unbodied—more fairy tale than truth as they traveled through the river birches and Jack pines, moving closer to our rumored camp, to the woman they could only imagine through hairless leverets and sharp-snouted kits—milk-dumb and blind.

They saw the omens and then—ten miles, five miles—just beyond the worst of the road, where three tote roads and a skid road came together, boughed and planked in places to prevent the horses with their cumbersome loads from slipping in the mud, they might've reached the edge of our cutting grounds. In the distance, sharp and deep sounds: axe bites, sleigh bells, a ring of hammer strokes on the splitting wedge, and then a man might've called out, "Widow-maker!" And a tree might've shivered and leaned ever so slightly before it began to fall—first slowly then with a rushing violence, snapping limbs off neighboring trees, before smashing onto the forest floor in a cloud of needles, sawdust, and snow duff.

From the stories, they knew to go on: just beyond the felling grounds. Camp 33. A little lean-cabin tacked onto the cookhouse where a window palely glowed like the light that sometimes comes before storms. I imagine they stood under our rough-edged awning. Song-catcher knocking twice and waiting as the rain came down and amplified itself on the

7

duckboards where Mama had painted hopscotch squares for Ivy. Maybe Song-catcher placed her feet on two and five, while Ebony stood neatly on ten. It was Ivy who opened our door that day and considered the women. She took full measure of them then stepped aside to let them in.

I imagine Song-catcher and Ebony standing at our threshold, their eyes adjusting to the inside dark. Our room close, lit only with oil lamps—their pie-tin shields reflecting loose light and the backlog fire that made everyone's eyes glow amber. Our walls papered with yellowy pictures from calendars and cowboy magazines, dried flowers and herbs strung above the window, and the beds—two troughs filled with fir boughs—made over with crazy quilts. A deacon's bench. A mule-eared chair. Our lean-shed typical of the camps in its meagerness, but not so typical in its occupants.

I imagine it was only after they'd stepped into our lean-cabin that Song-catcher realized she hadn't prepared herself for this at all. The long travel, the weather, and Mama in a rocking chair next to the fire, soot streaks running up over the chinked logs with the shapes of boneless faces. Our room would have held the afternoon dusk and the window light would have haloed Mama's slight form, and her bare breasts: an infant on her right and, on her left, just as the rumors claimed, a bear cub, who watched the women approach, though it did not stop its suck.

I'm sure Ebony's breath caught in her throat. *Jesus*, she might've whispered.

8

Deep-eyed and thoughtful, Ivy would've sat at Mama's feet. A groggy housefly buzzing in the burlap curtain's folds. She might've held up a cloth doll. A topsy-turvy. Now a little red riding hood, now a grandmother wolf with her spectacles and teeth.

"Look," she might've whispered, pulling at Song-catcher's pant hem with the wolf. "Look."

=

I saw it once: that photo of me and Bruno and Mama. We were part of Song-catcher's talks in the Outside about the woods. Recordings of both Bruno's cries and Mama's lullabies, so I've been told, have traveled through many parts of the world, of which I am unfamiliar. I did not have a name yet when Bruno came to live with us, though my parents and all the woodsmen deliberated on what I might be called. It was Song-catcher, on her first visit, who suggested Pearly Everlasting, a plant that likes to live beside shiny things. And from her wooden house near Smoke River, fifty miles away from our lean-cabin, in love a little with Mama for her kindnesses, Song-catcher later sent us a spoon from Bern, Switzerland—the City of Bears—with a silver bear attached to its handle and a bowl engraved with our names and birthdate: Pearly Everlasting & Bruno False Spring 1918.

everyone awake in the swamp

So Bruno and I grew up together on shoveled land, cut land, sawed land, and burnt land. Land gridded and hollowed, stumped, surveyed, and pulped as companies tried and failed to tame the place—forcing on it little resurrections. And we came to know certain things at those tusky edges of what most people thought of as "the woods," where night animals of the northern kind followed their own dark laws—their crooked paths secreting through tule ponds and high shoulders of snow. But during the summer months, when the season finished, we moved back up to our cabin on Greenlaw Mountain.

We were Greenlaw royalty, Mama used to say, because there's always been a woman up there, though not always a man because they sometimes died too fast or left for elsewhere, but a woman, a woman has always lived on the mountain. My eighth great-grandmother, Burunild Slaywrock, came from the Outside—the Highlands of Scotland—with her collection of herbs and salves and moved onto the mountain and never left. How she came to find it, no one knows, but Mama said she'd been honored by a king who'd fallen from his horse during a war. A strong man had lifted the armored king from beneath his battle-killed horse and brought him to Grandma Slaywrock. She'd mended the king's broken bones and he'd given her a gift in return: a gold double-horn necklace to protect her against the evil. Passed down from generation to generation, it now belonged to Mama. It was her sole piece of jewelry and she wore it with great pride. The king also granted Grandma Slaywrock and her six daughters safe passage to a Canada known then by many other names. In our woods, she met and became friends with the local Mi'kmaq women, and they soon realized they had some healing in common. She showed them some of what she knew and they taught her a bit of their language and how to draw cures from plants unfamiliar to my age-old grandmother—some Mama still used on camp injuries. But I'm not at liberty to say those words as they're not mine to share.

Every year in August, we came down from Greenlaw Mountain to stay in the camps with Papa. When the men built new horse hovels, bunkhouses, and a cookhouse, they also built us a lean-cabin—much like a den with a low roof of cedar splints that covered a frame of notched spruce logs, hand-hewn with an axe and froe and chinked with moss. With the scraps left over, the men built me and Bruno a tree fort and Bruno a den box for his wintering. Surrounded by two hundred kerf-cut stumps, cordwood, sleds, snowshoes, saws, axes, and whetstone wheels, we always lived near a trail that led to the felling grounds and then to a river, in most cases the Crooked Deadwater—a snarly piece of drivable water—where the men cut, skidded, yarded, and hauled the logs that would be pushed downriver in the spring. The wind never stopped howling around those camps back then. It could take a man to strange places as both companion and haunter. I asked Papa once, "Why's it so windy round here?"

"It's them wolves trying to blow our house down," he said, handing me a molasses cookie and shooing me out of the kitchen.

Men came from all over to work in the camps, most hoping to work in Papa's camp as he was the most famous cook around. Our camp was always made up of a mishmash of hungry men: quiet, broken ones who caulked ships in New York during the war, needle-jigged tattooed ones who made hardwood staves for molasses barrels bound for Barbados or stoked grain in southern Saskatchewan. Men who worked on one-lunger steam engines, in woodpecker mills and ice houses, who came from villages named after conjoined twins and wild pigs. Men from Scottish Highlands, Swedish hamlets, and Polish parishes, from hidden valleys and deep fjords, and smoke-blackened shacks with too many children. Province men. Shanty men. *Les Canadiens. Les bûcherons. Skogshuggare. Drwal. Nujatejo'tasit.*

For many, it took several days or weeks to reach the Walking Bosses who'd cut the men from their raggedy lines like horses and lead them into camps. Some had to sell an old milk cow to pay for their mail-order boots. And their picking was never easy. Bosses would take a harness apart and throw the pieces in a barrel of used motor oil, and make a green teamster scoop them out and put them back together again. When the crew was hired, they'd travel in knotted groups, hauling their turkey bags, duffles, and wanigans with them— each weighed down with chattels of wool blankets, socks, mittens, darning needles, axes, and Bicycle cards for stud poker. Together they followed the Walking Boss by twitching trail and wagon and flat-bottomed scow deeper into the dark woods where our camp waited. Over those winter and spring months, we'd become a makeshift family of sorts. All of us, with our bruised kindnesses and broken parts, looking out for each other because it was a matter of survival.

Papa didn't start out as a cook, though. And while many of his stories changed with each telling, two mostly stayed the same. Until he was eleven, he lived with his grandfather in an old farmhouse with the upstairs sealed off in winter to preserve that fall's deer meat. "Not a pot to piss in," he'd say. But when his grandfather died, Papa was chucked out of the house like an old dog. He said a neighbor or maybe a government agent, he couldn't remember which, put him in a rough paneled wagon and started up the road calling to the neighbors, "You don't want a boy for work, do you?"

Most would eye him up and down before saying, "No, no. I don't think I need a boy."

"Don't know anyone who does, do you?"

"No. Nope, 'fraid I don't."

Eventually, Mr. Beecher, a dairy farmer, came out and said he could use a boy. Papa stayed there three years doing farm work, pulling chickweed for the pigs, splitting wood, and getting the cows in at suppertime. He was good at milking and caring for the fifty sheep besides. Twice a week, Mrs. Beecher baked. Papa would stuff his pockets with bread and cookies on his way out to the barn. He had to have all his chores done before dark because the Beechers didn't want him fooling around with a lantern out there in the barn. When he was inside, though, Mrs. Beecher let him watch her get things ready in the kitchen and that's where he learned a thing or two about baking.

The boys in the farms around the Beechers' place were mainly of a rough nature—orphans and left-behinds filled up with nameless moods, bottomless angers, and humiliations. It made that corner of the province dangerous. As the boys grew older, they began to fight among themselves on Saturday nights when they were free from chores. Broken bottles, pocketknives, and fists. It was a world that Papa couldn't see himself fitting into. After a couple of years, a distant uncle of Papa's, a woodsman, came to take Papa away from the Beechers' farmstead. Some months later, Papa married Mama and joined the Sawdust Fusiliers.

That's how he found himself inside the King's Tree. In 1916, Papa was sent to England on the White Star transport *Justicia*. The government figured every soldier needed five trees: one for living quarters, one for food and ammunition crates, two for gun stocks, and one for their own coffin. Papa worked on the Clock Case Plantation at the edge of Windsor Great Park, in the forest around Windsor Castle. It was a forest and not a woods, and there were many age-old oaks first planted by some queen called Elizabeth I. One tree felled by the Sawdust Fusiliers was the "William the Conqueror Oak." It stood beneath the king's bedroom window and was thirty-eight feet wide. And since no one saw was long enough to cut the tree from the outside, the Sawdust Fusiliers hollowed out the trunk, making a hole large enough for one man to pull the saw from inside the tree. Papa was the man sent inside the King's Tree.

Now, every morning, Papa woke around four o'clock to cook because the men woke by the stars and came back with them at night. He'd send his cookee into the bunkhouse to wake up the teamsters first as they had to get the horses ready and then, at just-light, Papa would stand outside the door and beat a broken peavey against an old steel beam and yell, "Everyone awake in the Swamp!" He usually worked until eight at night. Only sitting down when the last skillet was salt-scrubbed smooth.

At night, lying in my bough bed with Bruno and Ivy, I used to imagine all them logs piled up in the skid yards float-ing downriver to the mills to be planked and built into things people in the Outside liked: pianos and spice jars and rocking chairs. Did their new owners wonder about us out there in the woods where Jack in the Dark—Mr. Many-skins—har-ried the deer at night and injuries oftentimes meant a man brought back to camp wrapped in a wagon sheet? Did they imagine that a girl and her bear could live out there beneath the spruce shadows—too tall for anyone to see the horizon beyond?

15

once rivered with light

In the fall of 1928, hellish sickness and injury hounded us. Ansell, a fourteen-year-old limber, was struck by lightning just as the season started. That year, his job was to smooth logs so snags didn't catch on the horses. The men were working fast in the felling grounds because the wasps' nests were built high in the trees. A sure sign, they said, of mean weather coming. One day, the sky gloomed while Ansell worked on a felled spruce. His breath sinking into the work. His limbing axe following its natural arc from behind his back, readying to bite down into the wood's pale muscle again. It was then a squall curdled the sky and a wiry bolt of lightning knocked him galley-west—his axe still held high above his head. The lightning traveled down his axe helve and escaped through the bottom of his right boot. Everyone knew its path because it left its dark trace against his skin. Lightning flowers. Strange scars ferning and branching across his face and neck.

"Did it hurt?" I asked him once.

"No," he said. "Not like how you mean hurt. It hurt on

some other level, more like I was watching it happen. And then . . . I was changed."

Some of the men claimed Ansell was different after that. But woodsmen are a suspicious lot to begin with. Some said he could feel storms coming. That in itself wasn't a feat. All the men could feel shifting weather. Poorly mended bones, arthritis, swollen joints—each told a story of weather. But Ansell could feel the air turn even before the animals. Before the crows stopped heckling. Before the horses, especially the Clydes, started pawing the ground, wanting to head back to the hovel. At first, Ansell predicted changes casually, but the men soon caught on to how much time passed between Ansell's predictions and the day's shiftings, and these predictions did not keep to weather. Some weeks after being struck, when the ferning along his face was still welted, he began to predict injury. That was when the men had had enough of Ansell's talk. There were rumors in the bunkhouse he'd turned to witching. There were rumors he'd always been witching and the lightning had perhaps honed it into a keener skill or curse, depending on who was surmising at the time.

In those days, there were as many charms against witching and injury as there were men in camps. Bewitching was fixed into every camp's mythology—each man from his own particular region, with his own particular understanding of signs and superstitions and sacraments. One morning, Ansell crawled out of his berth of boughs only to strike his forehead on a hagstone hanging from a makeshift joist above. Another night, he caught a man setting out an open set of scissors—its blades like an evil conviction pointed straight at him. Other times, he found small crosses fashioned from mountain ash in his coat pockets. And besides these strange talismans, there was also the sense that the world was edgy. Crows and jays mobbed him with rasping alarms as though he were an owl or hawk. He felt his very voice might spook the horses or crack the trees just as the lightning had run through him and left its mark.

After his time resting and healing, Mama thought it'd do Ansell good to work as a day man for a spell doing whatever needed doing—piling brush, shaking out road hay, splitting firewood—but instead he just wandered the camp, bunched inside himself, avoiding the other men. His memory, we'd been told, often faded or was too bright, just like Benoît Boudreau's, the buck sawyer, who'd come back from the war with a fistful of medals—"Just ribbons and cheap tin, Pearly"—and was calmest alone with a steel-shod pike pole or cant dog between his hands.

That fall, Ivy had taken to dressing up Bruno, making him wear old nightgowns and capes and scarves. She had a whole book of butcher's wrap filled with sketches of Bruno in costumes. One day, she put Bruno in a red bow tie Pa once wore for a photo Song-catcher had taken of him in the cookhouse.

The bow tie made me spitting mad. "He's no toy bear, Ivy!"

"Isn't. Right, Mama? He isn't a toy bear."

"That's right, Ivy. Pearly Everlasting, you watch them manners."

I stomped out of the lean-cabin with Bruno fast behind me. But after that, he took to swanning around the camp in that bow tie. If I tried to take it off him, he'd grow shifty and air-snap like a turtle. One day, me and Bruno both had the pink eye and were spending time alone, up in our tree fort, which Papa and the men made so Bruno had somewhere to shin up high if he felt inclined. When he was cranky, he'd climb up the hemlock and pass the day belly-straddling a branch, despite snarls of horseflies and cicada buzz. To make amends for the bow tie, Ivy fashioned me a new costume, attaching some shed antlers to an old earflap hat with some leather lacings. I'd done some of my own decorating too. With a burnt piece of kindling wood, I'd blackened my eyes and drawn vertical lines like stitches across my mouth and I'd done the same to Bruno, where his snout paled to cinnamon. We were playing up there in our fort with the little swords Thankful Robinson, a teamster, had whittled for us over a slew of Sundays when Bruno dropped his chewed and chipped one over the side of the timber wall.

It landed right at Ansell's feet. We peeked over and watched him pick it up, looking for where it came from. We crouched down so he couldn't see us, but then Bruno started bawling and I started giggling with my antlers sticking up over the top of the fort wall, so I hollered down, "Ahoy, boy!"

And he, smiling for the first time in a long time, asked, "You testing gravity up there, Deer Girl and Fancy Bear?"

"What's that?"

"What's what?"

19

"Gravity. Some kind of cheese?"

He shook his head in a disappointed way.

"You lonely down there today?" I asked.

"I'm pretty lonely these days, I suppose, yeah," he called back, and there was a catch in his voice.

"You want to come up? We've got the pink eye, but besides that ..."

"That bear gonna maul me if I come up?"

"Not if you give him his share of your cookies."

"Well, what's his share?"

I thought for a minute. "Three to your one."

"Bit steep, eh?"

"House rules. Bear's share."

"Well, if he'll have me ..."

He climbed up into the fort and gave Bruno his agreed-upon share of cookies and told us about his home in the Outside where winds rolled over the Highlands. *Les suêtes*, he called them. They liked to knock things down, he said. They could slip a barn off square or set it down in a neighbor's field. His grandfather, he said, had a *suête* rope attached to a hard-forged iron ring, strung between the barn door and the house porch. He tied himself in so he wouldn't get blown off his feet when walking from one to the other.

"I call bull on that," I said, and Bruno went over and sat on Ansell's foot to show his own disbelief.

"Come see for yourself someday," he said.

And I promised him then and there someday we'd do just

that. "No wind could blow Bruno out to sea," I said. "It just ain't, er, isn't possible."

He stayed a spell more with us and we never, not once, asked him about that traveling of scars across his face. And I wondered if all the things the men said about Ansell crossing Jack in the Dark were true, though I could see the bold markings of this trespass for myself. In the night wind, in the bogey-hole under the stairs, Jack in the Dark's shadow went to grass, went to the four corners of the night, but Ansell did not seem filled with his black stain as I had sometimes sensed in others. I sometimes wondered if Ansell felt differently inside himself after the lightning had finished its prowling. I knew Bruno was smitten with him. He approached Ansell crabwise, testing the air as though deep inside there might still be something smoldering like a poorly doused fire. The real reason, I think, was that Ansell was filled with static electricity that sparked and crackled Bruno's fur whenever they stood too close.

All this time, Papa had been outside splitting kindling—white birch, red heartwood—pretending to his own business, but he'd been listening. And in the early dark, as Ansell climbed back down to the hard ground, Papa whistled for him to come over to the cookhouse for a sec. The very next day, he became Pa's official cookee. Papa usually didn't take to training cookees because they were always the sorts of boys who didn't ask questions when they should or asked questions when they should know better. Ansell was different.

He worked hard-steady and never forgot to soak the cow beans overnight. And because Papa had once been inside the King's Tree and did not believe in superstitions and witch-craft, Ansell was able to relax back into himself. Papa even let him set up a bedroll in the far corner of the cookhouse, near the little door that led out to the dingle. And everyone began to point out how that boy's skin, once rivered with light, was beginning to fade. In his new form, he became an important member of camp. I thought he was the most beautiful thing I'd ever laid eyes on.

=

Just after Ansell's accident, I'd gone over to the bunkhouse one Sunday to see if someone might sharpen my little Green River knife, though no one ever would, claiming it was sharp enough for what I intended it for. If I bugged them long enough, they'd sharpen untrue, leaving it duller than it was before. Thankful Robinson took my little knife and peered down its blade. He gave Bruno an apple and we both watched him sit on his big furry rump and hold it in his paws like a teacup.

"You know, Pearly Everlasting," he said, "think we saw Jack in the Dark out there on his bone horse last Friday."

"You did?"

He nodded and some of the other men nodded too. "Yep. He's some Outside thing. He'll jump right on the back of a woodsman, you know? Knock him down and take his breath away."

"Just like what happened to that young feller," added Toby Tobique, a swamper who walked like a cowboy.

"Yep, just like our Ansell," Thankful went on. "You know, they say if Jack in the Dark stands outside your house with a rake, your family will live, but if he stands outside with a broom, a man might just be struck sick. He can call up storms and—"

"Just like that young feller."

"Yep, just the same as our Ansell. And he can ride his bone horse over the land and straight through your dreams. You remember that when you and Bruno are out in them woods, Miss Pearly," Thankful said, handing me back my still-too-dull knife.

And I knew that somewhere off in that place beyond our little lean-cabin, Jack in the Dark coughed like spoon rattle and made a kicked-up moan. Like a wild pig, he'd dig up and scatter the men's bones. He'd dig down to meet the dead. We had dead all around us and this fact made my nerve knots sting when Bruno and I walked through the immensity of that steep-sided land, those old felling grounds, haunted with what was gone. The traces were everywhere: forks and knives, milk cans shedding rust, a toothless two-man saw our crew called a misery. Most of those men had moved on, but I was always afraid, if Bruno grubbed too deep, he might find some of those gone-from-ground bones out of their resting places, their unmarked graves and forgotten plots. Of anyone I knew, Ansell had come the closest to meeting Jack in the Dark face-on. He'd seen him coming and maybe could see him coming still.

That night, I told Mama what the men had said. I told her to hide our rake and hide our broom, but she only laughed.

"Jack in the Dark is just a story, Pearly. The men were pulling your leg again."

=

Some weeks later, the croupy wintering months found our camp. December saw us storm-stayed. Bruno had woken up filled with smoke and small tantrums. He took to clambering around the stove to the cook pot that hung on the crane. He'd stick his head in, just to see if there might be some soup left there to his liking. At night, as I practiced my letters, he'd shin up the back of my chair and slap the book from my hand, sometimes raking a claw down through a page. Mama was fit to be tied.

"Some strange for a bear to wake up so much during the winter," she'd say.

She never caught me stealing around his wintering box, knocking on his roof, calling, "Two-Eyes, are you sleeping?" I just couldn't spend those long months without him near.

By late December, everyone was either sick or recovering from something catching. Ivy had an earache that kept her up all night. Papa rolled up a bit of birchbark and blew tobacco smoke into her stinging ear. I had a rattly cough and so did Bruno. Mama gave us sulphur molasses tonic. Bruno wanted more. She gave me boneset tea and balm of Gilead for the splinter I had that wouldn't heal up, but Bruno kept licking it off my hand. I gave him little stars of bread to keep him occu-

24

pied. At night, to get us to sleep, Mama would wave her gold-horned necklace over my angry splinter and Bruno's snotty snout and Ivy's paining ear and sing, "*Hovela, hovela kavela streck. Es morres a fri, is alles aveck.*" A charm, of sorts, she'd learned from a Lunenburg lumberman who'd found Jesus and quit the woods.

=

Howlish March and still storm-stayed. We tucked rags into the sills to keep out the wind. There were always three snows in March: Smelt Snow, Robin Snow, and Grass Snow. The first brought the smelt running through the loosening Crooked Deadwater. Papa would send Ansell down to net some for supper, which the men ate fried, bones and all. The second was the return of the robins and their rain songs. And the third covered the ground just enough to keep the ice winds from killing the tender plants below.

Mama darned socks while she told us stories about the lost boys. The boy with a swan's wing for an arm. The boy with donkey ears. And the boy who lived in the belly of a whale. *Tell us about the swallowed boy, Mama. Tell us about how the boy lived with a wing where his arm ought to be.* As the wind knocked at the door, devilish and wanting, she pulled a hair from her head to knit into the toe of Papa's sock, so he'd always come back from the woods. She worked steadily. A running stitch in dark yarn. A warp. A weave. A weft. Her darning egg the color of a wren. Every time she set it down to change out a sock, Bruno monstered around her feet dragging the balls of yarn away with him. Still, Mama knitted like she'd been fed spiderwebs as a girl, like that sort of gauzy world was easy to walk through.

That spring, we got better, but I kept losing baby teeth. Whenever I lost one, Papa would take it in his palm and ask if I wanted him to throw it outside. To test the animals, he said. If we threw it out and a fox got it, I'd be a child-fox, he said, and see best in the dark. I wanted to feed them to Bruno so I'd grow bear teeth, but Mama said no, that was all foolishness.

Once the cookhouse night chores were done, Papa often told stories of the creatures who lived in the trees. And always there was Jack in the Dark, riding through the woods on his bone horse, crossing between camps at night, listening for those he might be able to snatch away while they slept.

"Clip clop, clip clop, where will his bone horse stop?" Papa asked, slow as a horse considering.

He claimed to have seen him once—a slinky brown creature with a great split tail, a head like a man with horns. A ribbon of teeth like a pickerel. He took terrific leaps—twenty feet or more—and disappeared into the woods, giving off an awful screech. Gone by the time he was seen. He never left tracks. Papa said Jack in the Dark was strong enough to break through rocks and tunnel deep into the earth. He said he could live on land or in water and spent most of his time around lakes. He said Jack in the Dark left a dead goldfinch, soft-necked, at the door of the cabin one night. A gift. A warning.

"About Ansell, because—?" I started.

"There'll be no talk of Jack in the Dark in here tonight," Mama interrupted. "He's in his sleep-hole, where he belongs."

Sometimes, I had bad dreams, those long nights, where Bruno was trying to eat his shadow and mine. On those nights, Mama would get out of her bough bed and bring over a perfume bottle made from red carnival glass. Squeezing the little fringed pump, she'd spray a little bit over us, and whatever was in it smelled of woodsmoke and protection and faraway places. Some nights, I listened for the bone horse coming through the frost-cracked trees. *Clip clop, clip clop, where will his bone horse stop?* I listened for Jack in the Dark's long nails at our door. All night, I heard breathing at the window. I heard something running somewhere in the night and then I heard just the night.

darkness grafted to the tree's blue shade

It was just plain bad luck, when good weather finally came shining, that our camp boss got the double pneumonia and had to be taken to the Outside. The company sent in Heeley O. Swicker as the new bull of the woods. A hog-necked bravo, with a beard shot through with silver. He walked through camp with a cat-footed swagger. Some said he was so mean he had a double row of teeth. Never without a cigar locked at the corner of his mouth. Often, before he spoke, which was with a slow and peculiar drawl that marked him from away, a long, minky tail of smoke would shiver and linger about him.

At the beginning of each season, the company gave the camp boss money to run the camp, fight with straw bosses, feed the crews, and turn a profit. He was, generally, preoccupied with the swampers, planning new roads out to the chances and making sure nothing got out of hand and no one held a grudge too long. But when Swicker came, things changed fast. He was a big talker. He had opinions. He was happiest badmouthing the men and drawing out everyone's lesser spirits. The Mi'kmaq were untrustworthy. The Irish lazy. The Acadians sly with their words. The Downeaster border-jumpers spleeny in wet weather. And the Québécois nothing better than unsavory horse traders. He complained about any man who didn't speak English as his first tongue. He mispronounced names he didn't think English enough. He knew who was unlettered, who had a stutter or a shyness, and he made a point of picking on them too. Papa often had to calm tensions because the men knew where Swicker was shortcutting—cheapening food stocks, upping their daily quotas, making the woods unsafe, and forcing them to live in more crowded conditions. They let him deprive them in some ways, but they made sure to remind him from time to time that they were watching and they wouldn't suffer his blood-squeezing forever.

One afternoon, I was playing outside with Bruno. I had an umbrella—its bones long broken and its black wings laddered with holes—that Ivy and I liked to sashay around camp, taking turns spinning it on a shoulder. While we did this, Bruno liked to lend atmosphere with a game of his own invention we called Bruno's Wheely. It began with a quick spinning dance as though he were chasing his tail. Then, shaking his head from side to side he'd bluff-charge us a few times. After some minutes of this, he'd skelter in the opposite direction. Finally, he'd pick up a chip of wood or filch my umbrella, curl himself into a ball, and somersault down the slushy hill, not stopping till he bounced with an *oomph* into our shack or into me.

On this day, he'd done his trick a couple of times and had stopped to rest beneath a big poplar in just a way that his

29

darkness grafted to the tree's blue shade. I caught Swicker watching us from the doorway of the work shed he called his forepeak. While the other camp bosses had left us alone all these years, so long as Bruno behaved and kept to his wintering box in the coldest months, this one, watching us from below his fedora rim, had other plans.

"He's some hell on wheels, ain't he, darlin'?" he said as Bruno knocked slush from his ears.

My scalp stiffened. Swicker's words were slicked with something I didn't yet have a name for, but in that moment, I knew we were not safe. My childish sense of changelessness had been wrong. This was not how the rest of our life might run. Beneath that consideration, shame burned through me because I saw, for the first time, how he saw me, standing there in my meagerness: a raggedy have-not, twiggy with a broken umbrella, hemmed in by a wasteland of chickweed, a trampled yard, a slash of stumps. I saw for the first time the poverty that marked us. How easily ribby coyotes could steal into camp and take anything not tied down. Ivy's topsy-turvy doll went that way—half-wolf, half-girl, soundlessly carried off one night. She'd wept days for its thready loss. Though I knew it was against the rules, I tried to stare Swicker down, but then the wind picked up, stinging so bad I had to turn away. When I looked again, he was gone.

About a week later, when he was in the Outside at Black Sturgeon, sending off telegrams to the company office, he was approached by a man from Boston who managed an animal show. The man had heard about Bruno from Song-catcher's traveling lectures and had found a rough address for us at the tavern in town. The man offered Swicker fifty dollars right there, right then, for Bruno. Swicker agreed, plucking half the sum in worn bills from between the man's thick fingers. He neglected to tell us what he'd agreed to in Black Sturgeon. And it wasn't until some days later, when the man from Boston came into camp with a collar fit for a setter dog and a furniture crate, rumbling behind his seat on the supply sleigh's bed, that we knew. The man was dressed in a shabby Sunday suit the color of bad weather. He brushed out the wrinkles as he climbed down from the running board. Swicker knocked three times on our little door, interrupting our lessons.

Fearing the cold would catch on us, Mama opened the door just a crack. Camp should have been empty. Even Papa and Ansell were gone for the men's dinnering out. They'd snowshoed to the felling grounds, dragging a one-runner sled piled up with food, with more tucked into strap-baskets. It was about an hour's tramp and they'd had to leave early to build a fire to thaw everything out.

Swicker's voice was sore as he said, "'Fraid that bear's goin' tomorrow, Eula."

Mama fixed her eyes on him. After a time she said, "Mr. Swicker, I'm sorry, but that little bear's my own heart and I'd no sooner sell him than I would one of my own children."

Swicker kicked up a little snow around the door. He was not used to contrariness and it was clear he wasn't good with women. "You know a logging camp's no place for a goddamn bear."

Curious about Mama's visitors, Bruno had pulled himself out from his dynamite box and dragged his deer skin over to the door. Bruno was small for a black bear—more sheepdog than old boar bear. He hid behind Mama's leg, leaning in until her knee half-buckled. He chewed at the hem of her Mother Hubbard apron then worried his snout in the palm of her chapped hand.

The man from Boston cleared his throat. "Thought this was a done deal, Swicker."

"'Course it is," Swicker said, spitting into a clean patch of snow beneath our little window. He wiped the back of his hand through his beard and then, quick as fire, hooked his fingers under Bruno's leather collar—the one a teamster had made for him on his Sundays off some years ago—and yanked Bruno towards him. "Give 'im here now!"

Mama squared herself to the door and wrapped her thin arms around Bruno, so tight he started squealing, snagging his claws on her housedress. "I will not give you this little bear!" Mama said again. "It wasn't for you to decide."

By now, Swicker's dented nose was cold-scuffed and his breath was quick smoke, because this thin woman in a worn-out dress and a ravelly cardigan was defying him. He reached out his big hands and snatched at Bruno again, wrenching him from Mama's arms. That's when everything knotted up quick. In his panic, Bruno batted at Swicker's face, drawing five sharp lines of blood across the ridge of his cheek.

"God damn it to hell!" Swicker hissed.

Crows boiled up from a bare ash tree and put dark color

into the sky. Swicker dabbed at his bleeding cheek. His eyes depthless with the pain behind them.

Mama unlatched her double-horn necklace and handed it to Swicker. "Take this and let me keep my little bear, Mr. Swicker. Please."

The little crescent caught the light as it swung in Swicker's hand. He rubbed a finger along its bright backbone, then dropped it into his chest pocket, where he kept his cigars.

"Thanks. But he's still going." Mean-smiling, he yanked Bruno away from Mama, which sent him bawling again.

Just back from the dinner run, Papa and Ansell came out from Slapfoot—the trail that carried behind camp and the felling grounds—in time to see what all the noise was about. By now, Mama was crying and begging Swicker to leave us be. Bruno was racketing as though he were being torn in two. His long claws scratched at Mama's collarbones as he tried to find purchase where she kneeled into him.

Seeing all this, Papa pushed between Mama and Swicker. He trapped Bruno with his knee crooks, holding him astraddle. "Why're you trying to steal away our bear, Swicker?"

The man from Boston spoke first about the twenty-five-dollar transaction, half of the fifty with the promise of the bear. He pointed to the sled, reminding everyone he'd taken great pains to get out to the camp on one-haul roads, which was both a dangerous and extraneous undertaking at that time of year. All he wanted, he said, shuffling his feet in the slush, was to take that bear and get back to the Outside.

"This all true, Swicker?" Papa asked. Bruno had settled

around Papa's feet, licking a front paw wrenched in the argument.

Swicker eyed Bruno like he was the worst thing to cross his path in a long time. "That bear's been sold. Weather's turning squally, so this man's staying tonight and taking that thing with him tomorrow. Put it in the bunkhouse until then." He hawked another gluey bung of tobacco-stain into the snow.

Mama stepped closer to Papa. "It's not right, Swicker. He's mine!"

Papa looked from one to the other. While he could find work at any camp he chose, not all camp bosses would agree to a wife, two kids, and a runty black bear. So, he made his decision. He set his mouth, kept his eyes on Mama, and handed Bruno over to Swicker.

"Ten for the jury. Ten for the judge, eh, Swicker?" Papa spat into the snow too. "Never goddamn fails. You put him in the bunkhouse yourself," he said, before turning to Mama. I stood hand in hand with Ivy while my brother, my twin, was handed over to that traprock of a man who ran our lives, and then I let my anger be known.

I pushed out past them all and glared into Swicker's sorry ox-eye face. "You take my brother and I'll kill you dead."

Swicker and the man from Boston laughed. "Ain't she a little firecracker," Swicker said.

Papa led me back inside, venom still in my threats.

Swicker dragged Bruno—shrilling and spitting—over to the bunkhouse. He slammed the door and jammed it shut. Bruno's claws splintered the door's bottom sill, but not enough to offer escape. Swicker and the man from Boston couldn't have been too far down the path that led to the forepeak when Bruno blew into a tantrum. Often, when he got wound up, he'd try to calm himself by biting one of his feet. I suppose he might have tried that to no avail, which sent him into new fits—throwing himself around the bunkhouse, knocking over pots and cordwood. I cried so hard I felt like I was living inside a headache. All day Bruno went on, only stopping for short bouts, a brittle bark, as he listened for things and waited for Mama to come get him. But she was in our cabin mourning the quick loss of her little bear.

Mama kept us close to her all afternoon. But the hours must have felt like her heart was unpicking from her body—stitch by stitch. Ivy rubbed goose salve on the parts where Bruno had scratched deepest—her shoulders and neck—bare now without Grandma Slaywrock's double-horn necklace. Mama let the tears fall onto her dress for so long there were damp spots on her thighs and the skin around her eyes purpled and sored up.

Papa went over to the cookhouse to get supper on. But when Bruno's finer nature turned from fretting to rage again, no one could ignore him, hurtling himself with deep body panic at the bunkhouse's door again. His big belly pants. His breath short, clotted gasps, tattered gouts. There was not a moment that Papa wasn't aware of the injustice being done to creatures who loved each other very much. I spent that afternoon fit to be tied—the world had schemed against us again, hemming us in like a snare.

35

The storm went on and the snow caught and held the evening's unfinished colors. Just after dark, the men returned from the felling grounds. While the teamsters went on to the hovel to put up the horses, the others, soul-weary, headed to the bunkhouse to wash up before supper. The men paused outside their bunkhouse door, wondering why it'd been jammed with axe helves and wondering why cook's wife was weeping next door. As a young limber reached to remove the helves, Bruno got wind of him, sprawling the men back from the door. His claws caught rough wood. He threw himself at the spaces between the wall boards. Broken mother sounds. Broken bear sounds.

"That Bruno?" one of them asked.

By now, every man had become a silhouette to himself and to each other. All the men were fond of Mama for her healing. She'd once stitched up a man's forehead using a mosquito clamp, needle, and horsehair for lack of stronger thread—stitches so neat, the scar was almost invisible in certain slants of light. She never turned away from a shin bone snagged with saw teeth, arms glanced off tree cuts, dislocated shoulders, horse kicks, or lightning sparking through a raised limbing axe. She saw to each injury best she could.

The men sent an Acadian boy through the dingle. He knocked on our lean-shed's door. Mama opened it just a crack for fear it was the man from Boston, ready to take Bruno away.

"Why's your little bear in our bunkhouse, Mrs. Eula?" the boy asked, his voice gentle with youth and exhaustion.

Mama explained the deal Swicker had made with the

man from Boston. She told him about Swicker's hatefulness towards Bruno and the crying we'd done all day. The boy went over to the cookhouse then. Though the rules were that no man might enter until Papa banged the broken peavey on a steel beam, the boy thought this one time it would be allowed. He found Papa pulling biscuits out of the heat while Ansell set out pannikins and graniteware pitchers of powdered milk along the board tables—one for every six men. The boy asked again about what had happened between Mama and Swicker. Papa, in his calm way, explained that if selling Bruno was the only way to secure the lean-shed for his family, then he would have to let Bruno go with the man from Boston.

"You could protest," the boy suggested.

"How? Refuse to cook? That would harm you boys more than it would that son of a—" Papa sighed as our voices picked up our keening again next door. "If I'm to keep them with me, safe with me in the cuts, I'll have to abide by Swicker's dirty dealings."

The boy returned to the men, still standing outside their bunkhouse, their damp clothes crackling in the freezing air. He told them in so few words what had happened and who was to blame. Fleetwood Restoule, a giant of a cutter, led them over to the forepeak where a small circle of light cut through the flurries. Swicker and the man from Boston were in there. Quiet and sly. Many suspected Swicker drank in there, though no alcohol was allowed in camp. Window light ran through the men's shadows as Fleetwood banged on the door. Swicker's boots groaned the sash-milled floor as he stepped away from the rough desk to open the door.

"Why's the bear in our bunkhouse?" Fleetwood asked. "Why's cook's wife cryin' in her room with the *petits enfants* all around cryin'?"

"It has nothing to do with you," Swicker said, peering out into the murky light at the tired men. "It'll be done tomorrow."

"Swicker, there's a jeezless bear in our bunkhouse!" Wilmot Duff said, a man who had fifteen river drives under his belt and could win a wrestling match with his hands in his pockets. "Hell, he's probably destroyed things. Our things. And that little feller's crying for his mother. Cook's wife."

"You're a pretty brazen one to be standing there with us coming at you," another said, though Swicker couldn't tell who'd spoken. But the men knew it was Jimmy Split-the-Wind, nicknamed on account of his beaky nose.

"You give whatever dirty money you've made back to your Boston man and send him packing tomorrow. This bear weren't yours to sell. You had no right makin' that deal yes'day."

Someone moved a lantern closer to Swicker so that deep hollows marked his face. He still hadn't said anything, but chewed on the inside of his right cheek where his cigar smoldered. Considering. Everyone knew the men needed the money and would not be hired onto another crew so late in the season.

"Go on, Swicker. You have your goddamn ledger books and your money to make off our backs, but we'll not stand for this. Give Bruno back or we'll leave this camp tonight."

There was a round of raised voices. Swicker's camp was larger than most and this many men gone would mean trouble for him and for the company. Hearing all the voices, angry and tired, started Bruno bawling again. His nails scritched down the door's pine laths.

"What's it gonna be, Swicker?"

The bull of the woods tried to hide a shiver as the cold crept down his neck. He rubbed at the five long cuts across his cheek in an absent way and then his face settled into its habitual expression, an arrangement of narrow gazes: watchfulness and disdain. "Fine," he finally said. "Take the goddamn thing back over to that jeezless woman."

Without a word, the men walked back up to the bunkhouse. In a semicircle, the lantern held high, a teamster with hands warm with horse smells unwedged the axe helves and opened the door. Bruno was there waiting. He shoved his snout out into the cold air. His small eyes, caught glassy, momentarily blinded in the lantern's light. The teamster inched the door open, making sure he had a good grip on Bruno's collar. He led him over to the lean-shed like a lamb, like the weaker lambs he'd once carried as a boy into the warmth of his family's farmhouse kitchen in Donegal—newborn bodies almost blue in the early spring moonlight. The others lit lanterns and assessed the damage to the bunkhouse—everything pulled off their clotheslines and Jerry stove wood scattered around.

The teamster knocked until Mama opened the door. She couldn't see Bruno at first, because the light was gone, but he saw her and blatted as he tried to wriggle out of the man's grip. Mama let out a cry at his carry-me-home expression, nuzzling the wool of him. His cold nose against her neck.

"We gave Swicker a good shellacking, Mrs. Eula. He won't be coming around again for your little bear." He smiled shyly. "He might think it, but he ain't better'n nobody else 'round here."

He accepted her gratitude with a nod and sauntered back to the bunkhouse to wash up for supper.

Without much time to prepare, Papa still managed a swamp soggin for dessert to show his appreciation. And that night, Bruno was once again sleeping beside me in my bough bed where, Mama told us the next morning, we both snuffled and whimpered all night as though we were trying to play over everything that had happened. Out loud. In our secret language. I'll tell you we talked about killing that man dead.

=

After Swicker's dirty dealings, Bruno was reluctant to leave Mama's sight. He shadowed her everywhere and shunned outdoors, though the spring air was full of teetering smells. If I went out to pick flowers for Mama's Mason jar, Bruno hesitated coming. If I kept walking towards the felling grounds, he'd trundle back to the cabin—not even a see-you-ma'am glance behind. Snuffling and scenting, raking his claws down the door until Mama let him back in. One day, Mama sent us out to dig for dead man's toes—the cinnamon fern roots that grew along the edges of the woods. She sometimes added them to our supper, though Papa said we got enough goodness from what he fed the men. We ate the roots, roasted, peeled, pounded until the starch seeped out and tasted green. Everyone but Bruno hated them. While I dug, Bruno took himself off, down over the berm where everyone threw their old tin cans and unfixable tools.

After I'd filled a pint's worth of root, I wanted him to play "What time is it, Mr. Wolf?" but he had other plans. He was dragging the bootjack around, though Mama had warned him against this as he always left it out in the woods somewhere. Whenever he had the bootjack, he became top-lofty, so high and mighty he'd spank past us with his chest puffed out and his breath coming in explosive gusts as he champed his lips. Papa called him Little Lord Fauntleroy. There was no reasoning with him then.

Ivy went down through a cut looking for him while I called and called, but only our voices came back. As I was hollering again, a Swedish axeman came over—an apple he'd been slicing with a jackknife in his palm. He was missing his pinky finger and part of his ring finger. Björn. He was the only Swede in camp that season. Some said he'd come west from the Outside for a woman. I knew him mainly from the stories he told on Saturday nights. He'd come across the ocean, he'd said, on an Icelandic fishing trawler that moved up and down on dark Atlantic swells—a sea road, he'd said, that linked islands and archipelagos and wild, strange landscapes. Steam vents that smelled like struck matches. Orange and violet mud gummed around their mouths. Dark winters. Midnight suns. And pillars of stone where trolls had been caught in the sunlight while pulling their night boats ashore. When it was Björn's turn to tell stories, all the men pressed him for more.

"In Sweden," he always began, as he did now. "In Sweden, there's a song women sing." He squinted off in the direction Bruno had gone with his bootjack. "To scare off wolves and bring the cows home."

I couldn't imagine what sort of song that might be.

"Maybe it'd work to bring bears home," he suggested, cutting a slice of apple off for me. "I will show you." He set the quartered apple down, cupped his hands around his mouth, then top-lunged a sort of unnerving yodel.

It was no gee or haw like the teamsters used for turning the oxen right or left. It didn't have words and I could no more hum it back to you than I could recite Greek poetry. It spoke to something bottled up and released. A sort of sadness it hurt to hear. It sounded like a song wolves might sing of heartsickness and loss. One to the other.

The woods filled with the song's after-quiet. I sucked on apple seeds and waited for Bruno—still in the sheltered air beneath the alders where Slapfoot went on. With his bootjack locked in his forepaws, he peered our way. Björn sang out again. Bruno dropped his bootjack and trotted over and sat at Björn's feet. Bewitched.

"He ain't no ordinary no-count bear. He's high liver!" Giver McGee, a teamster, called over from where he'd been checking some tack and watching Bruno discover his song.

like deep water or ghosts

Next season, we were still on the Crooked Deadwater, in a new camp that looked just like the old one. Swicker landed a week before cutting began with his seventeen-year-old nephew, Miles, and Argyle Corcoran, a scaler man, clearly in Swicker's pocket. Nephew Miles, looking like a magazine woodsman, spent his first days in camp dusting sawdust off his coat, checking his sweaters for snags, and thumbing mud from his pant cuffs. He walked through the yard with a mix of swagger and disdain for the puddles and churned and cupped horse muck. I knew, if I got close enough, he'd have that new-store smell on him.

One afternoon, I sat on a nail keg outside our paintless lean-cabin with Mama, watching the three of them walk through camp.

"Now don't they look like the end-alls and be-alls?" Mama sighed, beating a rag rug shot through with Bruno's guard hairs.

"Aren't they?"

"Hmmm?" Mama asked.

"Don't they own the place?"

"Company does, Pearly. Not them three."

When Ivy poked her head out to watch them pass, Bruno started banging things around inside. "Smarten up, Bruno!" she snapped. "Oh, Mama, look at that one's boots," she whispered.

Mama play-swatted her with the dowel she'd been using on the rug. "I won't have no boy-crazy girls around here. You hear me?"

"Don't look at me," I said. "Me and Bruno got no use for 'em."

"Ivy?" Mama asked again in her counting-to-three voice. "You hear me?" Mama had been out of sorts for a few months now. She slept a lot, claiming her blood was low. She had little patience for Ivy's new foolishness.

Nephew Miles caught us watching. He waved. Ivy cringed behind me like she'd been scalded. I waved back like the men did: two fingers, a thumb, and a twist of the wrist. I had a fierce urge to give him another finger, one that Ansell had taught me back last year, but I didn't dare, what with Mama right there. Ivy wiped her hands down her patched-up skirt and smoothed her hair as Mama passed her in the doorway.

"You got ants in your pants or what?" I asked.

She only rolled her eyes and mooned some more from behind the door.

At the cookhouse, Swicker stopped to speak to Papa and Ansell, who were lugging supplies off a wagon. *That is my enemy*, I thought, glowering at Swicker. Me and Bruno were now fifteen and I felt we had more say in what might happen in our lives. It was my own undoing, I suppose.

As the men talked, Swicker's white-coated German shepherds, Duke and Duchess, came coursing through the trees and swirled around his legs like deep water or ghosts. Bruno gave Swicker a wide berth most days, but the dogs were something new. He poked his head around our rough-hewn door, just to see. That's all it took. The dogs caught his scent and highballed it across the yard before Swicker could heel them.

"Close the damn door!" I yelled to Ivy.

"Duke! Duchie! God damn it!" Swicker bellowed.

By then, the dogs were inside our lean-cabin and I couldn't hear anything over Mama's and Ivy's screams, the breakage the dogs were causing, and Bruno's clacking and jaw popping as he clambered to get away from the slathering things. He'd cornered himself in our bough bed, walling himself behind a flimsy pile of fir. The dogs air-snapped—their eyes starry in the window light. One leapt high and caught Bruno's paw. Bruno gnashed his teeth and grew fierce. By now Ivy and Mama were standing in the middle of the floor hugging each other. That's when Swicker found me with an axe helve, readying to stove in his horrible dogs' skull bones. He made to grab them by their hackled scruffs and drag them away, but the bigger one turned on him and put heat into a bite, deep into the meat of his hand. Swicker roared and gripped at their necks again. He dragged them across the room, their nails gouging long rills into our soft

45

pine floor. Outside, he struck each a blow across an ear, until they curled tail and settled in the mud to lick the smell of bear from their fur.

Papa was in the yard now, his voice cold and level as it was when he needed to keep his calm. "Swicker, them dogs are dangerous. I got kids here. Someone's apt ta—"

"Apt ta what? Hell, man, I let you keep a goddamn bear in this camp. My dogs won't hurt nobody."

"They're liable to tear someone apart!" Papa shouted. "The pair of them's ugly."

By now Swicker was rumbling like something tight with steam. "And I'm telling you they're just high-spirited."

Inside, Mama stood amid our sorry belongings. The broken and mended now broken again: the carriage clock that no longer kept time and the china dog missing an ear. The sum of our claim on the world.

In a little while, Swicker called all the men in from wherever in the camp sprawl they were sharpening tools, mending a hame's broken kidney link, putting a roof on the hovel. Miles brought out some crates and Swicker glad-handed bottles of Coca-Cola around. He might as well have been handing out gold. Within minutes, the men were swilling their drinks and relaxing against the wagon boards.

Swicker came back over to our lean-cabin. Mama met him at the door. "Please, just go," she said. "We'll clean it all up. But please just go."

"But I got one for you and your pretty sister too, sweetheart," he said, winking at me.

"Pearly, come help me with these supplies," Pa called over from the wagon.

I looked Swicker straight in his mud-colored eyes. Outside that smile was nothing—a veneer covering over all manner of meanness and lack of decency beyond. I could see, despite my blood whishing through my chest and ears, where his razor had nicked his cheek. I could see where he'd had a recent haircut so that the sunburnt skin met the pale skin at his neck. I could see the five scars Bruno had raked down his face last winter.

"Pearly Everlasting, not telling ya again," Papa said in his own counting-to-three voice.

An uncertain silence. Swicker held out the bottles. "Come on, little wildcat. They're not gonna bite."

Me and Ivy had shared a bottle of Coca-Cola just about twice in our lives. Swicker's smile reminded me of a leghold trap. Slow and careful, I took them. He glanced at Papa in a smug way. I saw then something elemental in my father for the first time. A rigidness to keep course, a firmness in his own convictions—as easy for him as trickery or vanity or two-facedness was for another man. And I wondered if I too might possess this trait, and it saddened me to think that I might not, that, should the opportunity arise, I might choose the easy mistake again.

Papa did not speak again to either of us but handed Ansell another bag of supplies. I saw that Ansell, who would not meet my eyes, had not taken a bottle either. Feeling shabby for being bought so cheaply, I turned on my heel and went back into our lean-cabin, slamming the door behind me.

"Let Bruno be, Pearly," Mama said. "He's fine. Just being a sook. Don't get him going."

I handed Ivy a bottle and then sat down with Bruno—still in the boughs, licking some small puncture wounds. We took glugs off my Coca-Cola bottle, though I wouldn't let him hold it. We sat there in the new-fir smell, listening to the men laugh and carry on outside, everyone pretending everything was all right. Jimmy Split-the-Wind. Fleetwood Restoule. Wilmot Duff. I could not hear my father. I could not hear Ansell.

Those first gulps burned my stomach sick. I gave Bruno the rest. In the mule-eared chair, Ivy took sips off her own, *ahhhing* between each swallow, pacing so the bottle might last forever.

Outside, Swicker squatted on his heels in the mild dust, he put out his hands to crown each panting dog's sharp head. One hand wrapped in a bloodied hanky.

the sky bloodish, the pines black

We were wrong to see nothing dark in the rain. Jack in the Dark was there, whistling up the October winds, coaxing out storms. The men kept pointing to the signs: raccoons fat and brightly banded, muskrat burrows high in the river's clay banks, and woodpeckers sharing a tree when they'd rather not. With Swicker pushing the men harder to meet cutting quotas, injuries were happening too often. I'd seen more than one man lying on the board table in the cookhouse while Mama tried to keep him alive. I saw Benoît Gagné near split in two when the crown of a tree caught in the branches of neighboring trees. The trunk fell untrue and kicked back before Benoît could get out of the way. Mama said it near broke every bone in his body. They took him out to Black Sturgeon on the back of a wagon and he never came back. And just a few days later, while Peter Athanase was peeling bark, a dry limb fell from a tree above and struck his neck, breaking off an inch below the skin. Mama got the six-inch splinter out with some needle-nose pliers and a good dose of cussing. She said the crews were working short. She said Argyle Corcoran, the scaler man, was also shorting the men's daily cuts, wearing everyone down. I'd seen the age in Mama's eyes these past weeks too. Almost every injury, she said, could have been avoided if Swicker hadn't been out in them felling grounds swearing at the woodsmen and the horses, galled and weary, writing their mistakes down in his little black book.

"Everyone's so damned tired, Pearly," she said with a sigh, rinsing blood from some bandages, forgetting her own rules about cussing in only the most dire of circumstances.

It felt like something was ending and me and Bruno didn't want no part in it. Ivy was also changing. Fast. One day she was one type of girl and the next someone different. Rather than help Mama with the chores, she suddenly wanted to try on her meager array of clothes and traipse around the lean-cabin. She wanted Mama to add lace to her Humphrey pants and house-dresses. She'd lately taken to mooning around mirrors and other reflective things—rubbing a smear of raspberry jam on her lips, staring at herself like she'd just met the girl staring back.

"Stop gawking at yourself, Ivy!" Mama warned several times a day now. "Help me roll these bandages."

Instead, Ivy took to complaining about Bruno. "No one else lives with a no-count bear in a woodshed," she whined one day.

"Say that again and I'll pop you one," I growled from the stoop where I was working mud from under Bruno's nails with my Green River knife. Over the past few months, I'd taken to tucking it inside my boot like a cowboy. I liked the feeling.

50

"That's enough. The pair of ya's," Mama said, her arms full of bedding that needed airing.

=

Most days now, me and Bruno spent our afternoons deep in the woods, just to get away from the men and blood and Ivy's constant complaining. After learning my bear call, Bruno kept with me, so we could roam, provided we stayed away from the felling grounds and the tote roads. To keep us safe, Mama dyed an old wool coat, one the smallest boy had left behind last year. She'd cooked the pitch out of it then cut it down to my size and colored it with a slurry of raspberries, mountain cranberries, and maple leaves—boiling off their bright varnishes and setting the scarlets with salt. For Bruno, she tied a clutch of sleigh bells to a braided bit of twine and knotted them to his collar.

Fall was ending fast. Soon we'd hear the steel sled runners rasping over hard-packed snow and the trees' heartwood shattering from deep frost. I'd miss the air's greeny smells, rivery smells, the pink-winks and wood-frogs. I'd miss Bruno, who'd drag himself away again to his wintering box. But for now, we wandered off the skid roads—muddy and deep-rutted with a thousand horse tramps. Bruno had sunshine in his eyes as he thought his own thoughts, turning sometimes to wait for me. Already well-larded, he still ate everything he found: horsetail, dandelion, lupine. We walked and I told him made-up stories about the City of Bears.

Off a trail the men called Thieves Road, we crossed an open

strip purpled with fireweed. The Burnt Land, where woods-men once buried a piano to save it from a forest fire. With Bruno dawdling behind—eating, eating, always eating—we crossed onto Slapfoot, the trunks there gouged where sleds had scraped past. We walked on over a sprung matting of pumpkin pine and hackmatack needles—bright, ticking rain around us. Papa said, at one time, the woods here were so unbroken a squirrel could pass all the way down to Maine without ever touching the ground. Swicker was changing all that, bulling through the chances, pushing the men like he had something to prove. Papa said one day men would bring in gas-powered machines to lumber faster. He'd warned me then that the land would be emptied like a coyote gut, filled with worms.

"They're coming, Pearly. You wait and see."

Yan, tan, tether . . . pip, azer, sezar. I counted our steps in old shepherd's numbers just as a teamster had taught me some years ago, while we checked our snares up along the Burnt Land's borders. Just as we were readying to come back down, we caught sight of Ivy sitting on the Crooked Deadwater's cutbank where the water wheeled around granite outcrops. It was a good place to catch brookies in July if you could avoid the crabby old bank beaver who lived nearby. The sun was just going down, making the sky bloodish, the pines black. The raw-edged air smelled of the sleeving up of chimney smoke and sprung water. It was getting cold and no time to be moon-ing on some rock. The wind caught up a swatch of china-dot material I recognized from Mama's ragbag, wrapped around Ivy's shoulders like a la-di-da scarf.

"Champagne taste and a beer bottle budget," Mama often said now about Ivy.

I made to yell something mean when Bruno hinded up and nosed the air. I imagined his meaty body prowling smells: horses kidney-sick with black water in faraway barns, a spit-threaded needle, a gun dog's leg set with an ash splint, hens stabbing at their lice, heat around a human lie.

"What do you smell, Brunnie?"

He huffed in Ivy's direction. She wasn't alone. Miles in the nice boots was there too, close enough their knees touched. He'd cut his leg with a grub hoe his first week at camp. Mama tended to it when it wouldn't stop seeping. "That boy's not geared for the woods," Mama had said after he'd left. "Too dreamy." More than a month later and he still carried a limp.

Crouching down in the leaf litter, we watched Ivy become another person. Now the two of them were talking with their heads nearly touching. Now Ivy was laughing in some high, practiced way I'd never heard before. Miles the nephew's hands balled in the pockets of his mackinaw—his face just this side of unwilling to smile at something she'd just said.

He spat a gout of phlegm through his teeth onto the goldy moss at Ivy's feet and then, slowly, unwrapped her makeshift scarf. It blew into the water—a shed skin carried away by the river. He stepped closer and pulled out the collar of her blouse with one finger and got an eyeful.

"Jesus, Brunnie, she's got herself Swicker's nephew." Bruno snorted then snapped a tangle of alder, so loud it had them both caging their eyes to see deeper into the woods.

Not wanting to make Ivy any more salty than we did on any given day, we took off with a great thrash, tripping through swamp seeps, hoping the sun, lowering into the water, might hide us. She'd cuffed me in the ear some days back for spying on her, leaving my head to ring the rest of the afternoon. She'd called me a baby for believing in Jack in the Dark and pulled Bruno's tail when she caught him napping on her favorite quilt. I sometimes wondered if she'd even miss us if Jack in the Dark and his bone horse came for us in the middle of the night.

"Where's your sister?" Mama asked when we came slamming into the lean-cabin. She was soaping blood from her hands into the basin.

"At the oughtn't-to-be place."

"And where's that, pray tell?"

"Mrs. Eula, we're not saying nothing against no one, are we, Bruno?" We climbed into our bough bed's darkest corner. Bruno had a good gash on his nose he licked in earnest and both my hands were skinned up from burdocks. I dabbed at them with a sock.

"Well, did she say when she might grace us with her presence?"

"You want to know what she said without the cuss words?"

"Yes, please."

"Then she didn't have nothing to say."

"Don't test me today, Pearly Everlasting Hazen," Mama warned.

54

Ivy was back at camp soon after, in a quiet mood for once. She helped Mama make up bandages without being asked.

"Where'd ya get up to today, Ivy?" I asked.

But she only scowled at us.

=

All that week, me and Bruno escaped to the woods as soon as we could. Tramping far enough away we could no longer hear the men yell, "Widow-maker!" We could no longer hear them holler for Mama to come quick with her tourniquets and yarrow salve to help stop the bleeding. One afternoon, we went down to the edge of Sawpit Bog. Its surface all circles where the water bugs fed. Bruno waddled through some thick buckbean, stirring up a plash from a slick-gilled pickerel prowling the darker depths among perch and silvery roaches and speckled trout. He found a punked tree with an ants' nest swarming blackly. He dredged his paws through the rankled insects and stoved their house in.

I walked out to where two fallen canoe birches made a V and shinned up one with roots still in the ground. I thought about Ivy and Miles. I thought about how Mama kept sending me and Bruno away because we got in the way. It was always Ivy passing Mama thread and scissors and bandages or holding one of the youngest boys' hand when fear got into his eyes. And now Ivy had a secret life. Then I got to thinking about Ansell. "You think he might look like a singing cowboy, Brunnie? Tumbleweed Baker maybe?"

Bruno was busy with a half-sprung pork barrel now, left over from last year's camp. A hole gaped where it leaned against an upright rock. Other bears. Wild ones. At the bottom were still some slabbered bits of salt pork.

"Yeah, me too," I said. And then, because I was beginning to feel a little uneasy, I hooped Bruno's song—my voice echoing off the cuts. I could've stayed out there forever. Alone with Bruno. Our world unharmed, unmade. And Bruno, my brother, my twin, was all that more ancient because bears are made of myths, constellations, deep hollows, and long stories of their escapes from men.

the kind that spooks the horses

Hear the woods. Something in the ground, in the air. Tree to tree. So that pine sometimes sang like steel wool buffing cast iron. Tree to tree. And then through the understory: lambkill, prince's pine, and ostrich fern, momentarily caging wind in their waxy leaves before releasing it to carry on farther into the woods where it pooled and changed as it traveled on and outward and then was heard no more. This was how Song-catcher entered the woods.

She and Ebony hadn't been on this side of the Crooked Deadwater in some time. She'd meant to, but her lectures had kept her closer to Smoke River. She'd given nearly forty talks that year on New Brunswick's woods and ballads, but Bruno's story was the most popular.

"We'll never get this son of a bitch out of here, if you don't push!" Ebony said from the back of the goat cart, where she was rocking a wheel out of a rut.

Earlier that morning, they'd done some fine recordings of the Knockwood brothers' paddling songs. But sometime between then and now, one of the wagon's axles had warped loose, and the wheel had bent itself at the nave, buckling the thing's underbelly. The wagon had started its life with a bench seat, where children sat while a bridled goat pulled them around. A pretty Victorian picture. Song-catcher had bought it from an arthritic Go-Preacher, an unaffiliated, unordained minister of sorts, who'd traveled the dark and wet miles between lumber camps, looking for the lights of fires, the soft parts in souls in need of Bibles and brimstone sermons. Three Newfoundland dogs had hauled the wagon back then. Each, the preacher claimed, knowing every spur and skid and tote road from Magaguadavic to Sainte-Anne-de-Madawaska. Song-catcher had taken the wagon to a shade-tree mechanic, who'd worked the whole of an afternoon beneath a candling horse chestnut, knocking out the little bench seat and walling up the front, making it a proper handcart, which now carried all her recording tackle beneath sailcloth: a hand-crank Edison Gem, wax cylinders, a Butcher's Cameo camera, an old army bell tent, and enough supplies to keep them a few days, if caught short between camps.

"This is some misery!" Ebony complained. The mud so thick on the soles of her skate boots, she had to keep scraping it off with a stick. "I really hate these woods sometimes."

A curl in Ebony's boyish haircut fell forward from behind her ear as she worked off the muck, and Song-catcher couldn't help but feel that now-familiar, but still shocking, sense of her. Part girl. Part boy. And sometimes, it seemed, part other. Like paintings of androgynous archangels, Ebony, in her overalls, shawl collar sweater, and felt hat, was multiple, mercurial. It was a quality that often drew people to her and opened them up to share their music. But if Ebony couldn't persuade them, the "talking machine" often sparked their curiosity, especially when Song-catcher played one of her wax cylinders. After listening to a song through, a weary woodsman might say, "Well, it weren't bad, but I got something better'n that." Those who might not sing still offered Song-catcher stories, stories about creatures fleshed in omens: birds swarming windows or strange dogs howling in a dooryard. Forerunners to someone waking up dead.

But according to some of her contemporaries, foundering goat carts and hand-crank Edison Gems were no longer the field recording tackle *de rigueur* for modern-day song-catchers or, as Dr. Toby Archer-Braxton frequently corrected her in his letters from the University of Virginia, "ethnomusicologists." Men like him, of course, had titles and positions. They drove old ambulances through Appalachia and the Ozarks with reel-to-reel equipment double-charged on half a dozen car batteries. Behind them was private funding; all Song-catcher had behind her was Ebony. But as she coaxed the wallowed wagon along, careful not to pin Ebony's foot again, Song-catcher knew they were part of something exceptional, something even Dr. Toby Archer-Braxton had never recorded before: the spirit of the woods.

Mid-shove, Ebony walked away.

"Break," she said, pulling two cigarettes from a tarnished silver case. She lit them both and handed one to Song-catcher.

Spills of rain. Poplars exposed their leaves' pale, furry undersides. The day had warmed, but in a few hours the air would seize up again. They stepped under a beech, near some mossed-up blowdown. Water swashed over rock. This province was practically a spring to itself, wetted into seeps and brooks and streamlets—fast-moving, dark as over-handled chain. Picking tobacco from her lip, Song-catcher listened closer, and yes, there it was. She pointed towards the tree crowns. Ebony nodded. Wind. Lately, Song-catcher had come to realize better the habits of trees and wind. Small resistances and drip tips: one perfect moment of brushed sound. She could not stop collecting for her dictionary of wind: the kind that picks up late spring dust and temporarily blinds, the kind that spooks the horses and the kind that spooks the men. But to take all their tackle out now, when they were so close? It wouldn't be worth it.

Ebony had her doubts about this new project. "Stick to songs," she often said. "Wind won't get us to the Chautauqua lectures."

Song-catcher stamped out her cigarette. "Ready?" she asked, anxious to find Eula Hazen and give her the little envelope of money she'd made from her Bruno talks.

"Just a minute more," Ebony pleaded, lighting another cigarette off her first. And then, over the wind's patter, she sang off-key, "In the middle of the journey of our life I came to myself within a dark wood where the straight way was lost!"

The air hardened. Song-catcher hunched down into her

sou'wester, the one she'd bought from a Pubnico fisherman in return for a couple of sea shanties some years ago. To the north, Greenlaw Mountain stood dark and whole and ringed with mist.

Ebony petted the wagon. "Poor ol' beast. You'll need a blacksmith to see you through."

"We've got to get on, Ebbie."

Ebony tossed the dog-end of her cigarette into the understory.

They heard the noise not long after. A wolfish circling.

"Now, what the hell's that?" Ebony asked. It came around again.

Song-catcher had one guess. "Our Pearly Everlasting."

They came up around a hogback to find a tarry pond, studded with bites of granite. Out on a limb, peering into an empty crow's nest, stood Pearly Everlasting. Legs scraped raw where she'd rolled up the hems on her fishtail pants, a ratty pair of suspenders holding the tattered things onto her thin hips. She had some godawful haircut and was singing and walking up the edge of a toppled birch, its root plate half in the air, its crown hanging low over the pond, while Bruno played nearby with an old pork barrel.

Just as they came into the light, Bruno caught sight of them and shinned up the limb, weighing it down until it snapped and he and Pearly, mid-yodel, fell neck-deep into the dark water.

"Damn it to hell, Bruno!" Pearly yelled, splashing him from where she sat scowling in the muck.

61

"Well, you're some sight for sore eyes, wild girl!" Song-catcher said.

Bruno scurried off with his prize barrel, watching the women approach from a ways away. Pearly Everlasting wiped scum from her eyes. "Well, I'll be damned, the devil makes house calls! Back from the Outside!"

"Your mama'll wash your mouth out with some of that Shake Hands soap she hear you talking like that," Ebony said, laughing because she loved a girl who could swear.

"Hell, Mama can't hear me! 'Sides, she's too busy stitchin' men back together here at Humpty Dumpty's camp," she said, pulling herself out of the water with a branch. "Thought you guys'd never get back!"

"What are you doing way out here?" Song-catcher asked.

"Who wants to stay at home and watch the rain?" Pearly said. "Swicker's got everyone racin' around like headless chickens and everyone's coming back into camp missing fingers and bleeding all over the place. It's some hellish these days."

=

Together, they walked back to camp through a bushed-in twitching trail—Pearly Everlasting's boots squelching as she pulled the wagon. Bruno led, stopping from time to time to shake water from the keeps of his ears or munch on kinnikin-nick and blackberries, though they were all seed that year.

"What was that you were caterwauling before?" Song-catcher asked.

She grinned, her cheeks streaked with dirt. "Oh me, oh my! Heard me, did ya? It's my bear song."

"You make it up?"

"Naw, it's from near Nowhere."

"Nowhere?"

"Yeah, near Swee-dish," she said, a touch of pride in her voice.

"Ah, near Norway?" Song-catcher asked.

Pearly shrugged. "That's what I said. Anyway, it's something Björn taught me last year. I was just practicing. Works on Bruno every time."

"And who's Björn?" Ebony asked.

"Just some guy from near Nowhere who used to work here."

They walked on, into the camp yard where the sun burned stronger over stumps and loose-strewn tools.

"Like to record your song, if I can," Song-catcher said.

Pearly Everlasting gave her a wink. She'd grown so much since last time they'd been out that way. "Thought ya might."

"You mind me asking about that haircut? Bruno cut it for you?" Ebony asked, pausing to roll a cigarette.

Pearly held out her hand. "It'll cost ya."

Ebony glanced at Song-catcher, then handed the cigarette to the little imp standing there like a miniature woodsman. "It's a good story," she singsonged.

To tame the sleep knots, Ivy had kept Pearly in a Dutch bob for the past five years after she'd found a photo of Mary Thurman in an old *Photoplay* magazine. Pearly toyed with the rough edges of her new haircut then dragged a match along her boot sole—another woodsman's gesture—and lit the cigarette. "Don't tell Mama," she said, coughing. "Sometimes, I filch shag when no one's lookin."

Ebony held up her hands in surrender. "And the hair?"

"Aw . . . well, me and Bruno got into some pitch and then we got into some burdocks and then we got into a skirmish with a skunk, so, well . . ." She gave a beauty pageant twirl. "Ta-dah! Bruno got the same treatment." She rubbed at some baldish patches around his ears and along his ribs. "Mama and Ivy mend up men and socks pretty good, but they're useless with haircuts. I tried to fix it with Ivy's comb, but that just ended up broke. Now she's got nothing for combing and she's pretty sore about it."

"I'll bring her a new one next time I'm through," Songcatcher said, laughing.

As they reached the lean-cabin, a man stepped out, his arm bandaged wrist to elbow. Pearly stood solemn as a funeral guest as he walked past on his way to the bunkhouse. "There goes another," she whispered. And then she shouted, "Mama! We're coming in!"

"You wipe them feet before stepping in here, Pearly."

"Don't know if that'll help," she said, winking at Ebony.

"If you and Bruno were in that stinking swamp again, I swear I'll—"

"Look who's here from the Outside," she said, rummaging in a wanigan for something dry.

Inside, the cabin's color came only from magazine ads

pasted to the walls and the dried herbs and plants Eula used in her healing. It took some moments for everyone's eyes to adjust to the darkness. Ivy, taller now than the last time Song-catcher had seen her, had not outgrown her shyness. She smiled a little at them before nudging her mother. Eula turned from folding bandages. If it was possible, she looked more worn down than the year before. She wrapped her cardigan tight around her bony frame.

"Well, look who's here," she said, forcing a smile. "We was wondering when you might make it out for a visit. And me looking like the wreck of the Hesperus." She led them into the tiny room and lightly touched each mule-eared chair to show them where they should sit. "Let me see if Edon's got something to spare." And before anyone could protest, she was out the door and over to the cookhouse. Ivy kept her hands busy folding and refolding bandages.

"Ivy, the one that just left? How is he?" Pearly asked. She sat in the rocker, getting it going hard enough to make the floorboards squeak.

"Oh, he's not too bad off, Mama thinks. Just a bruised bone."

"Ah, like Miles, then."

Ivy scowled but kept quiet.

Eula came back in with a pot of tea and a plate of molasses cookies the men called barn doors. After tea, Song-catcher and Ebony brought in the Edison and set it up on the little table the girls used for their lessons.

"You still using that old talking machine?" Pearly asked,

her face close enough Song-catcher could smell the cigarette reek on her.

"Pearly!" Ivy hissed. "That's not nice."

Song-catcher smiled. Yes, same old talking machine. Though Ebony thought she should be using something more modern, she felt confident with the cumbersome thing. Its parts all worked and it never let her down.

When it was ready, Eula chose "Ah! Si Mon Moine Voulait Danser!" She sang, *"Un froc de bur' je lui donnerais . . . S'il n'avait fait voeu pauvreté, Bien d'autres choses je lui donnerais."* She sat thinking a bit after she'd finished. "I only know a few of 'em by name," she said. "Most I just know the feel of. Like this dancing monk. I love he's always dancing."

"How about 'The Jam on Gerry's Rocks'?" Pearly suggested.

"Pearly," Ivy said, a little warning in her tone.

"Oh, I don't think we need any accident songs right now, Pearly," Eula murmured, and everyone could feel the men who'd been in here over the past weeks with their injuries and fear.

"How about 'Pretty Polly'?"

"Murder ballads, Pearly? Let's not." Ivy sighed.

"Song-catcher loves murder ballads, Ivy. But 'Polly' was best when Havelock Barrows played clawhammer banjo that year. You remember him, Ivy? He looked a bit like Miles."

Ivy squirmed like something in the bite of a trap. Pearly kicked at the deacon's bench with her boots, causing Bruno to whine in his sleep. Ivy gave her another sharp look. Pearly raised her eyebrows and made her ears wiggle.

"Anyways," she continued, "anything we sing's gonna be

so good someone might just throw a rock through our little window." She grinned and rocked her chair faster. "Just to hear it better."

Ivy gave another Hollywood-worthy sigh. But Song-catcher could tell no one really minded Pearly's new fast talk and mischief. She was no longer a bear cub. She'd been licked into her shape: sharp and rough, but good-hearted too.

At Pearly's request, Song-catcher took the talking machine outside and set it up on a wide stump. "I got to stand up for this," Pearly told her. "It's no sit-down song. It runs through the trees, see?"

Ebony managed to balance the talking machine on a ladder. Its wide horn close to Pearly's fox-sharp face. Ansell and Edon came out from the cookhouse to watch.

"You ready, Ansell? I'm singing this for you, cowboy," Pearly called over, just to see his ears pink up. She teased him mercilessly. He shoved his hands deep into his overall pockets and nodded at his boots. "And Pa, I think this one'll be heard all the way down into the King's Tree!"

For extra drama, she waited for Bruno to wander off behind the camp where stumps and broken rock gave way to Slapfoot. And then she filled her lungs, cupped her hands around her mouth, and sang out that strange, haunting song. The needle cut deep grooves in the wax cylinder. Bruno came scampering back and plunked down on a stump next to her.

After supper, before they left, Song-catcher gave Eula the slim envelope: two dollars. Though Eula insisted she stop giving them money, Song-catcher said she wouldn't have gotten half the support she had over the years without Bruno's story. And besides, no one was getting rich those days. In the past season, a cord had dropped from $2.30 to $1.34. The men said they were just working now to wear out their clothes: "They got ya comin' and goin' and pretty soon they're going to make us pay to work."

Song-catcher and Ebony said their goodbyes and promised to come back before spring. What Pearly Everlasting didn't tell them was that sometimes, when she and Bruno were out, she'd sing the bad luck songs. The ones forbidden in camp because they brought death with them. But she sang them sometimes, testing the bad luck for herself.

his worn out words and his worn out boots

Everyone felt it—the change in the wind—or said they did. And there was Jack in the Dark with his one good eye, waiting for us when we started to get sick.

"L'hiver s'approche, Miss Pearly!" the men called as fall lost its kindle and made room for a sore-throated winter that wouldn't stop testing us. Just a few weeks after Song-catcher and Ebony left, early snows came and Ivy took sick with a cough that wouldn't shift, no matter how many times she breathed over a steaming basin of balsam water. I slept beside her, listening to her lungs sounding sore.

Between injuries and caring for Ivy, Mama didn't get much sleep either. And then illness sank its dark anchor into her too and stayed. She wore her knobby blue cardigan wrapped tight against her ever-fading frame as she coaxed Ivy to take a little broth, a bit of toast. Papa wanted them in hospital, but Mama said no, we don't have money for the Outside. It's just a bad cold down in the lungs, Edon. That's all.

The winter held on. Swicker's dogs went missing and he

started putting pressure on the teamsters as they'd been the ones complaining the most about them snapping at the horses, spooking them walleyed. Anger started to build up in camp. Argyle Corcoran was accused of shorting the men of their cuts day after day, always counting in favor of the company. Everyone began to speak about that winter in the past tense, giving it history. On Saturday nights, the men made up stories about it. "Back in 1934," they'd say, "woodsmen cut through the lake ice and built wide stairs up into the black bones of the trees and men held red-hot skillets in their bare hands outside in the cold." The winter of 1934. The winter that would not end.

Papa made Mama and Ivy teas from aspen bark, red spruce gum, and boiled beaver kidney. They drank Buckley's Mixture, hot ginger, Dr. Daniels' Colic Cure—good for man or beast. A swamper suggested gunpowder and boiling water. A feller suggested fir gum, singed with a flame and breathed deep. Nothing worked. One afternoon—our two small windows ferned with hoarfrost—I found Mama asleep in her chair, her feet tucked beneath Bruno's belly. He'd come in from his wintering some days before and shadowed her everywhere. I took the little carnival glass bottle down from where it sat, neglected now on a shelf, and sprayed it over Mama—thin as antlers—to keep away the shadows, to keep Jack in the Dark from our door. I could almost hear him out there, digging down to meet the dead.

One night, he was there in a clutch of lumberjack birds— the kind some call whisky jacks and others the spirits of dead woodsmen—pecking at our window glass for hours, despite it being the fifth day of a raging blizzard. When night made a mirror of the window, I stepped outside, my lantern jinking light into the dark and endless woods. All the birds were gone. Though the night winds took shape and the pines creaked and sounded animal.

"I'll smoke you out yet, you bastard!" I yelled into the howl, and something like laughter echoed back, forcing me once more into the lean-cabin's shelter.

In short time, the fever stayed Mama and Ivy swimmy and bed-bound. Their chests rattled with thick rales. We learned later people from all over died from that same sickness. It was Jack in the Dark wandering into camps in his long black coat. Hanging around the outskirts of our clearings with his worn-out words and his worn-out boots, knocking on doors with a face like a mask.

"Me and Ivy know time differently now," Ma whispered one late afternoon, when she'd woken confused as to what part of the day we were in. Ivy was asleep, a cool cloth I'd soaked in snow on her forehead. Bruno wouldn't leave Mama's side. He brought his favorite toys over to her bed and set them around her. Fear stayed in my gut like some living thing that only slept a few hours a night before stretching out its sore hind legs. Turning and turning inside my chest.

"Read me something, Pearly."

I picked up an old copy of *Western Story.*

"Maybe something in the Bible there."

"How about Krazy Kat? I got a whole scrapbook of strips."

"Bible, Pearly. Please."

I didn't particularly like reading from the Bible. Nothing much happened a lot of the time except begat, begat, begat, and I wasn't half-good with its wordings. Still, I opened it to a place Mama had dog-eared. I read, "Your hands shipped me—"

"Shaped me."

"Shaped me and made me. Will you now turn and destroy me? Remember that you molded me like clay. Will you now turn me to dust again?" I hesitated.

"Go on," Mama wheezed.

I read, "Did you not pour me out like milk and cu, cu, cuddle?"

"Curdle."

"Curdle me like cheese, clothe me with skin and flesh and ka-nt, ka-nit—"

"What do I do most nights?"

"Knit. Oh, yeah, knit me together with bones and . . ." I sighed and tossed the Bible aside. "I don't know that word neither."

"Sinews?"

This gave me pause. "Cheese, Ma? I thought we were made from a shin bone and some ditch dirt."

She laughed a little. "Rib bone, Pearly Everlasting. Lordy, you are a character." The late day pinked up then and she stopped talking and turned to watch it relume the trees' black bones. Under the blankets, done up to her chin, she seemed both very old and very young. Ivy, with those haunting eyes, seemed halfway to elsewhere. "And the goat shall bear upon him all their iniquities unto a land not inhabited: and he shall let go the goat in the wilderness . . . And he that let go the goat for the scapegoat shall wash his clothes, and bathe his flesh in water, and afterward come into the camp," Mama said, almost to herself.

Not so much later, their breaths untied their strings. One and then the other.

Mama and Ivy died and Papa couldn't stand their vacant chairs. I stood in the lean-cabin, waiting for someone to take the clay of me and shape it into someone who knew what to do and how to be. Around me all our little objects shattered with meaning: Mama's mending basket, her knitting, and most of all her absence. Ivy's magazine photos pasted up around our bed, the dog-eared Sears catalogue she refused to give up to the outhouse—the T-strap shoes, the dress with the zipper up the side she'd wanted for Christmas. I could no longer see the edges to things. So, I sat by the stove and poked the sulky fire awake and slept in Bruno's spicy fur and dreamt of nothing until Ansell came and woke us.

He'd come to say we couldn't bury them on Greenlaw Mountain, where all the women in my family rested. "There's no way to get them horses up, Pearly. Your father's been looking, along with some swampers and teamsters. The ground's iron and the switchback's unpassable. It's one hellish winter." Ansell sighed. I knew what happened to a body in winter when the ground refused to split apart and take you in: you were wrapped in a sheet and tucked up high until the ground changed its mind. I couldn't bear the thought of them out there like that.

73

"They can't sleep there, Ansell. Not like that."

"I know, Pearly, but what can we do? Jesus."

He stayed with me and Bruno until supper. The cord muscles in my neck hurt from trying not to cry. I fell asleep again in Mama's rocking chair and woke to angry voices. Bruno whined at the door, wanting out, but it was near dark. "No, Brunnie. Stay inside." The voices rose again. I listened through a knot in the door.

"By Jesus, Swicker! Cook's family's gonna get the best burial we can give 'em out here in these damn woods!" one man said. "We're taking time to do this right."

Swicker's voice was low, warning.

"It's one day to bury Cook's family proper!" someone who sounded like Ansell shouted.

Swicker said something else. All at once, another collective wave of anger erupted that followed the men over to their bunkhouse. Soon after, Ansell brought me some beans and brown bread. He stood at the door, kicking snow off his boots.

"Close the door before the night gets in," I said.

He closed it and handed Bruno a cookie. "How ya doin', Pearly?"

"What's going on out there, Ansell? Why's everyone so mad?"

Now, Ansell was only a few years older than me, but I thought at the time he was a full-grown adult, someone who could fix things. He cracked his knuckles and stared at his boots. Bruno, pushing up against his leg, gleaning for more cookies, bumped Mama's rocking chair. Ansell jumped across

74

the room and stopped it mid-rock. An empty chair rocking brought bad luck. He sat down on the deacon's bench.

"Pearly, Edon ought to tell you, but the men are going to bury your family tomorrow. Swicker's threatening to fire the works of us and the men are threatening to put something sharp through Swicker's jeezless skull. Ground's locked with frost, so we're gonna burn it until we break through the frost wall, and then we'll hack out the rest with picks, and—" He suddenly looked scared. "Maybe I shouldn't be telling you this part."

"Naw, go on," I said.

"Well, hopefully, we'll be able to do a proper burial tomorrow or the day next." He rubbed at Bruno's snout. "They're gonna do the ground out behind the hovel. Best view facing Greenlaw."

We stayed quiet together for some minutes. I heard the men moving outside—a hard clang of shovels and picks biting into the snow crust and then the ground below. It sounded like the bone horse carrying Jack in the Dark into camp. "Hell, Ansell," I said, not trusting myself not to cry. "Hell."

"I gotta get back, Pearly. I told your father I'd finish up, so he can see to setting the fires. He'll be in when he can." He gave me a one-armed hug and then, shyly, wiped my face dry. My heat against his coolness. It was the first time he'd touched me.

The men, good to their word, kept those fires burning all night and all the next day. They brought out fiddles and played hymns and somber ballads. Their faces hollowed as those all-night flames shifted and spumed. Me and Bruno sat nearby with our dynamite boxes, in case they needed more fuel. Occasionally, Bruno got up to scratch at the warming ground like a dog might—the fire's woody breath confusing scents. Sometimes, he moved to the edges of light and then, for a moment, disappeared into a world his own color. I watched them fires and clumsily prayed my bad feelings away. And I took some consolation that Ivy and Mama had loved those men and those men had loved them.

I didn't want to sleep in me and Ivy's bough bed that night. It felt too big—marking where my body ended and hers was gone. All I could do was curl around her missing. Bruno slept under my baby quilt in my parents' bed. I curled up beside him and dampened his fur, letting it all give away.

In the early morning dark, half the men had not yet gone to bed. The burning went on. Once, Thankful Robinson stood where Bruno and I watched, because the men said I couldn't help. He stood beside us for a spell, patted our shoulders, and said, "What a sad, sad day for you poor little beggers."

By late afternoon, the men had dug deep enough to lay some cut-down barrels. They filled those with wood and the blacksmith nursed the embers and flames with his wolf-jaw tongs. When the ground grew gummy, they dug some more. But no sooner had they begun when they hit chunks of granite. The biggest near the size of Bruno. They trenched around it, then hauled over some chains and cant dogs and an armful of blocks. Ansell chocked it with wood blocks each time the others wrenched and hollered at him. And then two of our biggest Clydes worried it onto a stone-drag and hauled it away like a rotten molar.

The next day, as the graves were being finished, one man after another—hat in hand—showed me and Papa an injury Mama had healed. "I bet the whole damn world she's already helping someone somewhere else," Jimmy Split-the-Wind said. "And Ivy, helping as she always did too."

I can't remember who laid them down in the ground or said some half-remembered prayer or whittled their final marker or what Miles said when he stepped over to where me and Bruno sat. I can't remember when those rooms in my heart closed up.

IN LOVE AND FAMILY:
EULA MAGALIE HAZEN & IVY HAZEN.

I do remember the wolf moon came out that night, bright as jar glass. And in all that time, I never saw Swicker. Not once.

when it thundered but did not rain

Mama used to say bad things came in threes, and the winter we lost her and Ivy, it proved itself true. A week after me and Bruno turned sixteen, we woke to a confused wind—something that passed for midday warmth—that coaxed mist off the shoveled banks beyond our doors and froze the black bogs again before sunset. Over those fateful days, weather-dumbed chickadees flickered down for crusts of bread, softened in the gin-clear puddles of our melting or seizing prints.

Swicker was bulling the men to get the logs skidded in the yards before the snow grew too soft to support the heavy sleds. In the coming weeks, he'd start sending men home, calling back only the most cat-footed to work the river drive—those in the business of danger. One day, when Ansell was fighting a chest cold that reminded us of Mama's and Ivy's graves out beyond the horse hovel, Papa snowshoed out to the felling grounds. The men, too far out now to come back at noon, were dinnering out. Most had packed breakfast leftovers, but the teamsters had left too early to fill up their cotton pokes proper. Pa packed up the dinner sleigh's long box with roast pork and gravy, pies, beans, and biscuits. He left long before dinner so he'd have time to get a fire going and sit a spell with the men and listen to their grievances before heading back to camp to see to the afternoon baking. It also gave the whisky jacks and gorby birds time to pick the men's plates clean.

With the temperature flip-flopping, Papa took the Slapfoot east, where the land hogbacked and, in places, grew steep. As he duck-walked up the ridge, dragging his sleigh behind him, a teamster with a full sleigh-load started down. The sandpipers were working fast that day: heating up sand or scattering snow over the hill, depending on the weather's mood. The road had hardened up again since morning—slick now where it doglegged at the bottom. A teamster, impatient to keep going, started down before the sandpipers could treat the snow. The horses galloped like fury to keep ahead of the bobs, slewing over the slick road. Papa said later he could hear the pins and chains, full of frost, clinking and ringing out as the sled picked up speed.

The teamster had been around horses his whole life, but was new to the woods and Swicker's way of running things. Fear got into him as the horses came up on the dogleg and instinctively he reined them in too fast, forgetting to give them their heads. Just like that, the front bobs jumped one way, the back bobs the other. The hind ends of the logs whistled through the air. The sleigh overtook the horses. The log chains snapped, loud as rifle shot. With a whoop, the teamster jumped free.

"*Ça vâ le djâble!*" yelled P'tit Celestin Crispou, one of the camp's arm-wrestling champions, who was standing beside Papa.

The teamster shot off into the air over and over until he struck a snowbank some hundred feet or more from the road. The men found the horses, their legs skinned up, trying to kick loose from the few bits of harness still hanging off them. The bobs were wrapped around a spruce, and the logs scattered like spillikins. One man crawled back with a fractured arm, another with a dislocated shoulder. In the confusion, a log that hadn't been limbed properly flew off the side of the hill and struck Papa in the leg.

One second. Two seconds. Three seconds. Papa said later it was one of the worst accidents he'd ever seen up close. Weeks later, he still suffered from his injuries. "I can't get them horses out of my head," he often said. Their hellish panic. Their terrible cries. And then that haunting silence that happens just after an accident, when even the crows watch and wait. "Just like when it thunders but doesn't rain," he said.

The accident was another example of how the conditions in Swicker's woods were too dangerous for men just scraping by. It made everyone restless. Tempers flared. With the Depression ongoing, there was less demand for newsprint. Companies, some said, were putting mills on short time and stopping other operations altogether. The stories were always from someone who knew someone in Ontario. For the most part, the men felt the stories held some truth. Unionists had started tramping into camp, rattling the men's cages, soap-boxing about fair wages for fair work. They were mainly good talkers from Upper Canada. Ontario boys.

"They can't do it without us, fellas."

"All we're doing out here is wasting our time and wearing out our clothes."

"I have not been doing woods work all these years to have some jeezless company take food out of my kids' mouths."

Some had heard unions were working in other places, but unlike the coal miners in Queens County or the gypsum workers in Albert County, lumber camps were seasonal. And everyone knew you couldn't run a union with roamers like woodsmen.

=

Two weeks on and Papa's leg still hadn't healed up. He half managed to get around the cookhouse with a crutch Ansell had fashioned from an ash branch, though he couldn't lift pans or skillets with his balance off. Ansell had to take over as cook, while Papa ordered him around from where he sat near the stove, his leg propped on a stool. The medical care he needed so much was some fifty miles away. Though the doctor came out from Black Sturgeon twice every winter to check on the men, little help was gained when he did show up.

The doctor chastised Papa for using Mama's healing. Mama's mutton tallow with camphor and sulphur tonic weren't going to do the job, he said. He left some pills that Papa never took. Still, we kept on. At night, I slathered mustard poultice on a piece of bread—the fuming stink burning my eyes—and laid that over Papa's cut. He near kicked up out of bed from the spark in it. Some of the men suggested Papa had been witched by someone in Black Sturgeon when he'd traveled there with the supply wagon last spring. Some thought something bad had crept up and slipped beneath our door when we weren't looking. But Papa didn't believe that bunch of foolishness and he wouldn't listen to the men talk on about burying needles in glass bottles or boiling nails in milk.

While he dozed one day, I read to him and Bruno from *Peter Pan*. I paused just after Peter's shadow had been quick-stitched back to his body. "Do you believe in Jack in the Dark, Papa?" I asked.

"No, Pearly, I don't. But I suppose he's there, all the same," he said.

into the space between two straight spruce

After several cooped-up days with Papa, Bruno woke early, nudged open our poorly hung door, headed down Slapfoot, and didn't come back. It was unlike him to stay away for long, but the dull days inside had filled him with fuzzy static.

"Go look for him, Pearly," Pa said from the rocking chair. "I'll be fine in the meantime."

"You sure?"

"Good to get out a spell."

I slipped on my winter rigging, gave Papa a pannikin of tea and a dog-eared *True Crime*, then ran over to the cookhouse to tell Ansell I'd be gone just a short while.

"You head back soon, okay?" Ansell said. "Weather's turning." A sharpening in my heart when I thought about how Ansell had touched my face after Mama and Ivy died. It made me want to stay right there. All day with him.

Instead, I crossed onto a twitching trail off Slapfoot—the one the swampers had recently iced over to help the sleighs run smooth. Clotted snow fell thick from tree boughs with hollow clumps. Jack pine. White pine. Scrub pine. Holding their black-greens against the weather's no color. I snowshoed until I found Bruno's trot-lines mazing off. It was like following a sleepwalker: straight then a veer then straight again. He wouldn't find much out here to eat and he'd had his fill of molasses cookies and jam. This was more of a browsing trip—just to see.

The wind picked up again. Woodsmen called the rare day when the wind held back its tongue a "poor man's overcoat." A welcomed absence. But today, all its singing stayed in the tops of the trees. More snow coming. Scanning the woods for a bear in a grog, I thought about a story Amedee Lavoie once told to Ansell about a crew up north who had to sleep in tents after their cabin roof buckled one winter. The men had made a fire for tea. When it built up, a man in black appeared and kicked the fire out. Three nights running this happened, before someone asked, "Why do you keep doing that?" The man said, "You're making the fire on top of me."

Ansell had winked and waited for me to say something smart. I'd smiled to make him feel good, but all I could think was who'd be there to say, *Your fire's burning over our unmarked graves*? I stopped to catch my breath and sing out to Bruno. Something moved off to my right. Long and slinked. Not walking, closer to slithering or swimming. It stitched between the trees. It grew legs and then not. I walked on, slow. My snowshoes biting into the snow crust. More movement. The next road over. The one that led to the skid yard.

I was up near the Crooked Deadwater when it changed. A shriek like something being torn apart. I looked up, thinking first a hawk or a barred owl with a catch in its thorny talons—shadow-shapes of hares or voles. But there was no finish to the noise, nothing that carried deeper into the woods. It was the wet-sheeted silence afterwards, backfilling the space the noise had ruptured, that bothered me most. Because whatever made a noise like that also had to take up shape. I found my mind possessing no source or equivalent for it.

"Are you my death?" I asked.

When it came again, it was in a new place. I ran faster over Bruno's messy tracks. The noise circled then re-sounded behind me. I was smacked down, winded, onto the snow. Everything crackled like feathers or dry bones.

"Are you my death?" I asked again, righting myself. "Show yourself, you son of a bitch!"

I ran towards the next twitching trail, past a granite boulder mantling its own shadow. Finally, the trees opened and scribed the sky. I was near Thieves Road, the one that led down to the Crooked Deadwater's yard. At first, I saw nothing but the snow, grayed where the sleighs and horses had beat it down. Then, two small eyes and tufty ears poked up over a deep ditch. Bruno.

I called, "Two-Eyes, are you sleeping?" I cooed, "Come on, Bruno." A gnawing hurt still thrummed through my chest. My face burned where the snow crust had raked my cheek. Bruno's eyes cut about. He shivered and I could hear his teeth chatter. I tugged at a forepaw. A slick matted his leg. I rubbed my mitten across it: blood. "Are you hurt, Brunnie?" I checked him for snare cuts, stone slices, or rough ice between his paw pads. Nothing. That's when I saw what he'd been looking at from inside the ditch.

Some ten yards away, a shape in the road. Like a pile of rags or someone's dropped laundry. Snow already building over it. Bruno walked over to it, nosed and lifted a paw to almost touch it, then reconsidered and went wide of it. The conclusion was already unspooling.

"Bruno!" I called, half to get his attention and half to get him away from whatever it was.

He rolled onto his rump, glancing from the shape to me. He clacked his lips. He leaned back into the pines' shade, but some of the weak light still caught on parts of him. I was still some feet away when I recognized the fedora, blown sideways in the snow. A dark tie pulled loose from vest and overcoat. Only one man dressed that way. Out here. Face down. Arms out as though he'd stumbled and fell. Swicker. The bull of the woods. The wind picked up, pushing the hat farther away, lifting up the greeny scent of cut wood and beneath it the heavy reek of iron. I stepped closer.

The snow, not yet melted around him, crackled with blood seep. At its edges, tracks where Bruno had tried to rouse him, as he liked to do with us when we were sleeping. I grew up believing accidents were commonplace and unavoidable. Injury a condition of the woods. Trees were always leaning back the wrong way. Splitting up the stump, instead of at the wedge, coming back to strike a man. But this was not that.

He rested rough on his side. I pushed him with my boot toe and he rolled front-wise. A cut like a claw gouge ran from the left edge of his mouth to the corner of his eye, so that, in death, he looked to be smiling. Clownish as he was not in life. His cigar lay blackly beside him where it had singed the snow. The snow around his body was thrashed, giving mute witness to his attempts to rise before dying alone out there in the road.

Clip clop, clip clop, where will his bone horse stop? I felt Jack in the Dark step out, the whole of himself bitten back to winter's bone. *Wish it away. Wish it away.* Crows in their crowns. I looked to Bruno. He looked back with his animal eyes and his animal thoughts. Unknowable.

The sun would settle soon and disappear. Orion. The Plough. The dog forever chasing the hare. I could not quiet my thoughts, as the snow fierced through the trees, kicking up devils like ghosts of all the dead that filled these woods. My body calmed. I knew what I had to do. Before I could reconsider, I rooted beneath the layers of wool around Swicker's neck. Just to see. And there it was: Mama's double-horn necklace. I took it off the dead man and put it in my pocket. It was owed to me, to my family.

The wind shifted. Branches clattered their ice sleeves. "He's in the trees. He's in the ground. He's in the wind. He's all around." I said it to test the air, to make Jack in the Dark show himself, but only the wind washed through the trees, only my own heart pounded in my ears. Though I knew, as all people of the woods know, we are never completely alone.

And then sleigh bells, trace chains, and hard hooves

wrapped in ice shoes came down the tote road—a last turn before dark. I kicked free of my snowshoes and ran up ahead to stop the sleigh before it reached where Swicker lay. They were hauling off the lower ridges now, logs to lie boomed on the Crooked Deadwater's thick ice until the spring breakup. The roads weren't meant for cross traffic and so the sleighs, loaded high, were free to go as fast as they wanted. I ran forty, fifty, sixty feet more up the road until the teamsters, their beards thick with ice, saw me from where they sat on their dry-arse hay bags, high up on the sawlogs. Papa's accident and those short-reined horses fast in my mind.

A boy, a tender, the one who snigged out the logs, was the first to see me. He stood tall over the log butts. He hooted down to the teamster. I knew enough to get out of the road, which was banked high with snow and wayside trees. I scrambled away from the possibility I'd just set in motion another accident.

The horses exhaled thunder, and trundled their legs, pushing against the sleigh—its weight high and precarious. Backpedaling. Sharp-shod. Luckily, this wasn't one of the teamsters who liked to push things: the tallest load, the heaviest horses, the fastest run. Bunny Lizotte had been working in camps for years. In short time, he had the sleigh stopped, the horses—Spark and Lion, a Belgian and a Clyde—calmed, though Lion kept chucking his head, straining back on his neck yoke.

The younger boy was off the logs and running towards

us. Nimble in his boots, his high wool socks ice-hardened. "Pearly Everlasting? That you in them alders?"

Thom. Tim. Daigle. Something like that. He reached out a wind-burnt hand to help me up and out of the snow and waited for me to catch my breath. "You all right?" He was from far away in the Outside. Somewhere with long blue mountains, he'd once said.

"What the hell—" We both turned to see Bunny, still holding tight to the reins, squinting down the road to where Swicker lay, darkening his edges and outlines.

"What happened?" the Daigle boy asked.

"—something knocked me down," I said, my voice not right.

The kid gave me a strange look then yanked me fast out of the hip-deep snow. I couldn't stop shaking and I didn't have the language to explain it.

Bunny set the reins down slow—his left hand missing two fingers at the second joint—and whispered through his iced-stiff beard something that stilled the fidgeting horses. He stopped when their ears stood straight. The spirit knocked low in them now from the cold and the long day almost done.

"Jesus. That Swicker?" Bunny asked.

The Daigle boy looked harder at the body. "Your bear do them cuts?"

I stopped studying the battered edges of the sleigh. I looked down at my worn boots, rubbed pale from my snow-shoe bindings. Things were left to hang.

"He's got blood on them paws."

I slapped my thigh to bring Bruno closer. I could hear the two men talking. No one touched Swicker. The horses stomped their feet, snorted, and flung their heads back as they tried to rear away from the souring air. Another swell of dark feeling came rising in my chest.

"Jesus," the Daigle kid said. "Big tracks and one hellish mess." He squinted at Bruno, sizing him up as a killer. Bruno sat in the snow, biting at his back paw as he did when he was worried. "Hell, that boy's no more'n hundred pounds well-larded. No way he did all that. He's chickenshit, besides. Pearly's more wild bear than him."

"Jesus," Bunny said, rubbing at his frayed toque, thinking. "Mauled maybe? Cat?"

The Daigle boy stepped off the road and dry-heaved into a bank. Bent low, he cupped a handful of snow to rinse his mouth. He scraped his frozen scarf across his quivering face. He crouched for a minute more, back to Swicker, resting his forehead on his knees. Bunny said something, something that sounded, though I couldn't catch the words, kind. He hauled the boy upright, the bones in his knees cracking. He said something else and the boy nodded and moved back towards the sleigh. He ran his hand along the side of one of the twitching horses as he passed. Bunny stepped in front of Swicker, blocking my view.

It had started to freeze rain, which lifted the smell of horse and blood higher into the air. I stepped back a bit more from the men and from Swicker. *He died of bad luck.* And still I hated him. I closed my eyes. My heart shunted *wish, wish, wish, wish.* Mama's gold necklace burned inside my pocket.

"Love!" Bunny said, jolting me back to the issue at hand. "Love, I don't know what in Jesus's name went on here, but we've got to get that body back to camp. I don't suppose the pair of yous can make it back the way you came, can you?" His careful eyes stayed on me.

It was a stupid question. I knew every road through these parts, and he knew it too.

"Walk on, now," he said, waving his hand to get us going. "Git on home. That father of yours needs to know what's happening. You tell him straight away. Tell him Bunny'll be in soon's he can."

I snapped my snowshoes back on, whistled for Bruno, and we turned, without another word, back into the woods.

"And don't be telling no one else. You hear me?"

I nodded then slipped back into the trees, Bruno keeping so close his blunt forehead bumped at my knee. I didn't see the Daigle boy bring down a piece of sailcloth to wrap Swicker in. I didn't see Bunny crouch to compare the bloody footwork to his own burly hand. Nor did I see the men lift the body into the space between two straight spruce sawlogs Swicker might have been ordering the two men to stack faster that very morning. And I didn't hear the sleigh bells start again as the men continued out to the Crooked Deadwater to drop their load, before heading up the go-back towards camp, keeping company with a dead man much longer than either would care to. And I didn't see Bunny turn to study me and Bruno as we disappeared into the woods, half-lit like something filamentary. And I didn't hear what they said and what they thought and what they didn't dare say.

I did not see then how the moment would stay with each of us, in different ways, and change how we saw the world. There was a before and then there was an after. This middling space? On the side of a tote road? Overgrown in years to come, after the camps disappeared and the horses disappeared and we became something remembered through fallen-in camps, gutted sleighs, gouged tree trunks, stories, and songs: a girl, a black bear, and a dead man. And a shadow that moved like grease fire through the woods and left no trace in its wake.

a wind that collected souvenirs

I fitted my feet into Bruno's tracks, and we ran as the snow top-deviled, tilting and slackening and slewing until it blew itself apart. Our breath smoked and vanished, smoked and vanished. A stitch toothed my side and still we ran maze-wise into the alders and scrub.

Back in camp, I left Bruno in the lean-cabin and went over to the cookhouse. A drift of snow skittered the floor ahead of me. Papa sat at the edge of the stove's heat. A pannikin of tea, speckled like a crow's egg, between his hands. Ansell was there too, stirring a cauldron-sized pot of beans. I could see something had been under discussion.

"Oh, Pearly. Thought you was stepmother's breath spooking in." Ansell winked before turning back to cutting knobs of salt pork. He stirred them into the pot then replaced the dented lid, muting the beans' hollow bubbling. "That cold'll bite your face off today, eh?"

I was tied around tight.

"Bruno's back from gallivanting, eh?" Papa said.

Everything inside me cold.

"All right, love?" he asked, turning to look my way.

"There was some trouble up past Slapfoot."

"Where?"

"Out to the . . . um, the . . . Thieves Road."

Ansell raised an eyebrow at me but kept quiet, knocking bread from pans.

"Best be talking, Pearly," Pa said.

I stared some moments into the stove's fire, until its heat pushed me away.

I told them how it'd happened. In my thinking. And after I'd talked myself out, everyone stayed quiet. Only Bramble, a little three-legged dog Ansell had rescued from a snare last year, deep inside one of her running dreams, made herself heard. Her claws ticked the floor and her little yelps and whimpers broke the silence as both men considered my story. I worried they were disappointed in my version of the details.

Pa looked hard at his bandaged foot. His jaw flexing. "Anything else?"

He eyed me, waiting. And so, I told him about the noise that had circled and diminished, the quick shadow pieced out of the snow, the something that had sent Bruno into the ditch. And I showed him the cut on my cheek and the bruises on my knees where I'd fallen hard.

"Jesus, Edon," Ansell said, lighting his pipe. "What do you make of that?"

"Panther maybe came by him? Hard to say. The camp's

been a powder keg for weeks." Pa considered something for a bit. "You and Bruno shouldn't have been out there."

"We didn't do nothing!" My standing tears welled then slipped down my cheeks. I felt like a foolish baby in front of Ansell.

"It's not about that. Feelings are running high, too high, and there's no tellin' if someone else might get hurt," he snapped. "Now, like it or not, them fellas are gonna be coming back here with a story and a body. Swicker's body. And the pair of yous was out there. If something got Swicker, some of the men might feel a bit . . . There's no tellin' how they're going to take this and there's no way of knowin' what—"

"Who," Ansell corrected.

Papa nodded. "Who."

"Jack in the Dark," I whispered.

"Stop your foolishness, Pearly Everlasting."

Ansell handed me a tea—hovering his hand over mine for a moment too long. Before I could take a sip, someone banged at the cookhouse door. Ansell held up a finger. *Stay there.* It was the nephew, Miles.

"They in there?"

"Who?"

"You know damn well who. Bunny just brought back what's left of Uncle Heeley. Your goddamn bear sliced the man to shreds, it did!"

Ansell blocked the door with his boot. "You know as well as I do Bruno didn't do that."

More voices swarmed the yard.

"Someone's got to go out and fetch a Mountie!" someone said.

"It was that goddamn bear, I tell you!" Miles said to the men gathering now outside the door.

A tremor started up inside me I could not quell. Time was moving strangely. I was glad Pa had the only gun in camp. For a while more, the men shouted over each other. And then something heavy banged against the cookhouse wall.

When the men finally gathered into smaller groups, Pa took me over to the lean-cabin. He gave me some of Mama's calm-down tonic and let Bruno lick the spoon. My mind kept catching on bad things. I could feel Jack in the Dark, sung through with his traveling. We fell asleep while the air was still blue. And in my dreams, teamsters with their bells and calls and cutting sleds came for us from a great distance.

In the morning, Bruno had chewed the top off the calm-down tonic and drunk it empty. He'd gone back to his wintering box sometime in the early hours, dragging my favorite quilt with him. Before I could go out and check on him, Papa brought me in some breakfast. But I couldn't eat. He said things had settled down a little, though no one was trusting no one. He said he wanted me to take him out where it'd all happened.

"I don't want to go out that way ever again and neither does Bruno," I said, cocooning in my remaining blanket.

"Pearly, it's important. The men have been making up all sorts of stories. You know I'm a good tracker. I might be able to help sort things out."

It was true. Papa could tell from just a few tracks if a coyote was carrying pups. If it was young or old or blown up with worms. Soon as I got dressed, we left. Everyone was out at the felling grounds, though there were still small knots of those closest to nephew Miles in camp—bored and hardened men, and those inflicted with self-importance. Thankfully, their numbers were few. Papa said they were planning to send someone to the Outside to get the Mounties. They stopped talking when we walked by, but left us alone. On the way out, I stopped at Bruno's wintering box, dark and fuggy with bear breath. "I'm coming for my good blanket when I get back, Brunnie, you hear?" I said to his snoring shape.

We passed through the meander of twitching trails and over drifts, small hills, and sags. The camp smoke faded and soon we were alone. It took us near on an hour to get out there—Papa dragging his bad foot, his binding too loose at the ankle, his ash cane sinking deep in the unpacked snow. I felt to blame, though I knew he wouldn't see it that way. As we got closer to Thieves Road, I had the looming fear we'd find Swicker there and knew this to be the lingering effects of shock. We walked on until there was no question where Swicker fell. I was thankful the patches of snow, though pinky with blood, were no longer man-shaped. Papa flicked his jackknife open—the one he took when he worked summers as a guide—and pierced the blade through the bloodied snow. In other places, he near filleted it and studied these underneath layers balanced on the blade. Each gesture charged with meaning only he understood. I cut my eyes to the stain but then scanned the length of the trampled snow for signs of Jack in the Dark's cloven hooves, his split tail.

"What are you looking for, Papa?"

"Anything that might prove my theory."

"Which is what?"

He shrugged. "Cat, but maybe something two-legged with a grudge." He poked around some more in the snow then scented the air like Bruno might. A new wind was coming down from the boughs. "Feel that?"

I turned my face into the chattery flakes. The men called it the zigzag wind, but me and Ivy called it ZaZas. It was a warm wind that came up from the south. It scraped against everything like running a hand against the lay of an animal's fur. It queered things. Men were more apt to get injured or fight with one another. Teamsters grew impatient with spooked horses. And horses impatient with men. Papa said it was a sudden traveler, a wind that collected souvenirs as it swept across the world. Bruno always knew when it was coming, and I did too. It lasted only a few days and left nothing in its wake but our own sense of shame for unkindnesses done and words said that could not be put to right again.

"ZaZas," I said.

Papa nodded. "No wonder things are all upside down, eh? We're in the ZaZas again."

Standing there, in the ill-given wind, I tried to keep Swicker's ruinous face from my mind, but he was there all the same—his split grin, his lidless eyes. I felt the whipped-up woods watching. "Papa?" I said, my voice weak in my ears. "Papa."

He still had his eyes to where Swicker had fallen. "What is it, Pearly? You doing okay?"

The woods had started to swim a little, and everything was thinning inside me.

"You feeling faint?"

I shook my head, but my mouth filled with spit and I feared I might go under. I counted slowly under my breath, yan, tan, tether . . . When the blackness cleared, I came and stood by his shoulder to be, for a moment, inside his calm.

He eased back on his haunches and patted my leg. "What do you want to do? You want to head back?"

"Yeah. I think so."

"Well, I'd sure like to look around here a bit more while this leg holds out." He squinted up at the sky. "Them flakes are starting to stick. Everything'll be buried soon. You okay to head back on your own or you want me to come with you?"

I felt myself brittle and then, as I'd been taught, I drew myself up. "I'm all right."

"Okay then," he said, eyes back to the trampled, blood-ied paths the men and me and Bruno had left and the softer ones the crows had chattered, and the other, smaller ones that went out and came back and some that went only one way. "Straight back, you hear? I'll see you in just a bit."

I stepped wide of the bloodstains.

"And, Pearly?"

"Yeah?"

"It'll be all right, love."

I pretended to believe him. I waved and walked back

through the trees. The snow, aslant and hard, was already beginning to fill up the woods. I walked on, stopping whenever I heard a branch snap or something wing the air. After a while, the sounds began to gnaw at me so much that I stopped up my ears so I would hear no more. Yan, tan, tether . . . I wished I'd stayed with Papa. I was hungry for fire and homesick for last year when the world was weak-seamed but whole.

As I came off Slapfoot, I had to stop fast for a sled running its horses hard—a big wooden box on its bed. Beside the teamster, the one who'd caused the accident that injured Papa, was Miles. With nowhere to hide, I stood my place against the bank, chin held high, and waited for what they had to say. I knew that Miles would run his mouth off with lies about Swicker, though his saying didn't make it so. But both men looked right through me as they passed. They must be going to the Outside to get the Mounties, I thought. So, Bruno's in the clear. And then I chose to think no more about Swicker, somewhere in camp, his galled meanness wrapped up now in sailcloth.

=

I kicked off my snowshoes and sang out my bear song as I came into camp. Nothing. I went over to Bruno's wintering box to get my blanket back. Sometimes, Bruno didn't want to move much, especially in the ZaZas. But when I came around the corner, I could see that his box was flipped over. My blanket still there. Hay tattered the yard. An empty pie plate glinted beside his box. I pulled the blanket away, thinking Bruno was hiding beneath it, but it was only another pile of straw. He wasn't anywhere. I went into the cookhouse, but Ansell wasn't back from taking the men their dinner.

I found Jimmy Split-the-Wind out at the hovel, salving up a cut on a Belgian's hind cannon bone. The throaty smell of liniment reeked the cold air. Blue Babby was Jimmy's favorite horse, and Jimmy was often overheard bragging about how well-knit Blue Babby was, how he was probably a dancer in another life, though he often struck me as a strange horse—his eyes filled with thorny ghosts.

"Seen Bruno?" I asked.

He shook his head and small icicles quivered in his beard. "Nope, but it's been some busy round here. That young feller working with me just left with Swicker's nephew to fetch the Mounties in Smoke River. So, I'm short-handed. And someone's put the medicine in the box all wrong." He grumbled at the small lockbox where the teamsters kept a short supply of sedative, in case they needed to calm a twitchy horse while seeing to injuries or tooth rasping. He glanced up to the sky, big flakes falling fast. "Gonna get ugly today."

"His wintering box's flipped over."

He stopped babying the horse and turned to look at me. "What d'you mean flipped over?"

Something hitched inside me. "Have you seen Bruno at all this morning?"

He glanced over where the drug box sat and then to Bruno's den and then his gaze went dark like a put-out flame.

"Jimmy, have you?"

"No. No. Just my young fella and that Miles over by the—"

"Wintering box?"

Blue Babby replied with withering neighs, and Jimmy gentled him, rubbing a hand over his heaving chest.

I saw again that wooden box on the back of the sled. A ringing in my head started up and wouldn't quit. "They took him. By god, Jimmy, they took Bruno!"

Jimmy Split-the-Wind wiped at the tip of his long, thin nose where a drip stayed all winter. "Now, we don't know what's happened, Pearly."

"When I find that Miles, I'll kill him," I said, my head clouding up fast with anger. "Which way were they heading? Smoke River, you said?"

Jimmy shook his head. "Now, you just hold your horses. You need to speak to that father of yours. You can't be running—"

But I was. Already. Running back to the lean-cabin, trying to shape a plan.

=

Something happens. We walk through a door, step into strange light, cross a path a different way, and we're no longer who we were before. I didn't have time to get Papa. I didn't have time to ask for help. I'd grown up in the woods and understood how to get through the worst of them. I knew the soft parts and the sharp parts. I wiped my eyes with the back of my wrist and tried to think, but air wouldn't settle right in my lungs. I only had rough ideas where Smoke River was.

Song-catcher and Ebony lived there. I'd follow Slapfoot out and hope for a waymark to lead me to the Outside.

In the lean-cabin, I scratched together some supplies. I rummaged around Mama's little wooden box first, the one she kept on the side table—a lace cloth laid diamond-wise across its scarred surface. I found one of Song-catcher's letters to Mama so I'd be sure to know what the words for Smoke River looked like. Knocking things over, I raced to get out before I lost Bruno for good and also, though I wouldn't have admitted to it then, to get away before Papa or Ansell got wind of my meager plan and stopped me. If the snow kept falling the way it was, the horses would get hampered in drifts and sinks soon and the men would be back early. Fit to be tied, I felt if I sat down for a minute, it'd be the end of me. I'd just fall down and never get back up.

I went through Ivy's cedar box next, though this started my heart paining. Inside were some shiny curtains she'd wanted Ma to make into a dress, an old pair of T-straps that were just about the most impractical footwear a girl could get. I thought back to how Ivy used to model her getups. And me holding the cracked shaving mirror for her. *Higher, Pearly. No, higher. The other way. Okay, yeah, yeah. Hold it right there.*

And then I went through the cedar clothes trunk where Mama kept my things: a flannel shirt—soft-worn and thin from Borax and washings with melted snow—wool socks, wool cap with a drop band, two pairs of Humphrey pants, some Stanfields from the church box one of the Go-Preachers brought with him last year, along with a few pairs of old

Buster Browns, their laces mouse-chewed, three housedresses useless for tramping through the woods, and some Butterick pattern clothes Mama had taken in or let out. I ran my finger over the scarlet crow's foot stitches she'd added along the collar and sleeves to brighten up an old shirt, make it special. Under all of this, tucked up in newspaper, was Song-catcher's gifts to me and Bruno: our little spoon with the silver bear and the bowl engraved with our names and birth date: Pearly Everlasting and Bruno False Spring 1918. For just a minute, I felt Mama beside me again.

Jimmy Split-the-Wind called my name from somewhere beyond the hovel. I had to move fast. At the bottom of the box, odd leavings: a few primers, five dark pennies, some ragged Bicycle cards, and a red bow tie Papa wore once when Song-catcher took his photo in the cookhouse. It belonged to Bruno after that. The sum of my worldly possessions.

Just as I was shoving things into my rucksack and attaching Bruno's wooden trough to the outside, Argyle Corcoran, the scaler, came out of the forepeak, a pencil behind his ear. He called out something to Jimmy. He was a fixed grin, a man born to make himself felt. Already, Argyle had taken it upon himself to push as camp boss. From our little pane window, I watched Jimmy gesturing around camp, shrugging, and I knew he was telling Argyle about me and Bruno. Argyle frowned and spat into the snow by Jimmy's boot then shrugged at something else he said. I tucked my little Green River knife into my boot.

When Jimmy led him over to Bruno's wintering box, I

crept out of our lean-cabin and climbed up the creaky ladder, up and up, into our tree fort. Argyle came back around the cookhouse and knocked on our door and then went in. His heavy boots echoed over the floor, muddying up the place in a way Mama would not have liked. He came back out and squinted around camp. For a moment, his ox eyes went to the big hemlock and then to the ladder that led up to the fort. I crouched down but could still see through a knot Bruno had chewed into a Judas hole last fall. Argyle and Jimmy peered up at the fort for a bit and Argyle made to walk over to the ladder. I imagined myself down in the King's Tree. Hidden good. I said to myself, *If Argyle climbs up and stops me leaving, I'll put my Green River knife straight through his eye.* My heart beat into the roofs of my clenched teeth. He stepped on the first rung. *Straight through the eye.* I was squeamish at the thought of doing it right quick if it needed done.

A thump of snow and heavy boots. Argyle back on the ground. My hands unfisted. I peeked into the yard just as the two voices charged into the ZaZas—one sounding bored, the other concerned.

"Forget it," he said, whipping around to squint one last time at our tree fort. "Deal with it later. We've got enough going on."

And then it was Jimmy Split-the-Wind's turn to spit near Argyle's boot. "You know more than you're lettin' on, Argyle. I'm off to find Edon to sort this mess out. And you won't be stopping me."

When I was sure they were gone—Jimmy to find Papa

and Argyle to the forepeak—I shinned down the tree and back into the lean-cabin one last time. I stood a minute more in the middle of our little room, still uncertain, my heart skeltering in my chest. I fingered Mama's necklace. *Get on with it, Pearly.* My body moved forward, and it was like something was singing in my head, pushing me on before I could change my mind. One last time, I glanced at the space where my boots had been in the lineup near the door. Mama's. Papa's. Ivy's. And that empty space looked like a gaping hole from a yanked-out tooth. So much so that I pushed the others together to close it in.

I made my bed. I left a note. *Bruno. Miles. A few days. Sorry Papa. Sorry Ansell.* And then, like a common sneak thief, I stepped out into that hurry of snow, said a brief goodbye to Mama's and Ivy's graves, promising to be back soon. The little lean-cabin grew smaller and smaller behind me, like it was already forgetting me.

wind wolves, made of loose snow

I'd been walking against the ZaZa winds and snow some time before a sled came up behind me. Thinking it was sent to take me home, I scrabbled over a snowbank and hid behind a tree.

It stopped up short from where I crouched. "What in Jesus hell are you doing out here?" a man called. "Get on out here now!"

I bum-slid back down the drift and onto the road.

"And just who do you belong to now?" I could tell he was ill-used to talking to teenage girls.

"I'm heading to the Outside, to Smoke River."

He stared hard at me. "And why's that now?"

"You going that way?"

"Well, I'm heading thereabouts, despite these zigzags messing with us." The horses stamped and chucked their heads, impatient to get on.

"I'll keep walking," I said, picking up my rucksack.

"You never answered my question."

"What question?"

"I don't see a lot of young fellers out this way, quitting work in snowstorms." He squinted up at the thick flakes. "Someone's got to own you."

"I'm looking for my bear."

The man sat thinking. "You one of Swicker's?"

You'd think it'd take a month of Sundays to get news through those woods, but it didn't.

"I don't belong to Swicker."

"Bad thing that." He looked at me like something needing solving, then waggled a finger. "Hell, you're Edon's girl, ain'tcha?" he said, slapping his hat on his lap. "I seen you when you was just a wee thing, ol' angry fox you were, with that good-looking bear, eh? And I'm guessing Edon don't know you're out here."

I looked down at the torn eye of a buttonhole on my coat. *Don't send me back. Don't send me back.*

He sighed. "Well, you're near as far one way as you are the other. Suppose I'll get a strip tore off me, for doing something this stupid."

His name, he said, was Eight-Day Sam. He gave me a hand as I climbed up on the sleigh. "I'm going almost to Smoke River, to the Junction, but I won't be going in, 'cause I'm running out of day. You hear?"

I nodded. My stomach tight, knowing I was getting closer to Bruno.

"These two here are Starry and Bite," he said as the horses started up again.

"Bite?"

"Yep, she's some good at twitching, but stand close enough when she's in a mood and you'll know it. Near bit the ear off a feller when we were breaking her in. None of the other boys favor her much." He shrugged. "Guess I like nasty ladies, eh?" He stayed quiet a bit before asking, "Your father know you're out here being crazy?"

"Swicker's nephew took Bruno. I aim to get him back."

"That'd be the bear in question, no?"

"Yeah."

"Far's I know, bears don't travel easy on sleighs."

"He drugged him. And he's heading to Smoke River to fetch the Mounties for Swicker and I think do something bad to Bruno."

"Bruno have something to do with that? Swicker, I mean."

"Bruno's got nothing to do with that son of a bitch."

"Okay. Okay." He whistled low, thinking. "There was some guy flitting around last fall. Go-Preacher or some such god-bent fool. I gave him a ride to 15, west of you, and he was telling me about a fella who traded animals. Hell, he was even joking like about Bruno. Said he was out near Smoke River. Bought bears and raccoons and some such to sell stateside. Roadside attractions, he called 'em. Puts them in cages and makes people pay to have a boo at the poor little buggers."

My faith in people unlatched a little more. I could not imagine any animal, let alone Bruno, being used for entertainment, brought down to its lowest form. Mama always reminded me that Bruno and I would not live out all our years together. *Someday, you'll get to the bottom of that bear, Pearly. At some point, you'll have to go on without him.* But now was not that time. I clenched my jaw, feeling my teeth and skull bones grow sharper with my anger. "If he touches one hair on Bruno," I said, "I intend to kill him."

"Whoa, Al Capone!" he said, glancing down at me. "Hey, now. Things move slow around here in the freeze-up. You know that. You got time."

"Who's Al Capone?"

"Someone who shouldn't be tangling with the likes of you," he said, and then said no more.

At the Junction, the surprising emptiness of potato fields opened in all directions, where wind wolves, made of loose snow, ran. Nothing began there and nothing ended.

"I'm going on to the right," he said, motioning with his chin to a flat nothing that way. "For some garage stuff and then I'm heading straight back in." He gazed at the snow-filled horizon for a bit, thinking. "You sure you want to be doing this?"

I nodded.

"Wish you'd reconsider." He waited, but I didn't change my mind. "Okay, you need to get going to the left. That'll lead you Outside. Smoke River Road." I squinted in the direction he'd pointed. There was no tree or sign of life as far as I could see.

"I need to get to this house," I said, handing him Song-catcher's envelope.

Eight-Day Sam glanced at it then shrugged. "Can't help you there, kid. Words are not my strong suit. But you start walking thataway and you'll soon hit some houses."

He handed me my rucksack and Bruno's little wooden trough. All my joints ice-ached. "You be careful now," he said. "Hate to leave you out here. Can't imagine—anyway—I'll send word on to Edon, though I suspect he'll be lookin' to skin me alive. And I guess I'll see you in the funny papers." He paused to say something more but instead fixed his hat over his ears and nodded goodbye.

I watched the horses turn down the gray road. Straight and dark, with no indication that anything was waiting farther along to meet them. I watched until they became a dark spot on the pale horizon. With their leaving, a part of me emptied too. I was in the Outside. Standing, very much alone, in a wide field with only a dark slush trail to lead me to Bruno, I felt if I started down that road, home would get vaguer and vaguer with each step. I started walking in the direction Eight-Day Sam had shown me. Eventually, I found some streets. Smoke River was all spruced-up houses with front windows like eyes. Because I didn't know how to find Song-catcher's place from what was written on Mama's envelope, I stopped at a house on an empty street caged beneath bare elms. A boy of about twelve was shoveling snow from a driveway. The shovel was red and had a dinged-up, broken blade.

"You know where Song-catcher lives?" I asked.

He wiped a streak of snot from his nose onto his mitt. "I don't know nobody," he said matter-of-factly, "but you can ask my grammy. She knows everyone." He pointed to the house at the end of the driveway he was clearing. "She's inside."

I knocked a few times, until an older woman peeped

through the window. She looked like how I imagined a fairy godmother might look. She opened the door, releasing heat and air that smelled like soup.

"Does Song-catcher live near here?" I asked, handing her Mama's envelope with the address on the front.

"Who now, love?" she asked, as though there was a great deal of sharp air between us.

"Song-catcher. I can't remember her real name."

"'Fraid I don't know her. She related to that Minny Sears? She stole my bean casserole recipe some years ago and now—" She glanced down at the envelope then peered over my shoulder. "Clayton, you're supposed to be shoveling the snow, not fighting it."

I turned to see the boy whacking his shovel head down in a snowbank like he was trying to beat a snake to death. It was a dull part of daytime—late afternoon—so I understood a bit how the boy felt. After a moment, satisfied with his killing work, he got back, half-heartedly, to the shoveling again.

The lady stepped out onto the porch, careful not to catch her slippers on the salt bucket. She put on a pair of glasses that hung from her neck by a chain. "Camp 33? Where in the blazes—"

"The other address," I said, pointing to the left corner of the envelope. "Ebony lives there too."

"That rough-tongued one? That's who you're looking for? The one with the dirty dog mouth and her quiet friend?"

I nodded. She took me by my elbow and walked me to the edge of the porch and pointed down the street to a house the color of butter. "That one now, the yellow one way, way down there at the other end of town. Pretty dark over there right now. You want to stay here until they get back? Right through your bones, this weather."

"It's okay," I said. "If I get too cold, I'll come back."

"I'll be here," she said, "listening to my shows."

I walked back down the drive, past Clayton, who was stabbing the snowbank now with a huge icicle like a glass harpoon. Swicker crossed my thoughts and then he went away. I followed the icy road almost to its end and then sat down on Ebony's concrete steps to wait, though Mama would've said that's the best way to wind up with a stone in your kidney. I could not get the cold out of me. I crouched down for shelter and tried not to feel angry about everything that had happened and was still apt to happen. I pulled a near-frozen bacon sandwich I'd stole from the cookhouse out of my shirt. I'd kept it inside my Stanfields, close to my chest, to keep it chewable. I was so tired. Tired enough I kept biting the inside of my cheek as I ate. The bright pain of it made me angrier at my own stupid mouth and the mean-tasting grease.

By the time I'd finished the sandwich, it was growing dark—nearing on four thirty, I figured. So cold it hurt to breathe. I walked the road a bit, just to stay warm, though the snow wolves still grouped and skittered around me and sometimes stung my face. I waved at all the people watching me from their bright front windows as I passed because I didn't want any of them to see how angry and sad I felt inside. A few waved back. As I was punching the cold from my thighs, coughing it from my lungs, thinking about going back to the lady's house for some soup, a pitched whir climbed and fell. I peered over the high-set snowbanks but could see nothing in any direction. And then, I saw it: a car driving slowly backwards towards me. It stopped up short of where I stood.

"Pearly? That you?"

I stepped over to the driver's window. Ebony waved. "Got some crick in my neck driving like this, I tell ya!" She turned to Song-catcher. "It's Pearly Everlasting, if you can believe it!"

Song-catcher leaned over. "Pearly, love, what in all things holy are you doing in the Outside?"

Ebony stretched her neck side to side. "Yeah, your mother know where the hell you are?"

I started to explain, but she waved me away. "Tell us in the car. It won't be warmer . . . but it'll be drier . . ."

The car was an old McLaughlin-Buick. A gangster's car, Ebony explained, a ridiculous car with mouse-eaten Meritas door covers instead of metal. It felt like we were inside a creature's false skin. Something wanting for wings.

"—and on top of that, the transmission's shot. Been out to see that useless mechanic, Everette what's-his-name, three times this week. Three times! Driving this thing backwards—and this one"—she nodded towards Song-catcher—"is as useful as a drunk goose when it comes to mechanical situations." In the sourceless winter light, she squinted across the length of the car, past me, out the small ice-plated window to make sure we had cleared a pothole. She told me how the drive out to the mechanic's should have taken thirty minutes but had, driving backwards in blowing snow, taken near an hour. "A five-cigarette drive," she called it. All the while, I sat— jangly, on edge—watching the darkening town pass backwards. The car too loud for explanations from me. Besides, I worried they'd send me home.

=

In no time at all, we drove past the old lady's house, its windows lit up, Clayton's shovel abandoned in the drive, and soon after we were back at the yellow house. "Thank the cheese!" Ebony said. "We made it!" She sailed the car into her dooryard, heavily banked on each side with snow.

Many mothers ago, the house had belonged to Ebony's great-great-grandmother and had, Ebony explained, been handed down to firstborn girls ever since. "That, of course, will end with me," she said, stomping snow off her boots at the door. "But it was a very good tradition while it lasted." It was a house of half-rolled shades and breakfast plates still on the table at suppertime. It was a house that looked preoccupied with thoughts other than being a house. Books strewn everywhere. One wall in the living room dedicated to scraps of paper and magazine tear-outs. Everything stuck through with sewing pins.

"Ebony projects," Song-catcher said by way of explanation.

Ebony said she used to rent rooms, but then decided she didn't like anyone enough to justify the extra walking-around money. Now it was just her and Song-catcher and a stray cat or two who stayed as long as they cared to before moving on. I had a hard time focusing, what with my chafing thoughts and my eyes catching on all the things that filled those many rooms.

Ebony pulled a chain on the ceiling and the room lit up.

"Now," Song-catcher said, "let me make some tea and we'll figure you out."

Apple pie and tea by a little coal stove. I told them all that had occurred over that terrible winter. Mama and Ivy. The fevers and the burning ground. Papa staying in the cookhouse longer every day and the walleyed horses. I told them about Swicker and what he looked like when we came upon him and then I said no more.

Song-catcher said she didn't have words for what had happened with Mama and Ivy. She was truly sorry someone so kind was gone.

Ebony raised an eyebrow and side-eyed Song-catcher. "Men are always saying there's things out in them woods we know nothing about . . . all for a bunch of church pews, piano benches, and clothespins." She sighed. "But that doesn't explain why Edon sent you out here in a storm."

"Swicker's nephew and some of the men thought Bruno did it."

"And?" Song-catcher asked.

After a minute I said, "This morning, I went looking for Bruno and there he was, gone."

"And your father said, okay, daughter, go out into the jaws of winter and find yourself some bad men?" Ebony asked.

I said nothing and that nothing filled the room for a bit.

"Okay," Ebony said. "Okay." She pulled a road map from

an overstuffed drawer and traced a finger around Smoke River, looking for a name, a place that might fit. "Damn. I have no idea where to start looking," she said, her nose nearly touching the page as she studied roads and rivers. She sat up on her knees. "You know how we *could* find out?"

"Oh, Ebbie, no," Song-catcher said.

"Only way I see of finding this Bruno-stealing bastard." Song-catcher sighed.

"What's the way?" I asked.

"The blacksmith's place," they said together.

The blacksmith's was not so much an enterprise as a ramshackle woodshed that had been hauled out of the blacksmith's backyard and set down in someone else's. It had enough room for half a dozen men—if they thought to bring their own chairs—who drank something they called *rin gummy* out of old milk bottles. The sort of men, Ebony went on, who wasted an afternoon talking about nothing in serious tones, who shied from anything female. All it took to shut them up, she said smiling, was one woman to stop by and say *hello, boys*. It was enough to have them all staring at their shuffling feet. But Ebony was the only woman with an open invitation, she reassured me, half bragging. It was how she'd found her useless mechanic, Everette what's-his-name, and it would be how she'd find Bruno.

"But why would they talk to you?"

"Neighborly interest and 'cause I'll bring a bottle of some boughten stuff. That's why."

"And they'll know where Bruno is?"

"I suspect they'll know someone who knows someone who knows where Bruno is," Song-catcher said, fiddling with her teacup.

In a while, Ebony came back into the room dressed in a waistcoat, tweed knickerbockers, thick blue socks, and a navy bow tie. She looked like something sullen and swanlike all at once.

"Wow!" I said.

"*Exactement*," she said. She touched her sleek short hair then glanced back to my own. "Maybe we can do something about that head of yours when I get back."

"You look very elegant, Ebbie," Song-catcher said, straightening Ebony's bow tie.

"Well, we got a girl and a bear needing reuniting." Rummaging around a high cupboard, she pulled out a bottle of dark liquid. *Canadian Club.* Around its neck was a rabbit's foot on a chain. She tossed the foot onto the table and pocketed the bottle. With that, she flung open the back door. "Don't wait up for me! I'll be getting my woozy on!" All the little bits of paper and photos on the wall rushed up on their pins and rattled as she slammed the door behind her.

"She talks big," Song-catcher said when the house grew quiet again, "but it'll work. Oh, I wanted to show you something." She brought over a box I recognized. It held her wax cylinders. She hooked one onto her old Edison. And after a scratchy moment, Mama's unbodied voice ghosted into the room, singing as she once sang to us in the lean-cabin on storm-stayed days when we all just had to get along. It was

118

like coming home. *Danse, mon moine, danse! Tu n'entends pas la danse!* The wax cylinders made Mama's voice sound both sad and hopeful as she sang about the poor little monk.

As we listened to Mama, I toyed with the rabbit's foot. The metal band around its ankle read Good Luck. I rubbed its fur against my cheek, feeling its long, sharp nails.

"You keep it," Song-catcher said. "You need some luck."

I hooked it onto my overalls, though it wasn't luck I was after; it was the animal part. Bones and fur and claws.

===

After we'd listened to Mama sing a few times through, Song-catcher put away the Edison and led me over to the couch and weighted me down with some blankets. Half-asleep, I listened to the house creak with the winds carrying in off the open fields. Sometime much later, Ebony returned from her "wobbly pops with the boys." She kicked her boots off. They landed in a damp heap on the kitchen mat. She pulled the light chain, near blinding me with its bright viciousness.

"Men always want to keep things to themselves, Pearly Everlasting Hazen! Don't think they don't. They don't want to tell you where to get a deal on cordwood or a five-pound hammer. They don't want you to know the secrets of roofing a shed. They'd rather watch you do it wrong so they can tell you how they knew you were doing it wrong all along," she said, rolling her eyes at the thought of it. "And don't you be falling for it, Pearly."

I promised I wouldn't. "But what about Bruno?"

"So the boys say there's a guy who's been known to sell a bear or two stateside as a curiosity, a—"

"Roadside attraction."

"Bingo. Now these boys say there's a shed full of poor little buggers out behind Burnt Hill Road, across the lake, where no one lives."

I drew in a hopeful breath. "Are we going now?"

"Now hold your horses. The moon'll be full tomorrow night and I won't be so full of wobbly pops. Tomorrow Bruno'll be back." She gave me a messy kiss on the forehead and turned off the light. "Though damned if I know how, kid."

I listened to her bang and bump her way through the house until she found the bedroom and the house quieted again.

from a dead man to a storied man

The day after Bruno and Pearly went missing, three Mounties and a coroner closed in on Camp 33. Edon kept insisting he needed to get to the Outside, to bring Pearly home, but the Mounties wouldn't let anyone leave camp for any reason. From the beginning, they treated Swicker's death as suspicious, though the three Mounties were of two minds about this. Over the next few days, in a slow drizzle of rain, the men were questioned and re-questioned, causing them to shift under their clothes because most woodsmen had a passing familiarity with the law in the usual forms of drunk tanks and summer stints in county jails. In terms of alibis, teamsters spoke for swampers and limbers spoke for sandpipers.

"There's no goddamn way a swamper over in chance five knew what a teamster yarding in chance seven was doing all day!" Miles would hiss and spit from where he stood near a constable, accusing each man a worse liar than the last.

Tensions grew. The men worried about unpaid days as the

Mounties brought in another round of tired questions. They worried about the work not getting done and the lack of a foreman. Many were unhappy Bruno had been taken away and Pearly Everlasting was missing. The week's chaos affected how the men saw the woods as well. Some spoke, quietly, about something out there, creeping towards them when they were working. Something that might sit on a stump and be gone in a skewed way when they turned to peer after it. They took notice of how the horses spooked and scissored their ears, and how the wind picked up and set down noises in places they didn't belong.

The investigation took four days. The Mounties found a lone mitten, but no one took ownership of it. They came across some oval-shaped prints, like those from the butt of a rifle, but there was only one gun in camp and Edon showed them where his—an over-and-under Browning that didn't kick too much—had a chip knocked out of its stock so that it made a split-foot when tested in the snow. All the other prints had muddled into one.

The coroner—a chain-smoker with a bad mouth twitch—took his time inspecting Swicker's wounds. Ansell heard him say to a Mountie in a muskrat hat, "Them wounds are some strange. Could've been from some sharp tool, something long—"

"Well, no end to things like that round here," the Mountie interrupted, impatient to get back to the Outside, away from this ragtag of characters with their scars, missing fingers, and scarecrow faces.

The coroner coughed a long, phlegmy hack into the snow. A churchyard cough, the woodsmen called it. "All the same, damn things almost look like they were done by an animal. Long-clawed. Strong. Damnedest things."

"A bear? They had one around here."

"Have to be a big one."

"Naw, they say this one was a runt. A pet. Topped out at eighty and some change."

The men stood quiet for a few moments.

"Might do some damage, but kill a man this size? Doubtful."

"You gonna call it?"

The coroner lit a cigarette off the dog-end in his mouth. "I'm calling it inconclusive."

"Foul play?"

"Foul something but damned if I know what."

=

In this way, Swicker shape-shifted from a dead man to a storied man—the worst of the bull of the woods kept alive through rumors and suppositions. While the Mounties packed up and signed their reports, reasonably satisfied that none of the woodsmen were murderers, the company sent in a new camp boss. This could have gone either way. They could have sent in another bull of the woods to get the job done, but instead, wanting to deter any more uprisings, they sent in a soft-spoken man in his mid-fifties, who shook each man's hand after climbing down from the sleigh, saying, "I got a job to do, fellers, but I don't intend to let a rich man get richer off a poor man. I'm here to play fair and get everyone out in one piece come spring drive."

The next day was April Fool's Day. Twenty-one inches of snow fell, making the woods seven to eight feet deep in places. When they weren't clearing snow, the men were talking about Pearly and how a teenage girl might get through the woods at this time of year. A lot of what they were thinking, however, went unsaid.

A week later, spring budded misty green. Edon's leg was paining him less, and he was able to get up and about a bit more. Often now, he worked in the cookhouse peeling potatoes, greasing bread pans, and other kinds of sitting-work, all the while watching begrudgingly as Ansell deviled around his kitchen. Other days, Edon seemed elsewhere—turned inward, silent. He didn't sleep much. Ansell sometimes heard him in the lean-cabin, his crutch knocking on the uneven floorboards as he paced its small perimeter. He was alone over there for the first time and Ansell didn't think it was right: a sick man making himself sicker with worry.

"I'm going out to get them," Edon said one afternoon, as sleet pricked the windows like gravel.

"Where would you start?" Ansell asked.

"Smoke River, I think. Jimmy said she'd followed Miles out that way. Though that son of a bitch nephew's not saying much, one way or the other."

Ansell considered something for a moment. "You get back on your feet and I'll go."

"You'd do that?"

Ansell nodded.

"Well, I'm pretty near there now," Edon said, kicking his leg out a few times to prove it. "Hell, I'll drag myself around by my elbows tomorrow, if that'll get you out there looking for them."

back to their own quiet kingdoms

Just as Ebony promised: when the moon blued the next night, we drove backwards through Smoke River, past all the mailboxes with their slack overbites—the few cars on the late roads moving like catchlights through the trees. I lay across the back seat so Ebony could see what little she could out the back window. Sometimes, she drove with her head out her window, but then we tended to tail too much to the right.

We stopped when we met the edge of the lake. The animal shed, according to Ebony's boys, was on the other side, where people did not live. Under our feet, small gunshots where the lake had froze then warmed then froze, leaving pockets of ice weaker and full of air. Before we reached the shed, we could smell it: caged animal rank with piss and musk, fur and fear. The shed was a barely held-together thing made from crate-wood and stolen stop signs. We moved around it soft-footed so the animals inside wouldn't startle. I found an unchinked board and waved my flashlight beam into the deep of it. Every manner of wildness shivered in its poorly built cage. Red eyes.

Green eyes. White eyes. Half a dozen pairs of masked eyes and other creatures too—their faces patchy where they'd chafed against bars and chicken wire. Small animals shifting nervous on small feet.

None belonged alongside each other. Seeing them that way made me suspect the entire world, not just my own, had somehow been reordered, as though some unnamed god had shaken out the woods, upending all these bright and dark travelers. Leaving the world in a way we were not meant to know it. Bruno wasn't among any of them. I tried to gather the scattershot bits of strength left inside me, but the hidden turns of my thoughts said only one thing. *He's not here. He's not here. He's not here.*

"Just hold on, Pearly," Song-catcher whispered, "until we get inside."

On the lee side of the shed, Ebony whistled low. I came around with my light and she pointed at the door: padlocked with a chain going to rust. Song-catcher had thought to bring a cat's-paw bar, which Ebony hooked through a link. She twisted until it snapped the air with the blood smell of age. She slipped the broken chain off and threw it and the padlock into the alder bushes. And then we pried open the door.

Stacks of old tires, metal junk, stove oil, and dozens of animals. All skittery now, though little sound came from their ramshackle cages and crates as I walked down the length of them, shining my light into their flat eyes, but no, Bruno wasn't there. "He's not here."

"What?" Ebony snapped, her face close to mine. She

turned up her lantern's flame, so the mantle whooshed and brought flickery light closer to the cages. Each creature backed into the darkest corner and wished her away. "The Rin Gummys are never wrong about this stuff." She peered at the animals a few minutes more. "Be right back. Let these poor buggers go while I'm gone. They're likely to start a ruckus." She slipped out of the shed, to somewhere beyond where we stood—cold blue wind creeping over all of us.

I called out to Ebony a few times, but Song-catcher put her hand on my shoulder to still me. "Ebony's looking. If he's here, she'll find him."

We turned our attention to the others—beaver, otter, ermine, fox, and raccoon among them. I didn't want to be near any of their noising and hissing. I felt a sudden hate for them: the faces that were not Bruno. Still, we wrapped our coat sleeves thick around our hands. We carried each crate outside, and lifted the doors and splintered the frames, and let the spooked animals pass on into the woods or drift over the lake back to their own quiet kingdoms. And each of those who went pale in the winter months took on a bluish glow under the moon as it slinked away—some high-shouldered and proud, others low-bellied with the wrongs done to them. A new sort of sadness settled in me as I watched each disappear.

As I let the last ermine go, its eyes wet and passive, Ebony came back around the shed. "Think I found him," she whispered. "But it's not going to be easy."

"I don't care how hard it is," I said, because already everything else had come at a terrible cost.

The other shed was farther back in the woods. We walked in Ebony's tracks and then stopped at the door. "You ready?"

We nodded. She sighed. "I do not want to get ate or shot out here. We need to be careful."

Inside, Ebony set her lantern down on the floor so that it lit up two cages. In one, I could not see what make of animal it might be, but there was no doubt about the other, the one deepest in the corner.

"Bruno!" I ran up to his cage. He stood to meet me, but his eyes were those of a wild creature. "Bruno?" I said again. "It's me." He huffed hot, sour air into my face, spooked by both what he saw and what he didn't.

"What's wrong with him?" I stepped forward and then I could see, none of his mannerisms were familiar. "Brunnie?"

"Pearly, he's just wound up, he'll be fine," Ebony called over.

"No," I said. "There's something really wrong with him."

"Just leave him for a minute."

It was the first time Bruno was unknowable to me. It was as if he'd told me his secret, and I'd misunderstood it all these years. "This isn't Bruno!" I said.

"Of course it is. Just look at him."

As I waited for him to pick up my scent and come back to his senses, I shined my light down his body. On his chest was a cinnamon star. Not Bruno.

"This," I yelled over the caged noises, "is a *wild* bear!"

"Pearly, honey. You got to give him space, we got—"

"Oh, god, Ebbie. Are those wolves?" Song-catcher asked.

Ebony brought her lantern closer to the second cage. The creatures hid their faces, remembering some dark law against fire and light and humans. They bared their teeth and the flews of their lips snarled wide. "Close enough for our purposes. Damn," she sighed. "Coydogs and a wild bear."

"But where's Bruno?"

The shed was now a mess of noise and anger and loose fur and we needed to do something quick before we woke up anyone within twenty miles of that hellish place.

"Here, I think, here," Song-catcher called from the other side of the shed.

Bruno's cage was tucked behind those scraggly-pelted creatures. We couldn't get to him without standing close to the others.

"We got to move 'em out first," Song-catcher said.

Ebony and Song-catcher rummaged around in an old footlocker shoved under some rotten tarps and found army blankets and some sacking.

In another corner, stood up like bones, were several thick dowels. "Rake handles, Ebony!" I said.

"Bring 'em over!"

Me and Song-catcher threaded the handles through the first cage lengthwise and then draped some of the sacking over the top to blind the coyotes. "You ready?" she asked.

"As I'm going to be," I said, smiling off my fear.

We carried the cage like a sedan made for royalty across the slivery shed floor. All the while, the coyotes slavered and gouged. I could feel how much they wanted to break something in two. We brought them out into the snow-spitting air, their angry sounds following us. They'd managed to chew off some of the baling wire that kept their hatch shut, so it was easy for Song-catcher to pry the rest away with her rake handle. She opened the door and gave them a wide berth. They stepped out, low and considering. One slink-tailed and pissed there in the field and I felt I should look away from wildness brought so low. They side-eyed us once more before taking off together, crabwise, towards the woods.

"Pearly, you better let that bear go," Ebony said, hauling its cage with a rake handle into the light.

"Me? Why me?"

"You know bears."

"Hell, Ebony. I don't know wild bears!"

Song-catcher came up beside me. "I'll help."

The bear was bigger than Bruno, but still a yearling with fear-bright eyes. Its claws and gums bled free where it had chewed and dug at its cage walls. When we stepped close, it whirled, trying to pin all three of us in its sights at once. As we staggered it out of the shed, it could not keep its feet and this seemed to set it off further and near flip the cage. The haywire was twisted hard around the hatch and would not give. I pulled my Green River knife out and made to untangle the wire, but Song-catcher grabbed it from me.

"Let me," she said. Jinking forward and away from the cage, she stabbed at the wire like a buccaneer while the bear lunged. Finally, she loosened it enough that we could use the rake handle to jimmy it open. We worked on it a few minutes

131

more before the hatch gave and the bear sprang out. But instead of running into the woods like the coyotes, it turned, angry muscles ridged beneath its dull fur. It turned on me first, charging as I fell backwards.

Song-catcher banged her handle on the empty cage. "Git! Git! Git!" she said, giving me time to find my footing. Her handle caught on the cage and dropped into the snow. When she bent to pick it up, the thing reared up and came at her. Her long red scarf had come unwrapped and hung down to her waist on one side. The half-crazed bear grabbed on to that length and started yanking. Each time it pulled, the scarf cinched tighter around her neck. I could almost see the blood pulsing behind her eyes, her lungs going slack.

I took up my rake handle again, thinking it strange an animal we'd just saved from certain misery was now going to have its skull stoved in. "Let her go!" I brought the handle down on its snout. It felt like beating Bruno. I hit it again. Its face sparked with pain as it let go of the scarf.

Scarf strings hanging from its canines. It backed away until it could turn and then it bore off, directionless, towards the woods. I stood some minutes more out there in the blue-white field, rake handle raised, in case it had notions of coming back.

"You okay?" I asked Song-catcher, still kneeling in the snow.

She coughed then nodded.

"She was some werewolf ugly," I said, a giddiness fizzing up inside me I could not contain. "You wake up beside her, you got to gnaw your arm off to get free."

Song-catcher started laughing, which brought on another coughing fit.

"And hell," I went on. "Not even a how-de-do."

"Or nice scarf!" She hooted. "Guess she didn't want to put up much of a fight."

"You two coming to help out or what?" Ebony stood near the shed door, arms crossed tight against her chest. "I can't do everything around here myself."

I helped Song-catcher up and we walked back into the shed—the musk of wild bear still sour on the air.

With the others gone, we could see Bruno's cage better. By now he was blatting to take the roof down. He looked like he was wearing a slept-in suit. Unlike the other animals, his cage was made of metal. Soldered shut rather than chained. He huffed up against the back of it and then, catching my scent, ran to the front, whining and blinking. Bear eyes. Bruno eyes. He gnawed on the bars, forcing his snout out through the thin space between.

"Hello, Two-Eyes," I whispered into the black deep. "You're good now."

"There's no way to get him out like this. We have to move the whole thing," Song-catcher said.

"And then what?" Ebony asked. "We can't get a cage with a bear into a backwards-driving car."

"Let's get it down on the ground at least," Song-catcher suggested.

We shimmied the cage to the edge of the workbench. But as we moved it, Bruno also moved. When his weight shifted too far one way, the cage listed as though caught in a high wind and then tipped, crashing onto the ground and flipping twice. Bruno was in full tantrum now. As he uprighted himself, he bit at the bars, which had been at the bottom of the cage before. He whined and claw-hatched the raw floor.

"Stop with the racket, you little Christer," Ebony said.

"He's fetched up on something."

"Holy dying, he's angry!"

"What is it, Brunnie?" I spotlit him. The bottom of the cage also had a door knotted with baling wire. Not soldered. I held the light while Ebony and Song-catcher worked the wire loose with their frozen fingers and the cat's paw. It wouldn't give. I rummaged around the shed until I found some old pliers, and between the three of us we snapped it off and freed the latch. We had to flip the cage—over once, over twice—to get it open, which Bruno was not happy about. In his tantrum, his collar got snagged on the latch's sharp wiring. Ebony set down her lantern.

"He's hung up good on this wire. Why don't you two wait outside, in case he makes a beeline? I'll free him up."

"Shouldn't Pearly do it?"

"Yeah, but if he boots it out of here, we're going to need her to catch him."

We stepped a ways outside and waited for Bruno to come bawling out. While Ebony was fighting with the collar, Bruno managed to spin himself and the cage. This shot the lantern against the wall. The night's edges enflamed and then the rest of it hackled with fire. It happened that fast.

"Ebony!"

"Bruno!"

We grabbed the old sacking and army blankets and beat at the door. I saw Jack in the Dark hanging there in that dirty smoke—blady and fire-stung. If we hit the flames harder, if we yelled louder, everything would right itself again, I kept telling myself. More than once, Song-catcher had to pull me back from the flames. I couldn't remember wanting to be let in. And then the shed began to list and give way.

From around the corner, the fire and the keener dark beyond, Ebony staggered with Bruno stiff-legged at her side. Soot-coated and singed, they were like something newly resurrected out of those hot tongues of flame.

All of a piece, we lay quiet in the snow, listening to one another breathe.

"I'm about done in," Ebony said as she lit a cigarette. "There's not much left of ol' Ebbie no more."

When the shed collapsed whole, we drew ourselves up and started back over the frozen lake towards the car. Bruno at my side, the tips of his ears rough and warm.

It wasn't easy getting him in the car. Like me, he'd never been in one before, and was not open to the experience. I pulled him by his ruff and shoved at his fat bottom, but he shied and bawled and acted as though I was trying to bury him alive. I fell backwards a few times and finally, fed up with

135

everything, I did what I should have done in the first place: I opened a jar of jam Song-catcher had thought to bring, and put it on the far side of the seat. Shivering, we waited for Bruno to decide. He sniffed the air, stretching his tongue as far as he could towards the jar without getting into the car. Hunger won out in the end, and he climbed into the car and sat like a little lord on his big bottom, holding the jam jar in his sooty forepaws.

"If you're ready, your highness," Ebony said, "we'd best skedaddle."

Song-catcher handed me her red scarf. "A souvenir," she said, smiling.

"Right," Ebony said. "We're backing out of here in the dark with a bad luck bear in the back seat." She lit a cigarette and roared the engine. "Hold on, kids. We're in for one hell of a Sunday drive!"

The car's tires bucked and slewed and then spun free in the slush at the lake's edge. Ebony kept going. Driving backwards, we watched the final ruins of the shed burn just as the first world had limped to life from flint and forge. *One more broken place gone*, I thought. One more act of meanness and cowardice finished. Soon the shack became nothing but a thin glow behind the dark shapes of pines. Bruno stopped fretting. He found the bag of apples we'd brought and ate a few, sniffing and licking each one. I curled up on the seat with him, his breath heavy against my face. "We're almost home," I whispered. "Almost there."

=

All the next morning, Bruno wouldn't stop dogging me, gripping my ankles and soft-mouthing my hands when I tried to clean his sooty fur. "Gentle!" I had to say. "Be gentle, Bruno."

"So, how're we going to get you two back overhome?" Song-catcher asked. We were having another cup of tea, watching Bruno lie on his back and lick his wooden trough of pancakes clean. I'd already tried to take it away a few times, but he insisted on banging it around, snuffing it for jam stains.

"We're going to walk it," I said over the trough knocking against the wall.

"Walk it? It's still winter!" Ebony said.

"We can't drive in and we can't hitch a ride on a sleigh, so same difference." I shrugged because I'd already made up my mind. "We gotta walk it."

"You could stay until the roads open," Song-catcher offered, catching Ebony's eye. "If this guy gets some manners." In reply, Bruno knocked his trough across the room, where it clanged against a chair leg.

"We stay in the Outside and the Mounties'll be knocking sooner or later. And I ain't got nothing to say about Swicker. Besides, Bruno belongs back overhome." I petted his snout. "We'll take our chances, I guess." I didn't tell them how I feared Bruno was still to blame in the eyes of some. And I didn't tell them that I really needed to make things right with Papa and Ansell, who I missed more than I thought I should.

After breakfast, I packed up what little we had.

"What do you think about getting back home?" I asked

137

Bruno, drowsing in the stove's puckered heat. He opened one eye, caught ruby then amber in the fire's flame. He considered me briefly before his heavy lid slid back over his blurring eye. He breathed heavily with sleep once more, hoping to go unseen a while longer.

"Enjoy it while it lasts," I mumbled.

I shimmied out of my thin clothes and found a flannel shirt beneath Bruno's blankets. As I was pulling it on, Song-catcher came in with some extra socks.

She watched me struggle with the shirt. "That your mother's necklace, Pearly?"

I stopped fiddling with a cracked button. I stilled my breath, but I did not look up.

"How'd you get it?"

Something inside me loosened. She knew Mama had given it to Swicker in exchange for Bruno. I'd told her once how Mama told Papa she'd lost it. Did she imagine me taking it off a dead man? Still, I did not speak nor glance up for fear she'd read the wrong lie in me.

Instead, she crossed the room and touched my shoulder. "Let's get your stuff together, okay?"

"It was Mama's first," I said, tucking it back beneath my shirt.

"I know, Pearly. I know."

Once I knew she wasn't going to say any more about it, I asked, "How long do you think it'll take us?"

"Some time." She gazed out the window, where blowing snow blocked the view. "A few days, more if you don't get going now." She sighed. "I sure got a bad feeling about sending you two out there."

I nodded. Feeling unsure myself, I watched Bruno chew on an old boot. I knew he was watching me sideways, waiting for me to sneak up. Play keep-away. He was waiting for me and it made me ashamed, because there was no way to tell him any of this. There was no way to make him understand that we had to leave, and I didn't know when we'd be safe.

"Make sure when you leave here you take the tote road down to the twitching trail all the way to devil's rock," Ebony said as she handed me some rough-drawn maps. "Stay off the go-backs. You'll know them when you see them. Then, from there, take the stream on your left, the one that'll meet up with a stand of spruce bent in one direction. There may or may not be much of a trail there this time of year, but follow best you can. And don't forget your snowshoes."

"I got Ivy's."

"Okay, good. Now, don't forget to watch the sun. It falls some fast these days, Pearly. I know you know all this, but I'm half-sick sending you out there. Now, you find Ida's camp first. She'll put you up tonight and look after ya."

Ebony had the blacksmith mend Bruno's broken collar and he gave her an extra clasp, should the first one break. Song-catcher gave me a poke bag of dinner, a church key can opener, and some cans of milk and beans. She also gave me some millet to draw down the chickadees, if I should start to feel lonely or scared.

"If we're going, we'd better get going," I said, trying to

139

sound confident. I put on my red mackinaw and my felt hat and Bruno and me walked outside.

Another squall had passed. Bruno tested the air with gulpy snorts. At the end of the dooryard, I gave my three-finger wave and, just like that, we left Smoke River. I did not turn back around because I knew Song-catcher and Ebony would be watching. Later, miles later, before the snow and woods were done with me, I would come to convince myself that I had turned back one last time to wave or call something kind to them. That I gave them something: some comfort before me and Bruno walked away. But none of that is true. In the last windrowed field before the trail, I walked backwards for a bit, lifting each shoe high from the snow, turning once, then once more, trying to catch a glimpse of Ebony's house, but it had long disappeared behind the shielding trees.

like a come-loose hinge to the world

Ansell left early April, just before the haul-off finished. Edon assured him he was fine taking over for the few men still left in camp until the driving crews arrived. He promised to take good care of Bramble too. In the Outside, Ansell caught rides with woodsmen heading up into the dark ridges, the thin roads that would take them back to their farms and orchards in Damascus, New Zion, Beulah, or farther on to Skedaddle Ridge or Lac-des-Lys or Marshy Hope or Notre-Dame-des-Érables. During the day, spring worked itself into the land, splitting things open, prying into deeps and the wintering's sealed-off parts. He cut through fields, crossed open and covered bridges, passed through villages mispronounced by those from away, and tramped rough ridges that had no names and sometimes blocked out the still-weak afternoon light. He managed to find Song-catcher's place and knocked until his knuckles hurt and a neighbor came out to say she and Ebony had gone somewhere with their gear a few days before. And so he went on, stopping at gas stations, smithies, garages, diners, saddleries, hotels, dairy farms, sawmills, taverns, and other unlikely places, always asking after Pearly and Bruno. *A girl and a bear? No, no, sorry, son, never heard tell of them.*

The truck drivers and farmers he caught rides with told him about their struggles in the world they knew. They told him how long and mean the winter had been, how the wind had cut cold, costing them fuel, wood, and more feed for still barned-up animals. They told him that men had taken to riding on the roofs of trains to get to where they needed to be, if the nights weren't too bad off. Ragged work camps still marked parts of the province—one fifteen-hundred-men strong. And others hoboing new distances westward to shipyards, cotton mills, paving programs, or fruit-picking schemes. They told him of the daily shape-ups in New York where men stood before a hiring boss and were cut from the crowd like horses, just to earn a day's wages. All of them castaways. Homesick and lost. The world felt like a loose skin, shedding something Ansell could neither recognize nor name.

A week after leaving the woods, he started following the rail lines east as they took him through small towns. It was warming now—the snow gone out of the low land. He walked, and high-fevered starlings swung above him, skeltering to a roosting oak where the last of the light revealed the small violet fires in their feather vanes and under-colors. Somewhere beyond a heaved-up ridge, a train blew high, exhaling its dark, vaporous breath. Coyotes called in reply. And then it was upon him—the closest he'd ever been to a train moving like that through the night. He stepped off the verge, away from the suck of its undercarriage.

There was a locomotive and coal tender followed by ten steel-barred stock cars rank with animal air. These were followed by five, six, seven gold-gilt gondolas and flatcars stacked high with crates, tents, poles, and circus wagons. The emerald sleeping cars—Al T. Bassie painted along their sides—were just coming into view when Ansell turned to thumb grit from his eyes and the world filled with sparks. Horrible light and horrible sound. New stars wheeled. A moon-shaped hole in the eastern sky. Something dark came at him sideways then all went dark.

It was one of the gondolas that left the track first. Its front wheel arch-bar snapped nearly in two. With that break, the cars derailed as one great zigzagging wreckage of steel—some shunted off the tracks still upright, others aslant in various states of ruin.

Thunder far off. Sheet lightning flared the ridges. Something thunked like a come-loose hinge to the world. Cinder beds. Creosote. Sawdust. Animal piss: wet and dry. Ansell half woke inside a forest of dark trunks that blocked out the bloodied moon and backfires. Like no trees he'd known before. And then he woke more to something nuzzling his cheek. At first, he thought it must be Bruno, but no, it was—large with the moon behind it—workhorses beside a dark lake. No. Big-boned. Bluish. Cathedral-like in how they held together the space around them. The sky curdled with cloud and then cleared.

Eyes watery. Trunks penduluming. Three elephants stood round looking down at Ansell with dull wonder. They poked him with their trunks and made sounds like they were filled with steam. He stayed where he was, stiff as a window dummy, until his senses roared back into his body. And then he could hear. A pulse in his throat. Two in his ears. There was so much noise behind them, but for that briefest moment he heard nothing but the elephants' soft sounds, air escaping from those bellowing lungs, their feet scuffing the tracks' verge, their ears like net curtains billowing in and out with an open window's breeze. When he shifted up off the damp ground, a pain streaked from shoulder blade to thumb. It dropped him down hard again. With the back of his wrist, he wiped something gluey off his cheek, then tried again to push through the stiffness that held his body inert. The pain set him sober and the world filled up again with men hollering to be heard, and smoke and animal stench.

"Baby, baby, baby," a man called from somewhere Ansell could not see for all the smoke and steam and coal smut falling from the sky. He said something else in a voice Ansell recognized from teamsters—the kind that could tell what was wrong with a horse just by staying quiet with it for a while. From his place on the verge, Ansell watched the man walk around the elephants, running his hands along their hides, searching for injuries, while they in turn shied if he came too close to their long-lashed eyes, just as Ansell had seen a skittish horse do before someone shouldering a new saddle. After the man checked over the last elephant, the creature raised its trunk and pointed to where Ansell still lay. It trumpeted and Ansell felt the ground beneath him shiver. Everything he looked at wavered. He felt like he was looking through bad glass. He felt as though he might pass out.

"Goddamn," the man said in a hoarse whisper, still crouched beside the elephants, still moving as though his limbs were swimming through too-thick air. "You okay, pal?"

"Think so," Ansell said, righting himself. A sear of pain radiated out from a large gash across his forehead.

"Well, if nothing's broke, and if you could move real slow till I get these ladies settled . . . I'd sure appreciate it."

Behind the elephants, a smolder hung in the air like battle smoke, but they stayed there at the edge of the verge in a pocket of forced calm.

"Been a wreck," the man said as he reached a rope around one of the elephants' forelegs, stroking its barkish skin. "Hell's half acre everywhere, but we just got to stay calm over here. You got me?"

Ansell was lying a foot away from three elephants who hadn't taken their eyes off him. "Yeah, I got you."

"These here are the nicest African ladies you ever gonna meet, but even the nicest ladies, if they get riled up . . ." He reached down and wrapped the rope around the middle elephant's leg. "All jeezless hell might break loose."

"What are you gonna do with 'em?"

"I'm gonna take 'em over to that empty cargo car still

145

upright on these rails and put them in there for now." He pointed with his chin down the line to where the fore-cars were off in all directions, smoking at the side of the tracks, buckled and skewed. He pulled out a bag of something from his coat pocket and began handing them off to the elephants, who took handfuls in their trunks. Peanuts.

"I thought that was just some old myth. Peanuts and elephants."

The man smiled sideways. "Some old myths good as half-truths."

Sure enough, the elephants started to turn their big bodies around, tacking into the darkness. The man walked ahead, the rope in one hand and the quickly depleting bag of peanuts in the other. "Don't go nowheres," he whispered. He walked on with those high-shouldered creatures following him, and Ansell felt like he was watching the mountains come to the prophet. He wondered how the hell he was going to tell this to anyone in a way that might sound half-believable.

He scanned around himself. Men beating at flames with coats and blankets. Animal sounds. Something under a tarp not too far from where he sat. The entire scene frozen in a state of hellish damage. He got to his unsteady feet and followed the man and his elephants over to the car. He waited near the ramp while the man walked the elephants up into the car, despite the world shouting around them. He came back out as soft as he'd gone in. Ansell helped him hitch up the ramp and secure the door, so that the elephants could no longer see the chaos around them.

That's when the man turned his attention to Ansell. "You think you can run over yonder to where them lights are burning in them farmhouses?"

Ansell looked where he was pointing. They were closer to the village than he'd realized.

"Maybe get some help."

warrens and creep passages

All day we walked and all day we were hungry. Not yet weather-broken, the snow crust stayed hard enough to cross over without falling through. This couldn't last. But this was no country I had ever seen and so could not predict how the land might lie before us. Unsure where the boundaries were and knowing there could be horses, I made Bruno walk on his leash, though this insulted his better nature. Attached to me, his mood grew glowery and then, with every haphazard step, more contrary until his only thought was of slipping the leash. Stiff-backed, he muddled our pace, crossing in front, falling short, lurching ahead so that I might stumble off that trace of a trail. He pulled—left then right then left—sending me off balance. When that didn't work, he dove into the snow, rubbing the icy crust against his collar to work the thing off. He carried on like this for some time, face down, pushing himself along by his back legs, his rump high in the air. I said harsh things. I yanked his tail to make him behave, but this only made him uglier. Finally, while crows tacked above, whiffling over something cooling with death, I turned him loose but kept his collar on, in case I needed to re-hook him fast. He ran ahead. Lost to the trees.

I called once, twice. The woods quiet, but not in a good way. I thought about what leaves tracks: foxes with their puffed-out tails, owls lifting mice off the snow's crust, coyotes with their lax angles, wind over water, clock grass—its habit of inscribing perfect circles in the sand with its long, thin leaves. And Jack in the Dark: every tree, every shadow, every rock shuckling after him. My heart, a shuttering organ. I could have slipped down and slept right there. But I had to keep moving to stay warm and my anger at this made me wish Bruno gone, back to camp, safe and asleep. And with this feeling also came my understanding that I was now, at least until I found Ida's camp, completely responsible for myself and for Bruno.

=

A whirl of chickadees. A count of crows and there he was again beside me, matching my rough pace. I took off Songcatcher's red scarf and wrapped it around his neck to better spot him should he barrel off again. This I knew was risky because if he pushed through a blackberry tangle, the scarf might snag and I would be without. For now, I was willing to take the chance so that I could concentrate on staying upright. Ivy's snowshoes were wide, and duck-walking hills and wallows tired me. The snow, in the warming air, grew pulpy and stuck to the shoes' bentwood frames and weighed me down, forcing me to stop every few steps to scrape off the starchy buildup with a pine bough.

By late afternoon, I figured we'd walked halfway to Ida Pond's camp. I pulled out the dinner Song-catcher had made up that morning—was it only that morning?—and found a near-dry log to perch on. Halfway. Between. Thinking this way made me feel like we were at the edge of the world, teetering on the verge of disappearing altogether. Clackety-clacking through the underbrush, Bruno found his way back, still in his tattery scarf, and waited for me to share whatever Song-catcher might have packed. Two helpings of beans, two helpings of salt pork, two helpings of molasses cookies. Ebony had also tucked in a couple of cigarettes and a box of matches wrapped up in wax paper. Bruno tried to loosen his little wooden trough from my rucksack, whining when I batted his paw away.

"If I give it to you, you can't go dragging it through the woods."

He flicked his long tongue and would not look away.

"Fine," I said, pouring his share into the trough.

He sat down with his back against my log, and ate like a furry forest human, like a goblin short on time. I ate mine off my knees. It was all half-frozen and hard to chew. Each of us paused, mid-bite, if we heard something rattle the seed heads or creak the trees. We shared a milk bottle of slushy tea, over-sugared to keep the spirits up.

I pulled Mama's double-horn necklace out from my layers and held it up for Bruno to see. "We're the heirs, you know?"

He leaned into my leg, breathy and content, milk mustaching his snout. I thought about all the lives sleeping beneath and around us, all the things with thin roots—the warrens and creep passages warmed with slow-beating blood. I thought about Jack in the Dark readying to wake again. And that's when it began to snow harder.

=

All afternoon, the snow blew slantwise, so that I had to stumble forward, my face locked in a squint against the ice kernels that stung my cheeks and forehead. Bruno stayed close. The snow built on his back, face, and forelegs like a suit of armor and it gave me comfort to think of him that way. We walked on, towards the sun—pale as a peeled stick now. At times, snow devils walked beside us and then just as quickly blew themselves apart.

And would it be so strange to tell you that sometimes those whirling devils grew real in my imaginings before ghosting away? Would it be so strange to say sometimes they were as tall as Mama in Papa's old sweater? And sometimes they walked on beside me for some time, and they looked like any man in camp—some dead ten years or more—and sometimes like Ansell holding my hand. All the things I thought inside myself—the thickness of these devils and then their thinnings. Tangled up, half-formed, sometimes so thin I could see through them as they followed beside me, making sure I went on.

I tried to follow Ebony's directions, to not sink into my

fears: the fissures and holes. Climbing up yet another clumsy hill of snow-pelted rock, I sang to Bruno as the snow turned to freezing rain—vicious as pitchforks. It sharped on my skin and ticked on the long swag of spruce boughs. The way of our progress marked now with traces and back-traces between trails that might lead between camps but sometimes led nowhere and sometimes opened onto deer yards or seeps and went no farther.

Late in the afternoon, we stood in a wide field. There was no sound but the wind, everywhere at once. "We're altogether not in the right place, Bruno."

Some trees in our woods had notches or symbols, some were dented where sleds had slewed into them. Each nick and seep-scar told me something about the work being done and how I might find my way back to camp. But there were no signs where we stood.

"We need to get back into the trees!" I said. I felt too turned around.

In the trees, the snow mantled the boughs so that they almost touched, making a sheltering tunnel that muted the wind. We walked through for a while and then followed the curve of the land. Steep enough I had to take off my mitts and undo my coat so I wouldn't overheat and turn my clothes to ice. Bruno sat under a cedar out of the wind, licking ice from his belly, waiting. We came out at the rim of a deep-set valley. Tree line, fields, and the gray scarves of coming snow. The province spread out before us, much beyond my imaginings. But no real place to get out of the storm. I could think of nothing except hunching down beneath one of the bigger cedars. I didn't know how to do this part. From somewhere down in the valley's dimness, Bruno whined. I caught sight of his dark bulk belly-sliding backwards down the steep north-facing slope, blackened with frozen water. At the bottom, he fell on his rump then tumbled over backwards twice into the thigh-deep snow. He whined as he tried to right himself and then trundled back over to the rock wall, trying to catch his claws in the wet stone, but he could gain no purchase.

"God damn it, Bruno! You can't stay away from trouble two minutes!" I said, starting down the valley on my backside. "Can't look away for a sec without some catastrophe happening to you." Hand over hand, grasping at birch saplings growing slant to the rock face, I slid down into a scrabbled land. The foot of it darker than above. "Bruno?"

Nothing. The narrow valley ended with a wall of slick rock—thick blue ice sheeting its high ridge. It was a frozen sault that dropped from a jagged shelf some seventy feet above. Bruno's whines came from there. As I stepped farther into the valley, I tripped over something large and tined, half-buried beneath the snow. Two bull moose. Locked antlers. Their skulls conjoined. Their foundered bones collapsed in such a way that I could see how one had suffocated the other. They had died some time ago, and strangely nothing had disturbed their kill site. "Lost the battle and lost the war," I said, unwilling to stand too close to their deaths for long. With no way around them, I unlatched my snowshoes and clambered through their strew of bones. On the other side, I could see that the frozen sault hid a cave walled with a sheet of ice, except for a small gap. Bruno stood at its dark threshold, licking his frost-starred snout.

"Nice work, Brunnie!" I shinned the slick rock up to the cave's mouth. Inside, all sound disappeared where the rock angled into a deep wedge. There was just enough space for us to rest a spell behind the ice wall. "Maybe this was like your first mom's den, eh?"

Bruno sooked at the cave's mouth, licking at the thick ice wall, unwilling to step all the way in. Eventually, in his own time he shambled inside to watch me gather sticks and leaf duff from the cave's corners for a fire. He circled the dust and dead brush, making order out of the new scents.

"Stay here. Listen for once."

Outside, I cut some boughs with my hatchet. I dragged in some windfall and broke the small branches off with my heel for kindling.

Bruno was already knocking the wood around the cave, moving it elsewhere.

"Bring that back!"

I got a smoky fire near going. It sheened the damp rock and made the ice walls glow. I went back out to scrounge for some more boughs. Coming back with them shushing behind me in the snow, I paused outside the cave. The fire's pale light glowed like strange glass. A picture-book church window. Orange with fire. Bruno's shadow occasionally darkening the effect as he paced the small cave, poking his head out of the gap, waiting for my return.

When I'd settled us, I pulled out our blanket and some supplies for another dinner and let them thaw near our meager fire. A little more heat got Bruno steaming and softened my clothes. We ate what little we had, watching the snow fall beyond the gap. I wished Papa could see us: the only light for miles around flickering through the waterfall's ice.

"This adventure's just fine with me," I said to Bruno as I handed him the last of a biscuit with baloney. "We'll be home in no time."

We went to sleep that night to the soft sounds of melting ice and nothing bothered us.

===

In the morning, we woke to clear, bright sunlight. All the world's hard edges softened with snow sparkle. Ragged step after ragged step, we started out again. All day, we walked through the day's moods, sometimes in light and sometimes in scudding weather dark as horseshoes. In short time, the world no longer felt new and beautiful but aged and often strange in its indifference towards us. Finally, the spindling snow parted like a curtain, revealing Camp 32. Hunkered among the trees like a knot of toads. Its lights glowed as though underwater. Long before we reached the yard, a dog started up and Ida Pond herself came bustling out of the cookhouse. She watched us come closer. We made a poor show—a mess of wet and frozen mud.

"Where in tarnation is your iced-up little soul coming fro—"

She stopped when she caught sight of Bruno, now more polar bear than black bear—his scarf stiff along his back. "Oh, lordy. Only one gal around these parts is crazy enough to walk around in a snowstorm with a bear." She stepped towards us. "Pearly? What's happened?" she asked, wrapping her dishcloth around my neck.

I caught sight of woodsmen edging out of an outbuilding's lee to get a better look at Bruno. But they kept their distance, some nodding in a far-off way, unsure about a girl walking a bear wearing a scarf. Others paused mid-action: beating straight a piece of hoop iron, mending something split. Some smiled and others crouched low, resting their elbows on their knees to get a better look. Despite the storm, no man wore a coat. It was a rite of passage. A proof of strength. Still, one man came out from the bunkhouse and wrapped his coat around my shoulders.

"You're lucky to be alive, little one, out here in this squall," he said, his eyes wet with wonder and fear.

"Thought I'd seen just about everything, Ida," another man called over to Ida, wiping snow from his face with the sleeve of his shirt.

"Ain't that somethin'," someone else said. "We was hoping to see that little bear that's all the talk round here, but this is some dangerous time to do it."

"Ida, you get them warmed up first! Our supper can wait."

"I'm feeding you boys directly, so you best be getting ready!" Ida said, leading us past the dinner bell, creaking in the wind. "I'll be ringing for ya soon."

The crowd broke up, meandering to the bunkhouses to change into drier things. On Ida's orders, a couple of teamsters piled up some barrels at the back of the kitchen to house Bruno for the night, as far from the horse hovel as possible, though Bruno wanted nothing more than to look those tall creatures in their big windowy eyes.

"Now, you keep that guy on a leash, you hear?" Ida said, side-eyeing Bruno where he was exploring his walled-in bedroom. "And get that wet rigging off. We'll soon have you warm."

I handed her the damp note Song-catcher had sent along. "Just to explain a few things," she'd said as she'd scratched it out at the kitchen table that morning. Ida's lips moved as she read. She glanced at me from time to time then read on.

I sat on the bench, sock feet up against the stove, one of Ebony's cigarettes smoldering between my fingers. A radio played some love-lost song deep in the kitchen.

"Everyone's heard something about Swicker," Ida said when she'd finished reading. "No truth in any of it, maybe, but your bear? Well, more vinegar-fly than killer maybe."

"He's not," I said. "He's just a big baby."

"Sometimes feels this old world is set against us, don't it?" She sat down beside me and leaned in close. "Now, this didn't come from me, but I heard tell them Mounties have been crawling through here asking questions. Everyone knows that man acted plain reckless with his crews, but I never heard tell of men out here, and I know a slew of them, acting the murderer."

"We found him."

"What's that, love?"

"We found him. Me and Bruno. That's why Miles tried to get rid of Bruno." I felt my face color in patches when I swiped at my tears.

She gave me a quick hug and gathered up my wet coat and sweaters and Bruno's scarf and hung them from a beam near the stove. "The pair of ya's aren't to blame." She went back into the kitchen, letting me stay quiet.

"We'll be having some devil stew tonight," she said, "though I haven't a clue what to feed that one." Bruno was by now making himself at home. He'd found a shirt hanging from a nail and was twisting it around and around, drying off his face.

"I got some milk," I said. "If you got some bread or apples or molasses cookies—"

"Cookies!" she larked. "Well, I've never heard the likes of it. That little bear's been outside all day too. We'll find something hardier than that for the poor little begger, so long as he don't turn ugly."

I pulled his trough from my pack and opened a can of milk. He splattered through it then settled down on the blankets, his eyes goldy crescent moons. I sat near enough to the stove my clothes steamed. I was so tired everything had echoes, but I knew to keep out of Ida's way. I knew the rules of a camp kitchen. Stout and nearly the same height as me, Ida was a no-nonsense sort of cook. While the men often said they'd gone wind-deaf out working in the woods, Ida was the opposite. She seemed to hear everything at once: a pot boiling over, the radio, Bruno snuffling from his new spot. While her cookee washed up skillets and popped loaves from pans, Ida whipped up a little mixed beans and mush for Bruno. She peered down at it all, unsatisfied, then, snapping her fingers, came back with a glug of molasses to top it off. "He's a bear, not a king," she said, handing me his trough. "And you'll be next, my girl."

As she bustled around the kitchen, ordering her cookee about, I told her how Ansell was, and how Papa was since his accident, and then I told her about all the other accidents that had befallen the camp that year.

She smiled, thin-lipped. "It's some hard road you've got to go right now, love." She handed the cookee a wooden spoon. His whole arm almost sunk into the bean pot as he began to stir. "If I didn't—Well, Swicker made his own bed a long time ago," she said, but I knew she thought more than that. "Your father'll be some glad to have you back safe and sound. If we weren't down a sleigh and a few men recovering from injuries, I'd send someone out to deliver you in person, if I could."

"Bruno can't ride in the sleigh on account of the horses."

She handed me a heaped plate and sat down again beside me. "Wouldn't that bear be better off in the wild?"

I shook my head, my mouth full. "He's no good in the wild. Once, we was swimming and he got a leech pinned to his nose. He was running around blatting, bumping into things. Mama took a match to singe it off and you can imagine how he took that."

159

"And don't you look like your dear mama," Ida said, laughing as we imagined Bruno as a spleeny wild bear. That's when the men came in. While they ate, the sounds of supper washed over me in waves. My legs jolted from time to time as though stung with electricity, and my eyes felt lidded with grit. After thanking Ida for supper, I helped clean up a little.

"Batteries are dead in their radio, so there'll be music tonight. If you want to hear the fiddler, just come on back out," she said. "Some of the men are unsettled around here too with their wages and such, but our camp boss is a pretty good guy. We haven't had troubles like you folks have."

I thanked her again and, feeling swimmy, went back to the little camp they'd made for us. Bruno was curled up in some clean horse blankets, his forepaws over his nose and one of our three blankets pinned beneath him. I spread one of the remaining two over the floor and wrapped the other around myself. Wind leaked through the wall seams, but with Bruno beside me, I was plenty warm. I was asleep before Ida turned down the lanterns.

I'd slept only a short time when something clamorous brought me back to the room's deep darkness. Swicker and angry men. A room alive with birds. It took some minutes before the darkness gave shape to the sound. I came back to Ida's camp and the dull realization that Swicker was dead and we had miles to go through the snow again tomorrow. Checking that Bruno was still beside me, I got up, wrapping a blanket about my shoulders, and walked over to the men's bunkhouse, where the lights shone warm over the snow.

Though the two little windows were steamy from bodies and damp clothes, I could see a bit through one. Ida and her husband, Havelock, were there, sitting on a bench clapping at two blindfolded men down on all fours. One, tied by the ankle, pivoted around a peg driven into the floor. The other held a weighted sock. "Where are you, Jack? Where are you, Jack?" the man tethered to the peg hollered before leaping to the other side of his rope. "In the dark!" The other man answered, "If you die before I do, take that!" He struck out with the sock in the direction of the man's voice. I knew he had three chances to hit the tethered man or he'd lose his turn. This time, he hit the tethered man's shoulder, and everyone cheered.

All my life, I'd watched woodsmen play Jack in the Dark, but that night, standing outside the light and heat, I felt apart from it. It was as though I was watching from the other side of something now. I watched Ida clap with the men and thought of Mama and how we'd sit together on a little bench. I'd put the potatoes in the sock just like these ones, while Papa held it open for me. *I had. I had. I had.* I made my way back through the cold blue night to Bruno, who'd stolen the bottom blanket again. He snored softly. I burrowed close to his back. He smelled of musk, wet dog, wet stone, and pine soot. I listened to him breathe for some time, before drifting off again.

In the morning, I woke to a lightness of spirit I had not felt in some time. Home. In short order, we got ready to go.

bloodshot and worn low

All night, Ansell helped wherever he could. Sloshing in the bucket brigade. Pulling human and animal alike from crumpled cars. Triaging. All in all, three canvas men, two hobos, and two chimpanzees died. The village, he'd heard, had called in a local bear hunter to track down three missing kangaroos. When the fires were out and there was nothing left to do but wait for the coroner and the cranes and the heavy oxen teams, and those coming from the nearest houses with blankets and thermoses of tea, the animal man sat down on the verge with Ansell, where he'd crouched to catch his breath and still his shaking hands. He passed Ansell a bottle of something brown. As Ansell took a swig, he noticed the gash over his left eye had been bandaged. He couldn't remember anyone doing it.

"Damn, boy," the man laughed, "with scars like them, you sure could get a job round here."

Ansell had forgotten about the scars. They'd since silvered and were, to him now, just a mild curiosity, especially for small children who had not yet learned to keep their questions quiet. And how could he explain to a child or even to himself that his body felt unmapped and then remapped with light? His face no longer fit together in the way it was intended. He was not hard to talk to, but the scars made him, in others' eyes, he supposed, something composed of contamination or trickery. He took another swig from the bottle—woodsmoke and saddle leather.

"He didn't mean nothing by it, now, did he?" a woman asked, nettling in her voice. "Virgil?"

The man put out his hand. "No hard feelings there, young fella?"

Ansell shook his hand. Soot and ash.

"You gonna introduce me, Virgil P. Friday?" the woman asked, stomping her foot on the cinder bed and reaching for the bottle. She was closer to Ansell's age than Virgil's. Her hair a frizzy halo around her head. Ash smudges traced her sharp cheekbones. She wore a feathery scarf and her dress was edged with scaly green spangles.

"Apologies, darling." Virgil waved his hand in a magician's ta-dah. "Ansell, this here's my little lady and the circus's best seamstress, Zula Friday."

"Zula *Natchez* Friday," she corrected him. "On account I believe women should carry something men can neither own nor take away."

"She is," Virgil sighed, "a true-blue suffragette."

"And I will always be of assistance to any of my sisters. Any time," Zula added, knocking three cigarettes from her pack and offering them around. "Hell of a thing this," she said, almost to herself, as she curled up in Virgil's lap and smoked.

"Not as bad as Paint Lick or Altoona or Choctaw."

"Nah, not that bad. 'Member how we lost those gorillas in Goliad? Wonder what happened to them boys. Hope they all went on to have good lives somewheres."

"Hold on. You've been in train wrecks before?" Ansell asked.

"Honey, we are in the circus business. Half our life's on these rails." Zula blew smoke above his head. "Just part of show life."

The mist grew thicker, the ground damper. They small-talked for a bit, Ansell sharing a little about what he was doing out there, who he needed to bring home.

"You're looking for a girl and a bear?" Zula laughed. "And I thought our life was the strangest thing out here. Ha!"

A ropy-looking man strolled up to where they sat. His limbs crooked as though they'd been broken many times and wrongly put back together again. Ansell had seen some of that sort of healing in the camps, when the men took it upon themselves to set a broken bone.

"I hear you're the good Samaritan, young man?" His words, turned slantwise, betrayed his foreignness. "Much obliged," he added, extending a talonish hand. "I'm Tomaž Zalora, man-ager of Al T. Bassie Circus."

Ansell nodded but wasn't sure if he could trust his tongue—his heart still galloped and the whisky beating his blood shook his limbs.

"We come through these parts most years," he continued.

"Though I'm afraid this wreck will set us back a few dates. But listen, if you ever need anything. Accommodations"—he squinted at Ansell's scars—"a job, just ask for Tomaž Zalora and I'll do what I can to help you out." With that, he nodded at Virgil and Zula, straightened his tie—clipped at the knot with a diamond pin—and walked away. Zula skipped after him and had a few words, the crooked man nodding from time to time, before she came back and Tomaž Zalora carried on farther into the smoke.

"Sleeping cars are fine for now!" a man yelled from where a set of horses and a truck were hauling ribbons of warped steel off the track. "We're off on a spur! Get some sleep! We'll be heading out tomorrow! After the burials!"

"Must be hard burying your own out here," Ansell said, looking off across the flat fields, an occasional light out there at its edges, glinting low.

"Oh, hon," Zula sighed. "This is the circus. No one knows them guys. People come and go all the time. We're not all friends or family or nothing. That's just an old myth."

"Hell," Virgil said. "We had a trick rider here some years ago, Charlie . . . Charlie Frigoli," he said, snapping his fingers. "One day, we was setting up in Waupaca County, my big girls raising the tents, guy poles, whole shebang. Well, Tomaž gives Charlie five dollars and tells him to go into town, get some bread and milk and eggs. Frigoli pockets the money and works at a brewery for two years. When we came back through, he gives Tomaž a jug of milk, a loaf of bread, a bottle of beer, and change for five dollars."

165

"He got his job back," Zula added.

"He got his goddamn job back," Virgil said.

Ansell followed them up to the sleepers, thinking he'd just close his eyes for a bit behind one of the barns in the village, get the strength back in his legs before heading on.

"Ansell!" Tomaž called, one long, bowed leg toeing the running boards of a Ford. "Son, this man's going your way, I hear. Says he'll give you a lift far as Harland Road."

"You take care now," Zula said, brushing Ansell's cheek with the worst of the scarring. "Those'll heal in no time. And girl 'specially . . ." There was no finish to the sentence. On the steps to their car, she turned. "You'll find 'em. Your girl and her bear."

Virgil extended his hand. "Hope our paths cross again, Ansell. And good luck."

Ansell walked on to where a truck idled near the tracks. They drove away from the wreck in a low whine of gears, the driver rubbernecking all the while.

"Must be a full moon coming on," he said as they pulled out towards Harland Road. "Damnedest things going on around here." He plucked a cigarette from a pack sliding across the dinged-up dash and lit it. The tip of tobacco crackled and grew red. He offered the pack to Ansell.

"Thanks."

The truck rattled on the rutted road like something that might fly apart. "Just this morning a man tells me the god-damnedest thing. He'd heard tell of a bear in a scarf crossing a road up this way." He shook his head.

Ansell coughed smoke from his lungs. "A bear? There a girl with him?"

The driver cut his eyes Ansell's way. "Son, you looking for a bear with a fashion problem?"

"I sure am, sir," Ansell said, the whisky and nicotine running through him making him half-giddy. He laughed and his scars silvered and shifted anew.

Insulated in the cab's darkness, he told the man about Pearly and Bruno and he told him about the ruinous death of Swicker and he told him about Camp 33, fifty miles back in the woods, and Edon and the white-eyed horses screaming down the hot sand hill, and he told him about the circus and the elephants and Virgil and Zula, and finally he told him about the lightning that had silvered his face as it stood now. And when he was finished, feeling bloodshot and worn low, when he felt talked out, he sat empty in a good way and helped himself to another one of the man's cigarettes.

"Hell, son. Story like that might get some folks thinking you're soft in the head." He picked up the brim of his hat with his left hand and swept it back down over his head. "I was only going to take you 'bout five miles up the road, but with stories like them . . . I've already gone another ten just to hear till the end." He smiled and Ansell could see he was missing top and bottom teeth. "The added journey's been welcomed."

"I appreciate that, sir."

"And, if you don't mind, I didn't turn off where I should've, figuring you might need a good meal and a bed."

Ansell nodded. "I could sure use a bit of both."

"My wife makes just about the best pie around and I'm sure, once you tell her some of what you just told me, she won't be taking no for an answer."

Ansell leaned back in the truck seat, worn out from talking over its juddering. He'd find Pearly and Bruno in the next couple of days. He'd find them and bring them home. Damn. He felt it.

Good to his word, the man's wife gave Ansell two helpings of stew and pie and set him up in their son's old room, a little bedroom at the top of the stairs. And over the years, Ansell received many postcards from Zula and Virgil. From Dinosaur, Colorado; Placentia, California; Bacon Level, Alabama; Bitter End, Tennessee; and other places he'd never see in his life. Each reminded him of that black night, the broken people and withering fires. Each card was brief. Each with something interesting to say. And years later, when he heard tell of animal bones, lion-cage locks, and railroad spikes turning up at building sites, and when he heard stories about strange creatures that crept up on woodsmen or watched them from a distance—kangaroos or leggy birds that could mimic human speech, a town's fire whistle, an elephant's steamy sigh—he believed each and every one.

split with a glittering vein

All morning, my snowshoes broke through the crust. I rubbed a mitten against my runny nose and even this sounded like a file rasping against a saw tooth. Branches came out to thwack me cheek-wise, leaving sting lines beneath my eyes. Snow-choked boughs reached down to knock my hat askew or catch the pockets of Papa's sweater. No matter how careful I was, no matter how many times I reminded myself that these were *my* woods—every dip and turn and shadow— I still managed to miss an outcrop of granite, split with a glittering vein, sprawling me into the snowpack, the balls of my hands stung raw from the fall.

Tired of the woods' cage-work pressing around me, I lay there feeling how the trees moved. Not dissimilar, I supposed, to a sailor stepping onto a ship's deck or a horse handler climbing into a new saddle. It had to do with perspective. A certain sort of creak in the air. In the bone. Bruno nudged me upright again because, eventually, the wall of trees would open up to camp again. I tried for easy thoughts and sang to him instead.

Heigh-ho, the derry-o,
A-hunting we will go,
We'll catch a man and put him in a box,
And never let him go.

We'd been walking most of the day when I reached the crest of a berm. I waited there for Bruno to catch up. Crows knocked at unseen doors and clumps of bough snow fell from the trees onto the steaming wells below. It was one of the first times in my life I did not hear the woods being pulled down, tattered, and stripped from their shadows. There were many camps scattered throughout this area, but I had possibly found the only pocket refusing to be tamed and taken, refusing to be owned and destroyed.

To the left were through-lines and thin troughs, unstitched deer trails, and a lake with the skim ice gone to rot against the shoreline. We walked over to it and stared down at our own dark faces in a melt spot. Something large and shadowy swam past and I felt its ancientness. Its rightful place in the underworld's murk. I thought chain pickerel—its mouth spiky, its skin sharp. All muscle and mystery and long-kept secrets. Bruno sidled up to the lake's shine and leaned low, cracking the rime, admiring himself, maybe, in its glassy surface, until he batted it with a paw. We followed the berm down towards a clearing of trees that might have been, in better weather, a path. Bruno slid down the hill on his belly, stopping occasionally to lick trees where the winter-thin deer had peeled the bark away.

There was no path. Thigh-deep snow pulled at my snow-shoes. Bruno hopped out of each well his weight made. The air warmed and the snow began to smoke, so that it was difficult to see what lay ahead. I kept thinking, *We should see home. We should be home by now.* To keep from worrying, I told Bruno about Arctic explorers. I told him how they hauled sleds laden with bedroom slippers and candlesticks and carriage clocks across the icefields. I told him how they walked away from their ship, locked in the ice at an odd angle. A string of dark figures, burdened with useless junk, their rib-straked dogs following some distance behind.

Another hour on and I realized I was lost. Again.

=

Near dark, I couldn't stop fear from prowling my mind. We'd walked so long on the crusty snow Bruno was leaving pink prints, his pads chafed raw. We needed shelter.

Still, we walked. And our way took us up over another ridge, stumped from previous cuttings, then across blueberry barrens, so open they made the absence of wind in the trees spooky. The other side of a ridge gave way to a stand of maples in a sink of dusking darkness. Deep inside the stand, a brush-wood fire flamed and kept itself whole in the blue air. We walked on, breath-broken and shy, into the shade shift, until we came to a man, shirtless, in a raccoon hat, kneeling in the snow by the fire. He was rubbing something dark like dried blood over his chest and face. I could see, even from where we kept our distance, his breath smoke.

171

And to himself he said, as flame light slid over the nearest maple trunks, "Lord, you've told me to come and preach, and here I am!" He rubbed more of the dark grit onto his palms and face as he spoke to that empty place of footed trees. He gave invitation to the air to receive the Holy Spirit, and then paused. All his words sounded old from repetition. "There is a beast we shall not name amongst us!" I knew then he was a Go-Preacher.

Bruno stepped forward. As I reached for his collar, my snowshoe snagged a root. It sent me spread-eagle. As I tried to roll myself over, to grab on to Bruno for leverage, the man turned. His face-folds dark with the grit he'd rubbed over himself. He dropped the leather bag and stood. His eyes cut across the barrens and the black pine woods we'd just passed through, scanning the stunted alders outlined in frost. I thought he might be listening for the quick shapes that came out at this hour and spilled across their zones. Just out of sight.

"Where'd you come from?" he asked. His face hollowing in the fire's flames. He struggled into a faded drill shirt and then his mackinaw.

"I walked," I said, setting myself upright once more.

"Walking in the footsteps of Jesus?"

"Well, I don't tend to make saviors of my feet," I said. "And what are you doing out here?"

"I'm carrying the word of Jesus, but it's been a rough go so far. I started out near the Chic-Chocs. From there, Jesus sent me ministering to Camp 15, and I was ready. Ready for a revival crusade, you know? But I got into camp and there they were, gone!"

"Woodsmen work during the day," I said in my smart-ass voice. I watched Bruno crouch over the Go-Preacher's bag, surprised the man still hadn't noticed I traveled with a bear.

"That's what I'm praying about tonight."

"You still haven't found no one to preach to?"

"None to save and none to pray." The cold had him spacing out his words. "I suppose you could say, it's been a rough start to my ministry so far."

"And your face?"

He swung the little leather drawstring bag by a finger.

"Holy dirt from the foothills of the Sangre de Cristo Mountains." He paused, thinking it over. "You look like you could use some."

I waved away his offer. Anything that looked like blood was apt to turn my stomach these days. By now, Bruno had the man's pack open and was dragging little things away. His search spurred a throaty song—a private want and greed he shared with all animals. Sounds I was too familiar with to hear at times.

"Oh, lord Jesus!" the Go-Preacher said, tripping himself backwards in the snow.

"He's mine, mister!"

He turned, wide-eyed, strangely marked.

"Hell, he's a goddamn bear. Jesus, won't you forgive me. In your name, we pray."

"Bruno!" I called. "Leave that nice man's stuff alone."

"Enemies and beasts and the works of Satan," he whispered to himself.

Bruno shambled over but took his time.

"We've got to find some shelter before dark."

"There are few way signs in these parts but those put there by Jesus. He will drag us out of our dark places when he sees fit," he said, keeping distance between himself and Bruno.

I stared hard at him. My waning energy was beginning to make my legs weak.

"What I'm saying is, there's nothing round here," he said, something like joy in his voice now. "I'll sleep out here in a hollowed-out tree, maybe, and pray on the small, mean ways of men, and bears, and earn myself a ministry yet."

"Well, we can't sleep in no hollowed-out tree."

"There's a sugar shack some miles off that way," he finally offered, reminding me of Ebony's warning that men will never volunteer information readily. "I slept there last night and kindly left some wood for the next visitor." And in that moment, I realized we were standing in a sugar bush. Lidded pails and spiles bored into trunks all around us. Kept land. The woods had changed over without my noticing. It made my mind start running on with Papa's cooking: ham, bacon, sausages, baked beans, pork rinds, sugar pies, and snow taffy. *Stop that now, Pearly.*

"But not tonight?"

"Naw," he said, eyeing Bruno. "Jesus don't want me getting soft." He lingered with us a few more minutes, giving better directions, and then said, "Well, looks like we are in the prime numbers and though the number three brings me closer to thee, Jesus, my lord and savior, I will say adieu and leave you two to head on up that way." He kicked out the fire, wiped the red dirt from his face with a fistful of snow, and walked on without glancing back. Within moments, he'd slid into the darkness so that even his footsteps were gone.

=

Mile upon mile. Every star showed its best side through cloud scud. We crossed a river bridge and walked on another hour before finding the dim outline of the *sucrerie*, just as the Go-Preacher had described. I gave the door a hard kick and it creaked open, catching on its splintered sash-work and strike plate, where the Go-Preacher had broken the lock.

First thing I did was help myself to his cache of pine kindling. I built a fire, filling up the cabin with smoke and then clearing it away. Eventually, it cherried and spat heat. And then me and Bruno—below the cobwebs and the blackened window drafts, near the seeping flames and the burnt-sugar smell—ate our thawed supper and listened to the once-frozen flies—the kind that gather in sheds—reawakening. We curled up on a musty rag rug while the coyotes sang out there like hungry ghosts and soon afterwards we fell asleep. We slept until the day grew gray, until light came again—pearling pink.

In my rush to get a fire going, I'd left my rucksack outside the door. It wasn't until morning I realized my mistake.

Everything was still in it, except for three cans of milk and Mama's double-horn necklace from the little inside pocket I'd placed it in to keep it safe. That's when I knew, with sinking certainty, the Go-Preacher had not gone as far away as he'd let on. Nothing but a sneak thief. Just like me. Night-skulky and sly. The pair of us.

We worked the stiffness from our limbs and then we had to go on.

a ring made from a spoon

Ansell chose a stool at the far end of the Slow-Down diner's counter. A truck driver had dropped him off just outside town, recommending the all-day breakfast, neglecting to give Ansell the name of the actual town.

"What can I getcha, love?" the waitress asked, righting a coffee mug on its saucer with a click. On her left hand, she wore a ring made from a spoon. "Today, we've got—"

Crawls of coffee spilled over the zinc countertop. Ansell glanced up. She was staring, wide-eyed, at his face. The new gash above his eye. And his scars, which never failed to stir up weird energy in people.

"Fried potatoes," he said. "A big plate. With gravy."

She nodded, stepping back into the kitchen. He could see her hair was tied off like a horse tail's mud-knot as she side-mouthed the cook near the pickup window. The cook glanced at him, then away. He caught a few other men, singly or in pairs, turn on their stools to also stare. *Get a good look, boys. Gawk it up*. He let himself sink into the clatter around him: spitting oil, thick ceramic plates scraped clean with crooked-tined forks. He picked up a newspaper forgotten on a stool beside him. An almost rhythmic hiss and splash swept over him as cars drove through a half-melted puddle in front of the diner. Their tires flew out arcs of slush. Hiss quiet. Hiss quiet. Each time it happened, the men would look up from their plates and steaming cups of coffee until the sound faded.

A raw-boned man on crutches stopped up beside Ansell. This was the second sort of person who was drawn to him now.

"Looks like we're both pupils from the school of hard knocks," the man said with a tobacco-stained grin. He peeled up his pant leg to reveal a smooth stump in double wool socks and a pair of Stanfields, the same as Ansell wore. The man sat down on the stool beside him, close enough their elbows almost touched.

On the radio, Don Messer and the New Brunswick Lumberjacks. The cook turned it down. "Singer's only one that's ever been a real lumberjack!" he said from the serving window, gauging Ansell's reaction.

Ansell nodded vaguely. He didn't have much to say about it. Instead, he read an article about breadlines in New York City. He read about a sheriff up north who needed a hangman-for-hire to work two weeks from next Saturday. A double execution for triple murders: a backwoods-squatter, his wife and son. The criminals were brothers, set to be executed standing back to back. Apparently, neither their sleep nor their appetites had been affected by the sound of the men building the gallows outside their prison window. The sheriff claimed he'd been flooded with hundreds of applications, with payment quotes ranging from twenty-five to one thousand dollars. He was, the paper went on, still in the process of conducting interviews. On the opposite page was an article about a new board game where you used fake money to buy up property in Atlantic City with a token shaped like an old boot or a top hat—each piece belonging to a Rich Uncle Pennybags. Like all woodsmen, Ansell was often years out of touch with the Outside news. A king. A queen. A madman in Germany decreeing his own birthday a national holiday.

He scanned down the page. And there, in a small box near the bottom:

An argument over money between a scaler and a camp boss turned deadly on March 28th, spilling out from Camp 33 onto an empty tote road, new court records show. Heeley O. Swicker, camp boss, stabbed multiple times, was found dead by teamsters. Argyle Corcoran, camp scaler, was taken into custody on April 3rd and charged on April 4th with murder and first-degree robbery. The two men had been partners in several schemes to short lumbermen's daily cuts for some years. Corcoran will appear in person at court on Monday.

Jesus, Ansell thought. Ledgers and liens and these god-damn woods where so many have been broken for so little gain. And still they'll cheat you. Argyle and Swicker. All this time. He tore out the article and slipped it into his shirt pocket. *Pearly and Bruno have gotta come home now.*

"I applied for that job myself," the man beside him said, tapping the hangman-for-hire article. "I'd make as good a hangman as anyone else."

Ansell nodded but kept his eyes on the paper.

"Mind me askin' what happened? I'm guessing someone threw ya in a keg of nails as a baby or maybe your wife beat ya around the skull with a sack of polecats. Maybe for staying out too late." He started to laugh at his own joke, but this quickly collapsed into a long, wheezy cough.

Three quick thumps. Everyone turned to see the snow circles grease down the glass. The waitress, coffee pot in hand, whipped open the door, sending the bell above jangling.

"Mercy! Bobby! You break this window you're gonna know about it!" A few kids, some with snowballs still in their fists, ran down the street, laughing as they went.

Ansell returned his coffee cup to its saucer. Click. Since his accident, he'd grown impatient with those pushing friendship, their stories and hardships. He did not wish to belong to anyone's club.

"Lightning strike," he said.

The saying of it conjured up the red light of his blood dragging sparks, pouring its great god-weight back into his heart. The doubling never ended: the moment he was dead, the moment he was alive, and the loneliness that sort of untamable corrosion bred. The lightning strike had also shaped the resurrection dream that visited him often now.

It brought with it an exaggerated sense of returning to the earth more whole than he had begun: a better man, a righteous man. Each time he woke from it, he feared that if it one day moved on, its absence might leave his soul—in its new state—somehow diminished.

The man gave a low wolf whistle. "I heard of a lot of crazy stuff in my day. But lightning? Lightning doing that to a young feller's face?" He hovered closer. Peering. His crutches scraping against the tiles. "My accident wasn't nothing like that. But it ain't no charley horse neither."

Ansell kept reading the same line over and over. The game was called Monopoly and you chose a token to move around the board as you bought property: a thimble, a top hat, a shoe, a battleship—

"Shot myself in the foot. Done that while moose hunting." He eyed up Ansell, waiting for a reaction that never came. "Know what I learned from that?"

Rich Uncle Pennybags. Mr. Monopoly. "Nope, sir. I do not."

"You stop being bipedal, it's for life. A one-legged man stays a one-legged man. You can survive without some parts, but some things you can't make it right again. Mistakes, you know?" He fiddled with a crutch.

The waitress brought Ansell his plate of potatoes, his cup of gravy, and two basted eggs, a blood knot inside one yolk. She set it all down, then stood looking between the man and Ansell, who kept himself set apart, concentrating hard on the Monopoly article. Sentence by sentence.

"You about ready to settle up, Benight?"

It snapped the man out of whatever reverie he'd been locked inside of. He pulled a few coins from his pants pocket and slapped them down on the counter. He thumbed a soft pack of cigarettes from his chest pocket and handed it to Ansell. Ansell took it, waiting for an explanation, but the man merely gave him a Boy Scout salute before shuffling his way below the door's rattling bell, back out into the bright, cold day.

"He never closes that door tight," she said to no one in particular.

Ansell could see then that she was shortsighted—a look of uncertainty as though the blurry world beyond her was untrustworthy.

He wiped his plate clean with a potato then stared for some time into his cold coffee, catching both his own reflection and the dregs of grounds. But he could not see the two images at once. He thought about the past few months and how recent events had put a toll on his spirit and how he'd taken on a task he was uncertain he'd complete. Outside camp, the world moved differently. Everything was spread out, so that searching made no sense. He felt that Pearly and Bruno were existing in more than one place at the same time. It was wearing on him, choosing the right town, the right road. The one that might bring them home.

Wind churned up snow devils outside the diner's front window. The day was growing dim again. The diner was empty.

"Top-up?"

"What?"

"Top-up?" She shook the coffee pot a little.

"No, no, I'd best get going."

"Don't think I've seen you around here before. You a Watkins Man or gravel salesman?"

"I'm looking for someone."

"Ain't we all, love."

Unsure it was worth it, he pulled out a sketch. He'd drawn her over a number of nights, at one town or another, on an Outside-bound sled. He handed it to the waitress. But in that moment, he saw the sketch with a more critical eye and regretted showing it to her.

"Not bad. Your girlfriend, yeah?" she asked, handing the sketch back to him.

The word shook him a little. He'd never considered that before. He snugged the sketch into a coat pocket. "I'm looking for her and—" He hadn't drawn a picture of Bruno. *I'm looking for a bear* was probably enough information. A bear was a bear. What more useful thing could be said? "She'll be traveling with a bear."

The waitress lifted her eyebrows up. "And the punch line is?"

"No, no. I'm really looking for them. Together."

She exhaled, thinking. "Well, where'd you see them last?"

"Out at the camp. Out near where the Crooked Deadwater runs hard?"

She shook her head. No, she didn't know where that was. "Benight there might be the one to talk to."

"The man who shot himself in the foot? The one just here?"

"Weren't no gun accident, but yeah. He's our best customer. Everyone being on short wages these days." She set the coffee pot down on the zinc counter. It hissed as it touched the damp rings his water glass had left. She glanced around the empty diner. "His old man was a trapper. Sent him out to check the lines and Benight got caught in one of them big claw ones. Just a boy, you know? His old man was here in town. Drinking as usual. Took Benight's brother, All-the-Wishes, three days to find him and drag him back."

"What about his mother?"

"Oh, she hightailed it out of here soon's she could. Back to Jamaica or Florida where her people were, I think. She used to dress for January in July. Never warm, poor thing."

"And All-the-Wishes?"

She smiled. "Benoît and Aloysius. Kids round here used to have some teacher from Boston States, over at the one-room. He'd been in the war, yeah? Different-acting. Not much hearing left, neither. Teacher called them what he thought they'd said. Names stuck. Now we've got a town full of strange-named people." She laughed, glancing out to the street, hazed up with glittering snow duff. "Now Benight, he spends his days walking up and down the main street here. Up and down. Up and down. He's a fixture. If he stayed home, everyone'd be asking, Where's Benight? What's wrong? Where's Benight? If your girl's come through, he'd 'ave seen her."

"Where do I find him?"

"Well, he's either out walking around like I said or he's down the road with All-the-Wishes."

Ansell considered the shifty nature of finding lost things as the waitress busied herself drying cutlery before dropping it into a wooden tray. *Christ, they could be anywhere.* After getting rough directions to All-the-Wishes and a YMCA, he paid the bill, leaving extra pennies for the girl. She didn't come back out from the kitchen.

sparkled with carnival glass

We wasted the morning tracking the Go-Preacher, hoping he might have dropped Mama's necklace along the way or hung it from a tree branch—riddled with regret. But besides the black fire hole singed in the snow, there was no evidence he'd ever been there. This was why we hadn't gotten very far by noon. The snow was deep and the air spitting rain. And Bruno was in a salty mood again. He'd walk along beside me for a bit and then head-butt my thigh to get a rise out of me. He'd been doing this on and off for most of the morning until he'd sored up my thigh so that it burned with every step. Between not knowing these woods and imagining ways I was going to hurt the Go-Preacher, and ways I was going to hurt Miles, it took all my thinking just to keep us roughly in the right direction. From time to time, I could hear the Outside's noises—a factory whistle, a car horn—but they were far off and seemed to change direction depending on the wind.

"You cut that out!" I said, flicking Bruno's ear the next time he rammed me.

He did it again. So hard I lost my balance. I righted myself and shook the stinging snow from inside my mitts.

"God damn it, Bruno! You're nothing but a no-count bear these days!" I gave him a savage shove back. Hard enough the wind went out of him a little. I rarely lost my temper with him and he knew it. Sulkily, he stayed where I'd shoved him. He made some mewling arguments and waited for my reply.

"I don't need telling," I hissed. "*Halle ta frame!* Get going!"

He side-eyed me, but then sat down on his big rump, licking at his ice-caked chest.

"Bruno!" I called, but he would not look at me.

"Fine. See ya later." I marched on. Yan, tan, tether . . . pip, azer, sezar. We kept to our loose orbit for some time. Me marching and Bruno crashing through the snow crust behind me, grumbling to himself. After a bit, I turned around to make nice, but he was gone.

White fields. Tree. Tree. Tree. Something high-shouldered moved off to the right. A slow, dark thing stepped from behind a spruce, too vague to see clear.

"Brunnie?"

A patch of ravens boiled up from some cut stumps, crazing the air with their calls.

"Brunnie? Get out from them trees!"

Nothing. Still angry, I whooped out my bear song. Twice. And waited to hear his throaty reply, his barreling return through the trees. Something was coming. But my mind could not find shape for the sound that followed. And then, it tore loose from its tethers and Bruno poured out his alarm.

Everywhere at once. I ran towards him, screaming his name until my voice chipped and cracked. I came up over the berm and met a wall of darkness: a bear with a clouded eye reared up on its hind legs. It was taking swipes at Bruno, dwarfed a few feet up in an ice-bent birch. I'd never been near a full-grown wild bear before. It was nothing like the yearling we'd freed from its cage in Smoke River.

I pulled my Green River knife from out of my boot and kicked a rotten limb from the snow. The bear stepped into my path and I stepped into its. A black air without dimension. And though I knew it belonged out there more than me, it felt like the most unholy thing created. It was Jack in the Dark incarnate. Its wind-gnawed face gorging itself on my fear. Slashing feet. Hot breath. A hellish furnace. I was out of body, watching myself swing at its spade-like head, scarred deep with what looked like a witch's hex.

It swung its paw and my jaw answered. I heard Bruno nearby, but the world stayed black for a minute and then a minute more. I staggered up and the thing hit me again. *If I don't get up, we're both going to die.* I got my footing, and through my one clear eye I could see scratches raked down its snout. Bruno. It reared at me. Bruno came at it side-to, using up what wildness was still inside him. My eyes kept filling up with blood. The world slurred and in my mind I was already looking for the ending, the done of the thing.

It opened its deep mouth, inviting me to step inside. Inviting me to dance where nothing would be hard anymore. My rucksack lay beside my foot. I reached inside and found what I needed. Bruno was still biting and snapping. The bear took another swipe. Bruno fell from where he'd scampered up a trunk, loosely into the hard-packed snow, and did not move. I could feel my knees going soft. I fisted Mama's little carnival glass bottle, the one she used to spritz so bad spirits wouldn't catch on us, and with what strength I had left unresolved in my heart, I hurled it at the bear's mouth, its jaws readying to snap down again on Bruno's still form.

Red glass sharded its face and splintered inside its mouth and its one clouded eye. It made noises like a house coming undone and pawed the glass quilled in its wet gums and flaring lips. Just like I'd done for Song-catcher, I got the branch in hand and waved it around, screaming like a banshee, avoiding looking at Bruno for fear the thing had fish-gutted him. For fear he was already dead. Finally, the branch contacted its snout. Hard. And while it shook off the pain, I came down again axe-like across its dented skull.

"Are you my death?" I screamed. "You son of a bitch, answer me! Are you my death?"

I hit it another good whack and it backed down, woofing and teeth-popping. It ran bandy-legged up a low berm, bare except for some alders and sedge. I heard it go on, snapping through the deadfall, and then I heard it no more. I sank down in the worn-out air sparkled with carnival glass and blood and tried to figure out how to touch him.

The bear had gouged his shoulders and head, split the side of his mouth, clawed his stomach, and a back foot was welling with blood. In that fast-coming afternoon, with few options in front of me, I pulled out our blanket and rolled him onto it. By now he was glassy-eyed. Long streaks of half-frozen blood and snot and drool coated his mouth and chest. His breathing, hard, rapid. I found some peat moss down in a tree well, tore it from the ground, and packed the worst wounds and sponged up what seeped from his head into his eyes. I put both my sweater and scarf on him to keep him warm.

All that time, I tended to him from some distant place, because I couldn't stop shaking and couldn't look at those wounds directly. Sickness passed through me and then only dizziness remained. I couldn't look, not until I found someone who could help us. And I didn't believe that would happen. Finally, some part of me turned south, towards the work sounds I'd heard earlier, dragging the blanket, heavy with Bruno's near-dead weight, behind me.

a kind of horse without a name

Outside the diner, Ansell lit one of Benight's cigarettes and stood some moments watching the world shift from whiteout to light as snow swirled. Down the road came shouting. Children's voices, hooves, and something clattering and cracking sharp as it hit the frozen ground. He squinted into the icy air, unable to make anything out through the whiteout. And then a dark horse, walleyed, screaming, jinking away from what chased it. It reared up before the diner and tripped in the half-frozen pothole. Ansell could see then: a rocking chair bouncing, smashing into its flank. Two kids bellowed behind. Waving their arms. And then the horse skidded, sliding some distance, the rough ground tearing its flank and smashing the chair, as it tried to get its hind end back under itself.

Ansell ran back into the diner. "I need some flour!"

The waitress came out from behind the counter. "You what?"

"Flour! Lots of flour. Bring it outside!"

191

The horse, a gelding, lay on its side now, breathing heavily, blood seeping into the snow where the two girls stood as though at a funeral.

"We tied him to a rocking chair," the older one said. "We didn't know he'd run."

"Well, he did, didn't he?" Ansell snapped, taking the flour bag from the waitress. She stood shivering on the sidewalk a minute more, watching.

He hacked the frayed neck rope with his jackknife and sent the older girl to take what was left of the rocking chair somewhere down the road where the horse wouldn't catch sight of it. And then he managed to get it back on its feet. It was a cross-grained horse—a kind of horse without a name—one of the most common sorts in backyards all around those parts of the province. Inexpensive, quiet horses, with a sleepy sort of temperament, no great turns of speed, soft-mouthed, and small of stature. A child's idea of a cowboy horse. He ran his hands along its stout barrel and felt the bellowing force of its threatened heart. He let the horse lean on him while he checked the back hoof walls for ice-bruising and cracks. But besides the flank gashes and slight rashy malanders on a foreleg, it was without other injury. He walked around its front and stroked its soft cheek until its ears unpinned. Its mane was decorated with colored yarn and strands of old butterfly weed and those of another long-dead flower. Its forelock had been cut straight across, badly. *You poor old woebegone little bugger.* Ansell took some of the rocking chair rope and knotted up a rough hackamore and slipped it over its face. When he felt the horse willing to tolerate him, he started packing the wounds with flour.

"Someone tell you to tie a horse to a chair?" he asked.

"Daddy got us this horse just yesterday. Traded him for a couple of front axles. He didn't say where to tie him up."

One heartbeat. Two heartbeat. "Yep," Ansell said through clenched teeth. Fear is a horse's main emotion and here these damn kids—

"We didn't know!" the younger one shrilled. She wiped the back of her ice-pilled mitten across her snot-caked face and glowered at Ansell a bit more. "We didn't know!"

He glanced over the horse's croup at the child. Her face turned slightly against the sharp air. "Well, now you do, eh?" He finished packing the wounds so that the horse's dark flank was hatched with pink skinnings and ghostly handprints.

"His name's Santa's Sleigh," the other one said from where she stood near the uninjured flank, her face balled up in an anxious squint. She took a long study of Ansell's cheeks. "Someone put a hurtin' on you?"

Ignoring her, Ansell stepped towards the horse's face, speaking softly as it still breathed heavy and flared its huge, dark nostrils. He saw his own hatched face reflected in that deep, fear-bright eye and he saw the ageless fears its species kept written on its nine-pound heart. "You can manage to walk him back home, get your daddy to call a vet?" Ansell started to say more but shut his mouth. The horse blew gently now and rested its head on his shoulder.

The kids shuffled their feet in the snow in response.

"Where is your daddy now?"

"Sawin' ice."

"Since the mill closed," the younger added. "We don't got no more credit at the store."

The older one elbowed her hard in the side. Both turned their sharp faces towards him. He'd heard last year potatoes sold for ten cents a barrel. Thousands of tons left to rot in the fields. These kids' faces—hunger all over them.

"You take that horse home. Go slow and talk nice to it. Put it up in the barn with a blanket, you hear? And get someone to call in a vet. You hear me? Don't leave them cuts until it's too late. Go on. And get that malanders looked to, apt to spread into a worse rash. And," he added, half smiling, "don't be cutting that damn horse's forelock like that again. Looks like Friar Tuck."

It whickered in agreement and chucked its head but yielded to the children's gentle pull. One took the end of the now-frayed lead rope and the other walked beside it, one small hand solemn at its throatlatch, which sent its hide rippling. As they turned towards home, Ansell could hear her telling the horse, who carried its head low to the street, something lengthy, and secretive, and personal, and when the wind came up again over the fields through the bare apple orchard's dark, wintering limbs, all three were lost to that veiled winter landscape and, very soon after, gone.

Ansell brought the flour back inside and gave the waitress

a few more pennies for what he'd used. She pushed the coins back over to him. "You a vet, then? A horse whisperer, yeah?"

He shook his head. "Just met a few over the years."

"Well, still . . ." She fiddled with the bag's corners. *William Tell Flour. You Knead It.* "Good luck with your search, cowboy," she said with a wink.

He headed back out, averting his gaze from the pinkish stains weltering in the snow outside the diner's door.

between the dog and the wolf

Amaël Chanson saw the boy in the red coat first. He'd just come out through some rattled undergrowth that footed a pumpkin pine stand, which signaled his daily snow-shoe circuit was near complete. It was more than enough for one afternoon. He'd spent most of his day with the Fire Horse—a blue-black smoke eater that looked as though it had been forged in flame. Until he'd come to Bracken, Amaël had believed all fire horses retired. But the star of Bracken's team was down with a front leg bone splint. As Bracken's newest animal doctor, he was under pressure to heal the Brigadier because the horse pulled the hook-and-ladder cart and was a bit of a celebrity in those parts. A neighbor had told him how the soot-covered fire chief, well over six feet himself, often came into the Bracken Hotel, leading a smoke-stained Brigadier up to the bar. The dumbstruck guests waiting as the man said the now semi-famous words around town, "We're here for our after-fire drinks, Manny. A whisky for me and a beer for the Brigadier, if you please."

Amaël had been attending to the Fire Horse after an early morning house fire had sent out the pump trucks. Somewhere in the fray, the galloping had lamed it. With the Fire Horse resting in the barn, Amaël had come out to the woods to think about bones. Horse bones and how to heal them. This sort of thinking worked on him like a reserve of patience. It also kept his thoughts from straying to Raymond LaValle—the young man who worked at Broade's axe factory, who'd brushed his hand against Amaël's twice in the past week: once at the Bracken Hotel when Amaël had stopped in for a quick beer and once at the Reading Room, when they'd both reached for the latest *True Crime*. It was nothing. It was a nothing shaped like a thorn of light. *Keep snowshoeing. Think about the Fire Horse and not about Raymond LaValle.* His shoes bit into the crust. Lifting and falling. Lifting and falling. With the days still so short, an hour of snowshoeing could almost trick him into believing days would soon get longer and lighten. Days that often felt too full of sore mouth, ringworm, colic, and strangles. He was thinking about all these things when the boy in the red coat stepped out from the trees.

The boy walked towards the vet, his head down, his whole body angled forward as he closed the space—a continual upsetting and restoring of his balance with each step. He made no gesture of greeting. He dragged something heavy behind him.

"Ça va?" Amaël called. He was used to coming upon strangers stepping from the woods or walking down the cold, dark road to Bracken. Sometimes, he caught them with their

197

pockets heavy with poached hares—their silver snares toed under a fistful of leaves.

A broad-brimmed hat half concealed the boy's face. The skin under his untamed eyes stress-shadowed or hunger-shadowed. Amaël had seen both many times before. But it was when the boy glanced up and then through him that Amaël believed he was seeing something horrific unfold. The boy's face was greasy with blood. His left ear badly scratched. His knuckles barked and bitten with cold.

Amaël called out again. But the scarecrow creature in thready, oversized clothes continued to walk forward without seeing him. And there was something incongruent to it all: the way he, still unaware of Amaël, stepped forward, his snowshoes creaking as he forwent testing the snow to see if the crust would hold. He moved as a much older man might, one who'd worked his body very hard for a very long time. Stiff, over-heavy arms. Hands uncertain what to do with themselves without a saw or a five-pound hammer clasped tight. As he drew closer, Amaël could see that what he pulled behind was also covered in blood, leaving pink drag trails over the snow crust.

"Stop!" Amaël said, so that the boy stopped up as a horse might on command. His lips moved, and as Amaël came closer, he could hear him speaking strange words, *"Yan, tan, tether. Yan, tan, tether."*

Blood and something animal-sour came off the boy as though he'd been washed by death. Amaël glanced down at what he dragged behind him in the torn blanket. A figure in a sweater and scarf. *Oh Christ. A dead child.* The air slurred when he looked directly at it.

"I'm afraid he'll be dead if I look," the boy said, his eyes filled with terrible fear and terrible tiredness. "My brother'll be dead 'cause I got us attacked by a bear."

He shifted his weight to find purchase and stepped down too hard. The crust buckled and sank him up to his thigh in a sharp sleeve of ice. Without letting go of the blanket, he struggled to free himself from where a snowshoe had snagged beneath the thick crust. Ice rucked the woollen leg of his trousers, revealing a thin leg, skelped now with rune marks at the shin. It was then Amaël could see that the bloodstained boy was drawn down with exhaustion.

The boy slumped, his thin haunches resting on the tails of his snowshoes, and with a frayed sob said, "Bruno. He's Bruno."

Fighting both his imagination and revulsion, Amaël leaned down in the unstable snow and pulled the rank blanket away to reveal a small black bear. A black bear wearing a striped sweater and a red scarf. *It was the damnedest thing*, he thought, catching himself already retelling this to others, narrating through his own confusion. *I pulled back that bloodied blanket and there it was: a bear wearing clothes.*

The bear looked very much dead. Its body already cold and stiff. He leaned in closer to wipe some snow from its face and it was this warmth in his hand, perhaps, that revived the little bear enough to give a shallow sigh, a small sign of life that misted the snow with blood.

"It's alive," Amaël said. "And I'm an animal doctor." He took a minute to feel around the boy's face bones and looked to how the light set in his eyes. "You have a small concussion," he said, but the boy did not reply. He wiped some of the thickest blood from around the boy's ear.

"My head's full of bees!" he shouted, pushing Amaël's hand away. "Hornet stung."

Amaël wiped his hands on his wool pants and glanced again at the boy's face, half-shadowed in the turn of his hat. And that's when he saw it: not a boy but a girl—looking much older than she ought. The wind spelled over them.

"Let me," Amaël said, prying the corners of the filthy blanket away from her. The little bear stayed motionless. And the wind-galled girl followed along beside him. Silent. Ghostlike.

To those who'd lived there many years, these woods were unremarkable. But Amaël had not lived there nearly long enough yet. He felt that something else lived out there too—tricking his eye. He often felt set upon. A barred owl lifting, its wings throwing shape. A dark seep became an absence, then an animal, then an absence once again. *Un presque.* An almost. Dull shapes. Sliding eyes. Something carried away through the thick corridors of trees beyond his clinic's door. He felt this girl and bear were a part of that world and through some navigational misstep had found their way into this world. Out of place. Dispossessed. But he could not think of a single verb, in either language, for this sort of arrival.

"We'll go to my clinic," Amaël said, pointing towards

the empty fields beyond them. "And we will see how to help your bear." He smiled, though he felt a sense both of duty and of dread when he would have to explain this fairy-tale encounter to his other, less imaginative neighbors. And he feared what the death of the little bear might mean to this raggedy child.

The girl caught Amaël's eye then, her face set with panic. "Mine," she said. "He's *à moi*. He's *mon ours*, my bear." She turned and said something quick and unrecognizable and soothing to the still bear. "He's *mon frère*."

Amaël thought she'd said the bear was her brother, but it must have been the cool air playing tricks with his ears as it often did, making an owl's hew-hew, hew-hew come ahead and behind, behind and then ahead again.

"My brother," she repeated, her throat breaking into a sort of creak. She pointed to the bloodied form on the blanket. She spoke a strange English with broad vowels, wide inflections. *Mah brayther.*

"Okay then. We will hurry," Amaël said. Wrapping two corners of the blanket around his fists, he began to drag the bear towards Bracken. The afternoon was already hardening back into its frosts. They needed to get into town before it grew dark and the woods grew shaggy, and the little streams that ran through this part of the province, deep with switchery, began to conceal themselves once more. There was always danger of stepping into them.

As they came up on the other side of the hogback, dark smoke blunted the scape of the town. Amaël caught the girl watching it. "A house fire," he said. "Many hours ago. C'est très dommage." He considered saying more. "I have one of the fire horses in my care right now. Maybe you would like to see."

Again, the girl said nothing.

The air, weighted now with the acrid smell of the burning building, forced them to walk with their chins tucked down. They passed through the final field of rusty shrubs, reaching the clinic at the dusking hour—between the dog and the wolf. Amaël hung his snowshoes by their babiches from a spike on the wall. The girl did the same. "Come into the warm," he said.

Together, they carried the sodden blanket and animal into the examination room. Amaël got to work cutting the sweater away from the motionless bear. Below the scarf he found a thick leather collar, fashioned with a draw gauge from an old leather ox head harness. It had been made by someone with great skill. Two embossed bears and two hearts on either side of the name: *Bruno*.

"Do you want to help clean him?" he asked the girl.

She hesitated, still refusing to look directly at the bear. Her leg had not stopped shaking.

"No, never mind," he said. "You sit over there. I'll call if I need you." He gave her a soapy face cloth to clean her own wounds, but she only set it down on the chair beside her.

The bear had lost a lot of blood and Amaël was disappointed in himself for not having any training with this sort of care. There were rules, he knew. He did not cross certain boundaries, and in return, certain animals—the most elusive and wild—did not cross into his world. But this animal was out of place. Were bears constructed like dogs? Perhaps sheep? He thought again about the bones in things. *Pick an animal you know and work from there, Amaël.* He set his mind to his understanding of dog anatomy as he tweezed the bloodied moss from the wounds and wiped at the sticky underfur.

"It was very smart. The moss."

The bear had a good gash on its rump and back leg, a mouth like a busted zipper, an injured foreleg, deep tissue damage possibly. Most of the other cuts seemed superficial. There was blood in its mouth but not in its ears. Possibly no head trauma. Bears must bleed a lot, he thought as he began shaving around the jagged skin flaps. He fingered one of the largest cuts open—like a pocket, deep enough the bone glimpsed through. He syringed it with iodine, which pooled darkly over the floor.

"Just iodine," he said. "We can leave some of these open. Air will help close them up." He took a long time to say all this, leaving pauses between his words, so that the girl might say something if she needed to.

She gave a weak nod, but stayed, leaning forward, elbows on her knees, cracking her knuckles. Her eyes on her boots. "Learned it from my mama. She was a healer too."

"What?"

"The mossing."

He handed her the collar. "Very nice."

"A teamster done this. For us," she said, her voice fraying. "Some say the devil's dead, but we know better than that."

He was surprised how easily the devil sat on her lips. Such a strange child. "Yes, I see," he said, though he did not. He kept up a nervous chatter as he felt around the breath-frail bear's misshapen face. He pulled out its tongue and checked its gum color and flooded its eyes with quick light.

"Do you know?" But then he shrugged. "No. Nothing. *Rien. Rien.*"

The rangy child ground herself deeper into the old horsehair chair the vet cat often slept on, still studying her feet.

"And so he is Bruno and I am Amaël and you are who?"

"Pearly Everlasting," the girl said, leaving the vet unsure if she was saying a name or some half-formed wish.

"Pearly Everlasting?"

The girl nodded, but offered no more explanation.

=

By the time they'd reached the clinic, the village of Bracken had begun to talk, to surmise about the strange vet from away who'd been seen tramping through the hayfields with a boy, dragging something dark and bloodied behind them. Aldice Getchell, the mailman, had been finishing his rounds when Loftus Shaughnessy, who drove the bread van, stopped to say he'd seen the strange troupe up on Crocker Hill, tromping across the fields, beyond the rough-timbered barns, where dark, woolly moose were often seen moving north in the wick-lit mouth of autumn, away from their summer grounds. He'd picked up Goobie Drapeau walking back from Stedmans

Variety and had told him next. Between the three, word traveled. A scarecrow of a creature and some mangy goat. A tramp and a pony. A child riding on the back of a dwarf donkey. There may have even been a monkey or a raccoon with them. And so, from the door of Hazel Symmington, the chair of the local chapter of the Daughters of the Temperance Society, to Mr. Angus Scovil, the one-eyed butcher, who swore he could see perfectly from the empty socket during lunar eclipses, the village passed on the strange tale of the newcomers. The house fire already old news, though some suspected the two events linked—the strangers perhaps forerunners to future catastrophes. And those stories eddied around the village of Bracken that afternoon, all the way out to Frog Pond Road, where the poorer families lived in board-and-batten houses with too few rooms and too many children.

The rumors spread around all the framed houses except for the one house set off on the hill: the stone one, its windows blinded and dim. They traveled past cats in windows, dogs on chains, Connick's Drugs with its Sweet Caporal cigarettes, hair dye and hard candy, lemon soda and false teeth ads pasted to its pane glass window. They circled the pool hall, which some called Smoochies and others the Happy Birthday, though no one could say why because the sign above the door had only ever said Pool Hall: No Women, No Cursing. The rumors went on, past the Spoon Island granite cenotaph—finished in the rough for the war dead. All the names kin to those in Bracken and those buried behind one of the three churches, below the cemetery trees that made the ground around the graves rusty with long needles. Their grief-goods—their silk flowers and jam jar votives and soggy teddy bears—sometimes caught up in the winds and rain-veils like the leftovers of a parade or an enemy sacking.

===

Amaël finished tying off stitches along the bear's stomach. He stood back to admire his handiwork before it occurred to him. Shock. The girl's probably in shock. *Amaël, you damn idiot.* He went over to the wall phone near the door that connected the clinic to the house. Mrs. Pocket—pronounced only by herself as Po-kay, as she insisted her people descended from Huguenots—answered on the second ring.

"Mrs. Pocket, sorry, Po-kay, could you come in here a moment. Yes . . . yes, I said Po-kay. Yes, fine. Just come in here. Please."

Minutes later, the housekeeper came in, chattering about a barn cat that had been spraying the doorstep. "—and the mangy little—" She saw first the bear on the table, then the bloody clothes and rags and floor tiles, and then the girl. Each of them a thing out of place. "What in the—Is that a bear?"

"It's a long story, Mrs. Pocket, and I still have a lot of work to do here. Could you please take Pearly . . . Yes, this is Pearly. Please take her into the house and give her some tea with lots of sugar. I'm afraid she's had a shock."

A black sheen came over the woman's eyes as she took in

what Amaël was asking of her. The girl appeared an apparition of nightmarish proportions: the marks of her own bloody hands staining her face.

"Perhaps a change of clothes as well?" Amaël added, trying to keep his voice light. The woman's threads of order were the only ones that she abided by and he'd learned some time ago not to question how she ran the household, but this was different. "Mrs. Pocket, er, Po-kay? Pearly is waiting."

"Yes, Doctor," she finally managed. "I'll give Frances Boudreau a ring. She might have some things in the church box."

"And something to eat, of course."

"Molasses and bread," she said. No hint of invitation in her tone or manner.

"Fine. That's just fine. And Pearly," Amaël sort of hollered across the room at the dazed girl, who still sat studying her sorry boots. "Pearly, I'm going to keep working on Bruno while you warm up, all right? You come back when you're ready."

She nodded, her eyes brightening slightly. Amaël recognized the look: momentary hope, a brief question of the animal's future tense. It happened when he spoke to people about their cancer-riddled dogs and aging farm animals.

Careful not to touch any inch of the child, Mrs. Pocket led her to the house door. "Wipe them feet." When she spoke, her teeth were very small and square and sharp at the edges.

At the threshold, Pearly kicked off her broken boots. Then, remembering something, she turned back to the bear and whispered, "*Hovela, hovela kavela streck. Es morres a fri, is alles aveck.*"

Mrs. Pocket stood stone-still, her eyebrows raised in that way they did when she was judging something foreign and strange.

Pearly laid her hand on the bear's heart for a minute more, then stepped away. Climbing the three steps, quiet, as though her feet were shod in fur.

dirty little wood rat

Dirty little wood rat was what that house-lady called me. Blood-sick, I'd peeled off my mackinaw and Humphrey pants like I was peeling off skins. To make myself smaller, I rolled everything into the basket she held away from herself. Barefoot, my feet were pale and parboiled like a couple of blind baby mice.

Us walking in the woods and then a bear steps into my path and I step into his.

I knew how I looked: lost in my clothes and lost without them. Raising stink. Woodsmoke, sweat, horse, kerosene, something unplaceable that could've been the lard and pine tar the men used as fly grease every spring. Unshiftable and stained. It made me wish I'd brought some of Ivy's silly costumes. Something with a bit of shine on it. I knew this woman thought me and Bruno didn't carry no weight. But we carried a hell of a lot.

I stood there shivering while she and another woman, a church lady, rummaged through a box of clothes because *someone should have the good of them.* They shoved house-dresses at me, until I said over the buzzing in my head, my eyes watering in the electric light, "Hell, no! I won't be wearing no dress!" They eyed me like I was something wild.

Us having dinner on a log. I give Bruno the last cookie.

I'd never seen a washtub like that before and didn't know how to bring down the water. The two women snapped at each other over little things. But there were small kindnesses too, like when the church lady sponged the blood from my face. And those rare moments made me weep. I put on the clean overalls and flannel shirt and wool socks and found the kitchen. Mrs. Pocket moved from the sink, to the stove, to the kettle like she was fit to be tied at the whole world, like she wanted something to break. She glared over her shoulder from time to time, to make sure I was watching.

Us walking together in our woods. Slow snow. My hand in Bruno's fur.

She spooned Red Rose tea into a mug, settling it with boiling water. The room soured with orange pekoe, taking me back to the cookhouse where that same smell dragged the air all day. Shame cut through me, thinking how bad everything had gotten. All I wanted was to sit beside Ansell, the way we used to when I had all that anger in me and Mama made me go walk it out and instead I'd just go into the cookhouse to sit with Ansell and a cup of tea. And he'd look at them storms inside me for a spell like they weren't anything strange and that always, always made them go away again.

The woman did not offer milk or sugar. Still, the mug's

warmth seeped into my hands' sored-up places and calmed me a bit. When I was done with what little I could keep down, the cagey old bat gave me a backwards glance and led me to a room at the top of the stairs. She gave me an Aspirin to help me sleep. Sleep stepped forward then back then forward again. The buzz in my ear changed to something like listening to the world from inside a cake bell. The swollen claw-scratch over my eye felt almost numb. And though it was only the third night sleeping in a bed without Bruno beside me, I barely noticed. I was dead asleep before full night and everywhere hurt.

But just before I fell asleep, I heard what that old goat called me: *dirty little wood rat, Frances. Nothing but a dirty little wood rat.* And then the soft voices again. Scarcely there.

=

I dreamt I grew four-legged. Jack in the Dark watched, gnawing at chicken bones left in the dirt for the barn cats. He watched me meet that bear's hellish ground-shudder. Again and again, I fell into its long-jawed cave. I danced with it while Jack in the Dark buried something in a bloodied box in the field beyond the house. He pushed his hands down my throat and filled me with snow bright as milk.

I tried to unhook myself, but dreams carry themselves on their own legs. And when I woke in the dark air, I believed myself still standing in those bloodied woods where Swicker fell. And I wondered if the dead would always come to me in this way and, if I did nothing but stand witness, if, they might lessen and thin until I might dream the woods again—empty but for me and Bruno. And Jack in the Dark, in all his guises, would no longer take heed of us.

＝

I opened my eyes and everything was still dark. It was not the middle of real night, just that timeless, inward part. I waited for something to show itself, the gray to walk backwards from the room, the morning to fill up with teamsters calling out to each other as they backed the horses into their traces. And the horses calling out to each other too. Something, anything familiar to still my blood-sick heart. I laid there a few minutes more in the lemony-soap sheets and tried to figure out how I'd ended up there, and my heart rabbited with its remembering. I pulled Bruno's wooden trough from my pack, got dressed, and made the bed best I could.

I opened my door without a click. The old woman had gone to sleep, but she'd left a light on. I was learning quickly that electricity made me feel exposed. A mackerel-marked cat shot ahead of me. Left, right, right. I followed it back through the mazy rooms to where I'd begun, then took the stairs two at a time, not caring if a floorboard creaked under my socked step. Finally, I found the door that would lead me back into the vet's clinic.

One lamp lit up the clinic's starkness: a cabinet of glass bottles and metal tools. A lone poster on the wall of the inside workings of a cow. The animal doctor was slumped down in the horsehair chair, a ducking coat draped over him like a blanket. In the new light, he looked like a man in an advertisement for shaving soap. Through the window a lick of night and a pink sleeve of daylight. East, I thought. And everyone already awake at home. I stepped farther into the room. The table that had held Bruno was empty.

"Bruno?" His trough knocked against the man's chair. "Bruno?" I said again, louder.

Half out of the chair as if he'd been stung, he pointed to a far corner in the room, where less light reached. Bruno slept on several saddle blankets beside a boiler grate eking out warmish air. The window above him rattled in its sill when the wind picked up. I walked towards him but couldn't bring myself too near. Each time I tried, a prickly spark ran up my arms as though we were sharing pain. I worried my touch might loosen something needed now inside him, something not ready to be ruined.

The vet took a drink of something ambery from a short star-cut glass. He coughed a bit and then gestured to Bruno. "You're awake, Pearly."

I nodded, thankful my head didn't hurt so much now. "I dreamt that my teeth grew in," I said.

He took a long study of me, but I could tell he didn't understand. "Go on. Touch him."

Real careful, I ran my hand from skull bone to tail. Bruno did not stir, but just touching him, feeling his warmth beneath his cool-tipped fur, made my heart beat differently. I slipped back into myself and let the tears mackle my sight. Something was attached to him. A cord ran up to a glass jar.

"It's to give him extra fluids," the man said. He put aside his ducking coat. "Thought it best I stay out here tonight. To watch him, make sure he doesn't wake up wild."

"He's not wild," I said, as static built up between Bruno's fur and my palm.

"Right, eh. He's your brother."

"That's right," I said, readying myself for the hard question that squatted there between us. I swallowed a few times then asked, "Will he make it?"

The man fumbled with a pack of cigarettes, lit one, considered the spent match head for a bit, then exhaled. "Maybe. He was lucky." He smoked a bit more. "And he's strong."

I rubbed Bruno's back foot against the grain and he kicked out.

The vet shrugged. "The reflex." He offered me a cigarette. I took it.

"He's real tough."

"Et tu?"

"I give as good as I get," I said, jutting out my chin, exhaling smoke above us.

He gave a kind of spitty laugh and took another drink. It was then I realized he might be drunk. "You are—what? Ninety pounds, maybe, and this wild bear, six or seven hundred or more? I'm afraid your giving is not the same as your getting. You and you"—he pointed his chin towards Bruno—"are lucky."

I watched him consider me. "You going to call the police?"

He shrugged in a lazy way. "Should I?"

"No, sir."

"Okay. Let's talk. So where do you come from?"

"Camp 33. We, um, we had to leave. *Le camp de bûcherons.* We're Greenlaw royalty."

He nodded, but I could tell he didn't believe me. "And how far have you come? As a scarecrow boy."

"Yesterday, I s'pose a couple of hours."

This was not so much a lie as a way of feeling how the world had changed since we'd left the sugar shack. The Go-Preacher's misdoings and the bear attack had collapsed time and made it strange and there were wide patches in the day that had given way to something mechanical within me that kept my legs lifting out of the snow and my arms adjusting the rucksack that bit into my shoulder, leaving my mind to creep elsewhere in that desolate light.

"So how did you manage to find your way from so far?"

"We know the basic way," I said, "and then I followed a trail this Go-Preacher had taken before me. He was out looking to be evangelical. But he stole something important from us and when we find him—" I didn't want to mention Mama's double-horn pendant, though I'd all but settled it in my mind by then: the taking and the taking back.

"Go-Preacher?"

"Yeah, them border-jumpers call them Sky Pilots or Two by Twos from the No-name Church, because they travel in twos, sometimes. This one, though, was alone, and he wasn't very good, I don't think." Some small noise upstairs stopped me. I lowered my voice as I told him about the Go-Preachers:

the ones who believed in divine healing and those who spoke in tongues.

"And this all happened a few hours from here?"

There were no camps a couple of hours' walk away and I could tell the man also knew this to be true.

He paused, considering. "But you've traveled long?"

"Yeah, I guess."

"How have you slept? How have you found food?"

"Camps. Sugar shacks. Ice cave."

"Ice cave?"

Bruno's shallow breathing marked the silence.

"You said *from here*, but where's here?" I asked, waving my hand around the room. And this question seemed more diffi-cult for the vet to answer than I'd expected.

=

Over the next few hours, Amaël—as he reminded me—slept in his chair. The sky bled out its reds and seeped blue, while I sat on the floor beside Bruno and ran a cloth soaked in salt and sugar along his gums from time to time. I waited for a sign, sometimes nodding off with my head beside his.

When it was almost light, Amaël went to change for his house calls. In a short while, he came back into the clinic with a tray: tea and toast. He put on his ducking coat.

"I've got to see about my famous Fire Horse and a few others this morning. Milk cows and goats, goats and milk cows. I'll be back for dinner. You stay here. Talk to Bruno. It might help." At the door, the cold morning air leaking in, he

turned. "Just use that telephone on the wall if you need anything. Mrs. Pocket—" He stared out at the yard. "Just pick it
up and she'll answer, okay?"

And then he was gone. His footsteps crunching over the
crusty yard, heading out around the side of the house, where
the Fire Horse rested. I flicked the fatty electric light off and
on, just to see, and ran water in the sink until the pipes high-
pitched and rumbled hot. *Well, I'll be damned.*

I put some goose salve on the cut that ran up the side of
Bruno's mouth. I read to him from a dog-eared Zane Grey I'd
found in a cardboard box of books. Some of the stories were the
same we traded in camp: ranch hands on the run from a sheriff,
a pioneer woman good with a gun. I read until my legs went
to pins and needles. I thought maybe Mrs. Pocket might have
a curry comb somewhere so I could brush Bruno's matted fur.

I picked up the telephone as I saw Amaël do the day
before. As I waited for something to happen, I heard Mrs.
Pocket say, "Filthiest thing you ever saw, Zella. The clothes
hanging off her like rags and smelling like, well, you can just
imagine. And another thing, how's she going to pay for all
that care? For a bear, no less! You think someone like that's
got money to burn? Thing should just be put down."

Her voice raised and hard, Zella said something about slit-
ting a throat while Mrs. Pocket was sleeping, about burning
the house down around her ears, but I was already replacing
the telephone. I hadn't thought about money.

==

217

I finger-brushed Bruno's fur, digging hard enough under his chin to make his back leg kick. A reflex. I talked to him and sang to him and watched for Amaël's return past the houses and houses and houses—their walls filled up with big glass windows. When I saw him coming down the empty road, eyes to his feet, I crouched down on my haunches like the men in camp did when they had something important to say—my hand resting on Bruno's side.

Amaël shook sleet from his coat. He kicked the door closed with his heel. "Damn this weather," he said. "Ah, Pearly! How you making out? Any changes in our furry patient?"

"How much's this all going to cost?" I asked, eyeing him like I'd been taught.

He held his coat over the hook but didn't hang it up. "Cost?"

"You're gonna want some money for all this helping, I'm guessing?"

"I'm not doing this for money, Pearly." He squinted at the bloodied side of my face. "And you ought to have Mrs. Pocket put some salve—"

"I don't want that old dragon anywhere nears me," I said, filled up now with spit sparks. "And," I added, "some turpentine and sugar should fix us both up. We gotta get home."

"Now, no one's drinking turpentine and sugar," he said, shaking his head at the idea. He knelt down to check on Bruno: his gums, eyes, and tongue. "Good," he said to himself, before striding over to the phone. "Mrs. Pocket . . . Mrs. Pocket, I don't have time for pronunciation lessons today. Can you please just come in here?"

We could hear her dithering around in the house, her footsteps loud in the hallway. "Yes, Amaël? I'm in the middle of—"

He spoke at length to her, quietly so that I could not hear, except when he said, "Do you understand?" and "I won't have any more of it," when Mrs. Pocket tried to convince him of something.

And then he turned to me. "Pearly is going to be in Bracken for a while," he said. "While Bruno recovers."

Mrs. Pocket nodded but would not look at me.

"Now, she has it in her head that she and Bruno will be turned away because of money."

Mrs. Pocket, her face heating up, stared out the window, over Amaël's shoulder.

"I'm wondering if you know of any jobs she might do around town."

"I think the police—"

"I'm not asking you that. Since you're in everyone's business, I'm asking about a job for Pearly while her brother, Bruno, gets knitted back together."

"I believe there might be something at that boardinghouse . . . Broken Hill House," she said, her voice bruising the air between us.

a weather vane in the shape of a pig

On Monday, Amaël walked me over to Broken Hill House—our boots making muffled growls against the hard snow as we followed a path into Bracken. A low wind traveled over the fields, numbing the left sides of our faces. A headache settled near my temple where my cuts ran deepest. The wild bear still with me. Folded inside my pocket was a note from a Mrs. Alwyn Prue. Since its arrival two days earlier, I'd studied the shape of the letters several times, trying to determine what sort of person might invite me to stay and work in her boardinghouse. Mrs. Prue's letters were formed up and down with strikeovers and ink stains, and a short, stabbing line beneath the *Mrs.* The words often ending with something soft and tailed, as though she was apologizing for an earlier mood.

At the river, we paused to watch a knot of people calling to a big black dog that stood unsteadily in the middle of the iced-over water. Waving sticks, some children cooed, making up names for it as they called, but it only barked from its place on the ice. Held there by some unseen force.

"It is difficult to travel with a bear, *non?*"

"Yeah. It's some hard. He's lazy by design and just wants to eat all the time. He'd dinner out five times a day, if I let 'im. And he's some bold and foolish-acting most of the time."

"Me too and me too," Amaël said. He'd become quite taken with Bruno being awake in winter, living in a lumber camp, and had borrowed several books from the library on the inner workings of black bears. He had a lot of questions, but their answers weren't in books.

Unlike the woods with their roads like rabbit runs, Bracken had sprung up around four or five streets. Everything led to somewhere thought out in advance. Here, the left road led to a church with a fang-like steeple. Amaël said its stained glass had been shipped from France in vats of molasses and its wooden steeple was the highest point for miles around.

"What'd they do with the molasses?"

"What?"

"After they got the windows out. They use it for cookies? Beans?"

"I don't think anyone's asked that before."

We walked on. They were playing a film called *Watch Your Step* at the Dominion Theatre. The poster said: "A comedy in which a city slicker in a hickory shirt battles a country hick in tailor-mades." None of which made much sense to me. The roads to the right of Bracken led to the axe factory and we could see the charred uprights of the house that had burned earlier. The other two roads, I suspected, led out to more farmland, a scattering of houses, and then our woods again. We walked down one of these roads then up to Broken Hill House.

"You could stay at the clinic," Amaël offered.

"I'm all right," I said, though I had no notion of what I was getting myself into.

Broken Hill House looked like a neglected dollhouse set back off a potholed lane. Its gaze unnerving. Near the chimney cowl was a weather vane shaped like a pig. Its fixings, seized up with wind-worked rust, rattled and squealed. It leaned eastward, so that the pig looked to be either running away or peering down onto the ground below. I wondered just how far it might be able to see from up there. Maybe all the way home. Occasionally, restless snow passed over us as we stood there, revealing the late afternoon sun, which fell over the house's windows, lighting them up like little fires. The lid of an ancient mailbox, pocked with weather, clacked as the wind lifted it then dropped it back down into its hollow base.

As we stood there taking the house in, a girl with two sprung braids came from the side. She sang some small song, waving tatty death cards splayed like a hand of cards—photos of children, drowned or fevered into death, with the words *Hail Mary* printed above their small dead faces. Wrapped in layers of scarves, the girl looked like a pile of walking laundry. She came to the spade-headed gate, stood up on the cross metal at the base so that her boots squeaked against the uprights and cage-work, and stared hard at us. She pulled a lint-covered barley candy from her pocket and popped it in her mouth. A green hen missing its head.

"Is Mrs. Prue home?" Amaël asked loudly, as though speaking to someone much older.

The girl hopped down from her perch and took little running jumps up the wooden steps. One. Two. Three. "Only Jehovahs come to front doors!" she called behind her.

Amaël shook his head at some small disappointment I could not understand. "Let's go see for ourselves," he said, leading me by the elbow through the stiff gate blistered with black oil paint. He pulled on a frayed bell cord hanging out of its wall socket.

A shadowy figure grew clearer in shape as it came closer to the door's diamond pane window. The latch clicked. A reddish woman, much out of breath, stood framed in the open door. "Oh, for the love of Might. I told that flittin' and flyin' Zella that I needed a girl around here." Her stare swallowed things up and made them small and lesser-than. "And from the looks of that face, he's nothing but a little scrapper."

Neither Amaël nor I said anything for a few moments.

"I am," I said finally.

"What? You're what?"

"A girl."

"Takes all sorts," she said, peering hard at me. "Well, I guess you'll want to come in." She stepped aside to reveal a dark hallway. "Now, I don't speak no French," she said, waving her hands before Amaël as though language floated in the air like a shoal of minnows. "Can't keep none of them foreign words in my head."

"No worry for you, Mrs. Prue, my English is good enough

for the job," Amaël said, turning to me, still lingering at the door. "This is Pearly Everlasting. By the way."

Mrs. Prue's eyes roved over me. My cropped hair had dried strangely the night before and I knew I looked a scarecrow in my oversized clothes, the blue swelling over my eye, my face hatched with claw marks. Despite it all, I took out my letter, still folded in thirds, and held it out to her. Proof I'd been invited.

"Let's not heat the outdoors, then," she said. Only her mouth smiled a bit and I felt that she was someone who often suffered from poor sleep. "Come into the winter room, where it's warmer."

She led us into a side room, heavy with a sweetish smell. In the setting gloom, the room felt like the day had gone there to die. At the far end, one tree's shadow showed through a blind. And everywhere, dark, thick-footed furniture. In the corner, a man's shirt sleeve hung like a snared tongue, half-fed to a laundry mangle. In the opposite corner, a small black dog with long, shiny ears sat with his back towards us, staring at an empty, napless chair.

From a tombstone-shaped radio fiddling music played. "*Jean Étienne Thibault*," the voice said, "*présentement en comp sur la Rivière-du-Loup, de la part de son amie de Sainte-Anne-de-Portière.*" Girls requesting country and western songs for boys.

"I can only get the French in this weather," Mrs. Prue said, turning it down. She had a pronounced limp that made her walk with a rolling gait. "Got the cold in my hip," she said by way of explanation. The little black dog whined at the chair as she spoke.

"That's Chummy," she said, pointing at the dog with the shirt sleeve she was yanking from the mangle's rollers. Its seams crackled with her efforts. "Mr. Prue died six months ago, bless his soul, and Chummy spends his days waiting for him to come home. It's enough to break a heart."

We watched the dog watch the empty chair until the girl appeared again. She threw herself in it, singing, "Chummy bummy bummy boo!"

The dog, his view now blocked by the girl, still wrapped in her layers of scarves, kept repositioning himself so as to see around or through the girl.

"What'd I tell you about tormenting that dog, Ruby Mae?"

Ruby Mae sat some moments, thinking perhaps, then slid off the chair, leaving its cushion off square. Chummy nosed it back into place and continued his vigil.

Mrs. Prue tut-tutted then turned to me. "So, you're the one everyone's been nattering on about? The one that came out of the woods with them circus bears all cut up from wild dogs or something. Dark as the devil, I hear?" Her voice had taken on a know-it-all tone. *Dirty little wood rat.*

"I came out of the woods, yeah." *Hard-founded and brave.* "And I got a bear, but he's no circus bear. He's my brother."

"Well, we all have different names for the same things, don't we, eh, Doc?" Mrs. Prue said, winking at Amaël.

225

Amaël reddened around the ears then regained his composure. "How do you get on without any French, Mrs. Prue? So many speak it here."

"Oh, Mr. Prue done that work. He speaks some and writes less."

It was a nonanswer, if Mr. Prue was now dead. But neither of us mentioned this.

Ruby Mae returned holding a white cat. "And now I'm gonna perform a play!" she announced to the room.

"No. No, you're not, missy. Skedaddle right out right now. The pair of ya's," she added, eyeing the cat growling low in the girl's clutches. "And leave the Persian alone."

Ignoring Mrs. Prue, in a way that said she'd done so many times before, the girl sashayed over to where Chummy was holding his vigil for the badly used-up chair and tried to get the cat to walk along the dog's back. The cat howled and backpedaled and Chummy sneered a fine row of thorny teeth before he turned back to the chair.

"No needling, Ruby Mae! You leave him be!" Mrs. Prue said, loud enough to send the little girl out of the room again, the cat growling in her arms. "Lordy, lordy, that one's a little Christer," she huffed. "Gonna be a handful in a few years. You mark my words. Lordy. Lordy."

Mrs. Prue was like something capable of fizzing over with just the slightest shake. There was something not quite tame, or tame in ways that mattered less, about her. The wrong word. The wrong step. She made me nervous, and I knew this made me more apt to make mistakes.

A blast of cold air. Heavy boots at the door, first kicking off snow then dropping—one, two—onto the floor. "Mother Prue?"

"In here!" She looked directly at us. "Doing everything myself, as usual."

Like an Old Testament prophet, a man, not much taller than myself, shuffled into the room. Curls of wood clung to his gray hair and soft-settled dust coated his shoulders and glasses.

"Oh, Mr. Prue," Mrs. Prue cooed. "There you are, just in time to inspect the new girl."

Amaël stepped back, surprise running through his gaze. "Oh, I'm sorry, Mrs. Prue, I misunderstood. I thought—" He waved his hand, indicating the dog, the empty chair.

"That was *old* Mr. Prue," Mrs. Prue said. "Mr. Prue's father. Prues have lived in this house six generations. And my Mr. Prue, Alwyn Junior Junior here, is very much alive. As you can see."

"Yes, I can see. Much alive. Very nice to meet you."

"Can't see a jeezless thing," he replied, looking for some piece of cloth free from grit to clean his glasses.

"Oh, give them here," Mrs. Prue said, snatching them away and huffing hot breath over them and wiping them clean with the corner of her housedress, where the flowers were brightest at the hem. She held them to the light to check her work before passing them back. There was stubbornness in her hands.

"Mr. Prue is a woodworker," Mrs. Prue said as explanation

for her husband's appearance. "He makes signposts for new roads and also for old roads, if they should get washed out or knocked down by them winos." She announced in his general direction. "We have the animal doctor here, eh? And the orphan I asked for."

"Who's the orphan?" I asked.

They all turned to look at me.

"Why, you are, aren't you?"

"I come from Greenlaw royalty. Eight generations," I said. "And my papa is the most famous cook in the woods. No way in hell am I an orphan."

Mr. Prue gave a quick chuckle. "Might have finally met your match, Mother Prue."

Mrs. Prue stared daggers into me then turned her attention back to her dusty husband. "Must be some cold out there in the workshop today. Eh, Mr. Prue?"

"Oak," he said, half surprising himself as the word hiccupped from his mouth. "Gotta look for a straight grain. Not too many knots or whorls. Because I don't want them patterns competing with my lettering and . . ."

We waited for him to say more, but he'd finished for now, his gaze sliding again to the floor's skirting.

"Most words out of himself in years," Mrs. Prue said. And then to the room, she said, "Mr. Prue is in charge of the signs for New Codiac, where that circus train crashed."

"Cain's Crossing," Mr. Prue corrected.

She put an end to the argument by turning her small eyes back onto me, making me wish I'd sewn the missing buttons onto my sweater. "You ever use one of these?" she asked, pointing to the mangle.

Mama only had a washboard, but I didn't want her to turn me away. "I've used one twice as big as that one," I said, concentrating my face muscles not to twitch. Mrs. Prue eyed me up, roaming around my battered features, looking for a catch of a lie.

"Maybe you could explain what you might expect from Pearly Everlasting, Mrs. Prue, and then we can get out of the hairs, as they say," Amaël said.

"Well, what else can you do?" she asked me point-blank.

I took a deep breath and thought, because most of what I'd been taught wasn't really holding up in the Outside. "I can wash all the lantern chimneys and get all the lamps filled up with oil for the morning. I can chop kindling. I can sharpen an axe and bust a hole in the ice and lug all your washing water. I can cut cardboard to fit inside your shoes for Mondays. I can kill them chickens outside—"

"They're laying hens!"

"Still."

"Well," she said, thinking. "I don't have much need for them things, but I do collect the eggs in the morning and I've got a trout to clean."

Amaël shook his head. "Tomorrow, Mrs. Prue. She can help you with all that tomorrow."

"I'm sure she can learn something off me. Just cleaning up after boarders and Mr. Prue's endless shavings and dust is a full-time job in itself."

Mr. Prue, still leaning on the door frame, stopped brushing the dust from his sleeve, nodded in agreement, then occupied himself with unrolling a pigskin pouch and tamping tobacco into his pipe's fire bowl. He ran a wooden match across a deeply ridged thumbnail. He took several deep hauls on the stem, each time reddening the tobacco. Ruby Mae had come back into the room, without the Persian or death cards. She leaned against Mr. Prue's leg, two middle fingers in her mouth, and watched us—awkward strangers standing around a laundry mangle.

Mr. Prue broke the moment, tying up his boots at the door.

"Best to button up if you're going back out to the shop, Mr. Prue!" Mrs. Prue called over the snap of a shirt she was shaking straight of wrinkles.

"Mr. Prue, god bless him, took a spell some years ago," she said, keeping her voice low. "Needs some help remembering from time to time. Anyway, I should tell you about the boarders. That girl—" She glanced around, but Ruby Mae had disappeared too. "She's one of them ones that got burnt out couple days ago. Well, I look after her when her mother Loretta's at work in the factory."

"Oh, she's not yours?" Amaël asked.

"Get your eyes tested, Doc! I'm as old as Methuselah!" she said. "Descended from thieves they are. The husband up and left them just before Christmas." She paused, waiting for a reaction. When none came, she sputtered onwards. "Then there's Mr. Nevers and a couple of others who flit and fly through here more than they should." She rolled her eyes towards the ceiling. "And what about you? Pearly, is it? Where are your people? Out in one of them camps? One of them big outfits? Working everyone half to death? I heard one of them was killed a while back. Chopped up, axe through his head. You hear about that?"

I felt a shaking start low in myself. "No, ma'am. No. We're at a different camp. My father's the cook."

"Well, why you out here, then?"

I held the tremble from my voice. "My bear ran away. I had to get him."

"Kids sure get attached to toys, don't they?" she said.

I glanced at Amaël, ready to explain things better, but he shook his head.

"Guess you'll be a good help in the kitchen, maybe," Mrs. Prue went on.

Just then, one two three four short-footed steps ran across the ceiling. A light hanging from a water-damaged medallion rattled in Ruby Mae's wake. Her footsteps ran back in the opposite direction. Chummy ticked his ears with each bang but did not turn from his vigil.

"Well, I'll see you out," Mrs. Prue said over the clatter. Walking and pitching like her shoes were too tight, she waved us into another dim hallway that ran the length of the house. As we followed, doors slammed—angry ghosts making their presence known. Mrs. Prue said something under her breath after the third door slammed. Just before we reached the front door, Ruby Mae came rushing out from a room near the back

231

of the house and streaked past us. She slammed into the wall and ricocheted off, collapsing onto the floor. Her eyes closed. Her breathing shallow.

"*Ma p'tite*," Amaël gasped, leaning down to check her still form.

"Oh, she's right as rain," Mrs. Prue said, stepping over the child. Hesitantly, I did the same. Her face still slack, though I could see her eyes moving behind her lids. Amaël walked around her body, touching her shoulder as he passed.

"Well, it won't be boring here," he whispered as the door closed behind us.

=

By the time we left, the lower fields were in shadow and soft glows marked where Bracken's houses were densest—the three churches' fanged steeples competing at its center. Sadness settled in me as we turned from Bracken's lights to carry on back over the gray-blue fields to the clinic. I missed the night-side of the camp. On the river, the black dog was still there. We stood for a moment with a small group gathered at the edge, where the ice had buckled.

"Out there four days now," a man said. "Someone even sent out some canned ham tied to a string, but it just don't got enough sense to come in out of the cold."

bare trees in their dark wells

The man was in the yard. His gray hair roached up beyond his forehead like something roused from rough sleep. He spoke to himself as he worked, hauling scrap metal around the littered yard into patterns clear only in his own mind. The sign above the door said Kingdom Scrape Yard and below it were countless examples of this in various states of disassembly: engine cranks, car bumpers, joints of old pipe, buckets and cooking pots with their bottoms burnt dry or gone to rust, corrugated metal, bedsprings, telephone insulators, and twisted colters.

"Help you find something?" he asked, waving his hand over the displays.

"I'm looking for your brother."

"Which one?"

"You got more than one?"

"Nope."

"Well, then I'm looking for that one."

"Benight just went out for a sec. Off to get a few things."

The man lifted and groaned as he set things down else-where in the strewn yard.

"This isn't my enterprise," he said. "It's Benight's. I just come by to help him shift inventory so he can maneuver around it with his crutches. I'm a teacher."

Ansell pointed to the sign above the man's head.

He held up his hands. "Not my handiwork. Benight hired a guy. I let things be."

In a while, Benight came back down the road, a bag hooked over one of his crutches. He did not seem surprised to see Ansell. "Got some corned beef and potatoes. Gonna make hash." He smiled, but Ansell could see a private sort of sorrow in his face, caught in the hollows and wrinkles. The kind that had settled there a long time ago.

Ansell thanked him for the invitation, though he'd only just eaten, and he followed the brothers into a tar-paper shed with a potbelly stove in the middle, a car seat in the corner, and a card table with three chairs beneath the opposite win-dow. The window was draped in a frilly curtain that matched nothing else in the room. Except for that curtain, it was not so different from camp, Ansell thought as he took in the room, lit low with a kerosene lamp.

"Pull up a stump," Benight said, pointing to the three rickety chairs.

Benight busied himself frying everything up in a cast-iron skillet. He served up portions for Ansell and All-the-Wishes and ate his own out of the pan. While they ate, Ansell told them about Pearly Everlasting and Bruno and, despite his reservations, passed around his sketch because, besides saying her name over and over, this drawing was the only other real, bodily way he had for keeping her close.

"She's got something feisty about her, hey?" Benight flicked at the corner of the paper, thinking. "Seen some girls get on the Mersey Road Coach Line. Seen some get off."

"Yeah, but he says she's got a bear with her," All-the-Wishes said.

"Bear! Well, I hope he got himself a ticket. Them drivers get pretty testy about freeloaders these days! Ha! Ha!" Benight said, his laugh threatening to shatter into a coughing spell.

In a bit, he got up from the table with the empty plates and rummaged around in a cupboard. He brought back a quart bottle of something dark, a stub of a pencil, and some much-creased butcher's wrap. He gave All-the-Wishes and Ansell green celluloid glasses that said Hotel Beauséjour along their sides in fancy script. He drank his share out of the bottle. "Rum," he said when he caught Ansell sniffing his glass. "Put hair on your chest."

For the next hour or so, the men argued over their rough-drawn map, over where they were and where Ansell had come from and where a girl and a bear might go. Ansell told them he'd been around Smoke River, where Miles may have met an animal seller, and this information was also included in the debate—part of which was due to some places hiding behind different names and others having no name at all.

"You ask at Smoke River?"

"Yeah," Ansell said, the rum working fast on his head. He

told them no one had answered at Ebony and Song-catcher's door and the neighbor could only say they'd gone on a lecture circuit and had left no date for their return.

"Maybe your girl and bear are back already?"

"Maybe, but I don't think so," Ansell said. "It doesn't feel like they are."

As the map grew in detail with railway crossings and junctions and pieced-together farmlands, Ansell could see—how had he missed it?—Pearly had come a different route out of the woods. He was very much too north of where she would have started.

"If she's out around Smoke River or back into the woods now, she's got a few days on you," Benight said. "But if you get over here"—he circled a more southerly section of the map—"you should be in good shape to find them, cut them off at the pass, so to speak."

The night continued like this: Ansell's green glass filled and emptied, filled and emptied. For the first time in weeks, he softened into himself. At some point, Benight played something fast on a harmonica and Ansell thought, from the way the man danced, his foot must have grown back. The room shifted. People arrived, others left.

At some point, he found himself elsewhere, with other strangers—outside and then outside town. There was a fire in a cut-down barrel and someone swung the shadows of the flames, a thick bearskin mantling their body. Swooping low. Rearing up high. Someone strummed a guitar and crooned cowboy songs. A voice, off to his left, which reminded him of the waitress from the diner, kept asking, "Is that what your bear looks like, yeah? Is that like him?" Someone jumped over the fire. The fields. The bare trees in their dark wells. Strangers' laughter and others that sounded just like his own.

Ansell, his tongue too thick, could only say, "No, Bruno's nothing like that. Nothing like that."

But he couldn't be sure if the woman beside him could hear over her own cackling laughter.

"Now? Like that, yeah? Is he like that?"

Later, she may have been sitting in his lap. He felt very warm. Unable to move. Later still, he'd stroked the fur the man had worn across his back and head, and he'd tried to explain how it could not belong to a bear. But the voices kept up: *Is this yours now? Not like last year, before she died. Imagine! All that over a woodshed and a gun dog. Christ, you can barely pronounce your own name.*

He'd had a queer sense then of unbelonging. How different and separate he was from these people who knew each other, or thought they knew each other, in ways that mattered. Sadness sank inside him. He wished for nothing more—though he felt his face tight, smiling still—than to be back in the woods among those who also knew him. He wished to be in the cookhouse listening to Pearly tell one of her tall stories while Bruno got into things. He wished he'd had that chance again, on one of their last days together, to lift up her face and kiss her. She'd stood ready, but he'd turned away.

complicated world of bone

So I began my life as a cleaner, fire starter, occasional baby-sitter, and potato peeler. Every day, Mrs. Prue pointed out something else I didn't know. I did not know how to handle money or soup tureens or cheese graters or decorate a bed with small, lacy pillows, or remember to turn the lights on when the rooms grew dark, asking instead where the lanterns were kept. *Dirty little wood rat.* On days when I felt like I just wasn't part of anything, Mrs. Prue would find me out in the woodshed, cutting kindling or sharpening knives or oiling gardening tools because those were things I was good at.

"Pearly, I want you to go on down to Connick's and pick me up a few things."

"Where's he live?"

"Who?"

"Connick."

"He's not a he."

"Well, where does she live, then?"

"Pearly, it's a drugstore. They got them all over." She'd huff out of the room then, sweeping the floor, pounding at the bread dough like she wanted to punish it for something, just to show me how backwards I was.

Still, I worked hard. Over that first week at Broken Hill House, I woke at five and ran in the dark over to the clinic before I had to start my chores at seven. We'd moved Bruno into a large cage at the back of the clinic. Amaël liked to sit there and read to him. Sometimes, I laid my head on Bruno's chest and listened to the mechanics inside him. His heart—twice the size of mine—working its leathery bellows. His complicated world of bone. Everything slowing in his sleep. *Two-Eyes, are you sleeping?* I counted heartbeats and waited and counted again. It was what my heart was doing too. Wintering and waiting.

Each morning, when I had to return to Broken Hill House, I feared it would be the last time I'd see Bruno alive. Amaël said recovery was like that. It took time and animals often slipped from good to bad to good again in a run of a day. Bruno wanting to rest was a good sign.

"There's still fight in him, Pearly."

Sometimes, Bruno snored and we sat beside him, listening.

"I wonder if he dreams," Amaël said.

"He's dreaming of us, before we came to the Outside, before the woods felt watched," I said.

One morning, after I said goodbye to Bruno, Amaël walked me back over to Broken Hill House. He asked me more questions about camp and Bruno. He wanted to know what it meant to grow up beside a wild animal. But I couldn't answer those things. As we crossed the bridge, I held one nostril and blew snot into the snow, just as I'd done my entire life.

239

"Pearly! Here!" Amaël said, his ears mottled pink. "Mrs. Prue see you doing that, she'll have a fit." He handed me a hanky. "You keep it. And use it."

We walked on. Me playing the hanky across my face like a dainty lady. It made Amaël laugh and shake his head. At the river, the black dog was still pacing on the ice, its tongue spooning along its long jaw.

"You should try, Pearly," he said, nudging me down towards the river, where a few people stood watching. "You're good with animals. Try with the river dog."

I walked to where the water and land became confused and the larger pieces of coughed-up ice had buckled along its boundaries. Taking a deep breath, I sang out Bruno's song. At first, nothing. I hooped again, loud enough to echo off the wooden houses. The black dog scented the sound passing and reshaping the air, then, quick as quick, it came skeltering over the ice.

"That's the saddest song I've ever heard, but," Amaël said, laughing, "it worked."

I tried to hide my smile, but the dog licking my face kept bringing it back. We stayed with it until someone brought out a length of rope and led it away, it still turning to watch us. I told Amaël then about the King's Tree and how Papa said it'd felt and how he'd said it'd sounded. And for a few minutes, I too felt like I was inside the King's Tree where nothing bad could break through and touch me or Bruno again.

=

While we slept that night, the Tent of David went up. I woke to its white vastness down the hill, in a field that usually held a few horses.

"Holy rollers," Mr. Prue said.

"Bunch of foolishness, those revivalists," added Mr. Nevers, who'd left an arm behind at the Battle of the Somme, deep in the Guillemont mud, and wore his empty sleeve safety-pinned above his elbow joint.

"Carrying on down there. Speaking in tongues. Rolling around on that hard, damp ground, apt to get kidney infections, they are. And throwing hard-earned money at some bandit from the States for all we know," Mrs. Prue grumbled.

"Don't forget the snakes, Minnie dear," Mr. Prue added, winking at me.

By now, I'd gotten good at running errands for Mrs. Prue and I never got tired of looking in shop windows, amazing at all there was to buy in the Outside. Mrs. Prue sent me that day on a couple of errands, which would still give me time, despite the blowy weather, to visit with Bruno and see the holy rollers. I went to the tent first.

A hand-painted sign at the edge of the field read:

Blazing Fire Church Revival.
Showing the Darkness of a Millennial Dawn.
Admission Free. All Welcome.

More cars parked in the field grass than I'd ever seen before. They looked like beasts put out to pasture. Grilles like wide snouts, slow smiles. Trucks with meaty tires and mud splash along their sides. Crowds of people milled around in their Sunday best. I knew my overalls and flannel weren't good enough, but when the wind cut cold, I stayed warm, unlike all them ladies in their wool dresses. They side-eyed me, but it didn't matter. Above the tent, grackles sat up in the bare trees' high air—faces like spent match heads—and sang their song-less tunes. I walked around the edges of the tent to where the wooden pegs were stoved into the ground to keep the ropes taut. I found an opening that gave me a pretty good view inside. Rain in the branches fell hollow over the roof tarp. At the tent's front stood a man in a poorly built suit. Long-jawed and breathless, he preached over the crowd.

He skipped across the stage, shadowboxing the devil. "I carry the most important message here this morning to this holy of holy tent of meeting!" he said. "And I bring this to you clothed in its purest language! And some may wonder how I can preach on hell like this and I will tell you, my brothers and sisters, it is because I was born and raised there!"

He talked about Jezebel and King Ahab and their plan to steal Naboth's grapevines. He talked about godless acts and meagerness of spirit. "Are your burdens heavy? Well, cast them upon the Lord." His voice suddened the air and made the crowd murmur in return. "Because the rain shall bring the floods, and the floods shall bring the holy deluge!"

As he went on about bad weather, I had some recollection. And there, in the turn of his eye, in the way he snapped words straight, I recognized him: the Go-Preacher from the rock maples, crouched at his fire with his bag of holy dirt and his want of a congregation. And here they stood stupefied beside their fold-up chairs, making nonsense about God, like they wanted to start a fire with their voices. I'd never seen so much foolish faith and commotion. Though in the corners, I could see some—more curious than filled with the holy ghost miracle—whisper to each other from behind their hands. While others pocketed doughnuts off the back table.

He shadowboxed the devil some more and smashed a chair to purge the tent of temptation, he said, before raising himself up like a crucifix. "We are tabernacling today in this tent of meeting, tent of God!" He spoke like he was readying to collapse into a heap of empty clothes. And as he turned to preach at the far corners of the tent, I saw it: Mama's necklace.

Eventually, he mopped sweat from his forehead and declared a fifteen-minute break. Everyone, he said, was welcome to tea and sweets brought courtesy of the kind ladies from the Temperance Hall. And for those who might see it within themselves to donate to the Blazing Fire Church Revival, collection plates would be passed around.

I followed him past the outsized cross, to the side of the tent. He stood with a foot jacked up behind him on a tent peg. He lit a cigarette and gazed off across the pale open land beyond.

"Hey, Go-Preacher!"

He turned, squinting at me.

"You've got something that belongs to me."

"Beat it, little girly. I'm on my break."

"You stole something from me."

He breathed out a long snake of smoke. "I have given all my earthly possessions away in the name of the Lord."

"You stole my double-horn necklace," I said. "And if you don't give it back, I'll tell everyone in this tent about you out alone in the woods, feeling sorry for yourself."

"Git," he said. "I'm on the road to Damascus."

"Like hell you are." I pointed at the necklace, dangling against his cheap tie. We eyed each other for a few seconds and then I yelled as loud as I could, "This Go-Preacher steals from children!"

I watched him redden up, glancing into the tent to see if anyone had heard. But everyone was at the far end hoarding tea and buns. "Ah, the brat with the dirty bear."

"The very one."

He glanced back into the tent and nodded at someone. "Be right there," he said, thick smiling. He reached under his badly knotted tie and unclasped Mama's necklace. "Thing's not worth nothing anyway," he said. "Just an old piece of Cracker Jack junk you probably stole off someone yourself." He peered at me. "Yeah, that's what I figured." He drew deeply on the last of his cigarette, flicked its dog-end into a pile of slush, and held out the necklace so that it caught on the pale light.

"That is not an old piece of junk. It belongs to my family and we are Greenlaw royalty."

He jinked it out of my reach. Yo-yoing it until I had to jump to snatch it from his finger.

He made the slightest of gestures: a wave, a salute of sorts before slipping back through the tent flap. "Hey kid, it's just showbiz, eh?" And then he was gone.

I wiped his smudges off while the tent people clapped and sang. And then I walked back down the hill, thinking how Mama's necklace might pay for Bruno's care. I couldn't imagine life without it, but I was short on options for Bruno too. I went to the butcher's for soup bones and then to Stedmans Variety to pick up some green thread, some laundry bluing, and a package of thimbles as Ruby Mae kept stealing them from Mrs. Prue's sewing chest.

"Them things don't just up and disappear," Mrs. Prue had mumbled to herself that morning, eyeing Ruby Mae for a reaction. "Just grew legs and walked away, eh?"

Though stores like Stedmans were mazy with too much stuff, I managed to find everything on Mrs. Prue's list and, thinking I might have some extra time, I wandered through the aisles, past the lunch counter with its leather-topped stools, until I found myself near the hair accessories. As I was admiring a hair clip with pearls along its edges—something that Ivy would have begged, borrowed, or stole for—I saw a woman doing that very thing. She wore a red frogged coat of boiled wool—something fancy someone might buy from the States. Around her neck was another one of them dead fox scarves. I didn't know foxes could be used up that way until I'd gotten stuck in the trap-like sense of Bracken. While I was admiring her coat, she picked up a tortoiseshell barrette and dropped it into her pocket. Before I could look away, she turned to me, her eyes dark with something it would take me

245

some time to name: a wanting, even in theft, to be seen. She turned on one well-shined heel and walked down another aisle. I stayed a while longer in the store, putting distance between myself and the woman. I slipped over towards the lunch counter, but a cop sat there, hunched like an owl over his cup of coffee. I backtracked a bit and then took my things up to the cash.

I asked the cashier if she might know where I could sell a necklace. "I need to pay for my bear, er, my brother."

She eyed me, considering. "Aren't you a little young to be selling things?"

"I'm older than I look." I kept my eyes on her, in case she thought about calling the cop over.

"Uh-huh, sure ya are. You might try Little Egypt."

"Where's that?"

"When you leave here, go left, out past where Devlin's dairy used to be, then past where Shuggie used to have his smokehouse. It's out near Frog Pond Road, I think. Over where the old train station café was? The one that used to sell that real good potato hash? You can't miss it."

As she explained all this, the woman in the fancy clothes walked by without glancing our way. The little bell above the door jangled in her wake. Tucking Mrs. Prue's things under my coat to keep the damp off, I walked in the direction the cashier had given me. Uncertain how I'd find things no longer there, I walked, out to where the houses thinned. The air grew mizzly with cold spring rain. I thought about me and Bruno home again with Ansell and Papa.

All over Bracken, I caught glimpses of Ivy. Standing outside the Happy Birthday. Stepping off the Mersey Road Coach Line bus in basket-weave pumps. Sometimes, I thought I saw Ansell watching me from a diner's front booth, smiling his small, crooked smile my way. The one that always left my insides rabbit-kicked numb. And sometimes I saw Swicker leaning in a doorway, sitting in a truck. But when that happened, I kept my eyes on my bootlaces and thought about Bruno until Swicker disappeared. I imagined how Bruno was finding this strange place made of rags of scents: smoke and choke and oil, tongue thrush, gripe water, and poachers' pockets.

After passing a scattering of mean-looking houses where sometimes a dog barked from a yard or a rooster shrieked, I reached a sign I could not read in full. Little something. I recognized it as one of Mr. Prue's signs and thought the next word one from the Bible: Egypt. It stood out from the paintless shacks with a goldenrod-yellow frontage—its walls covered with mirrors and other shining things. Each surface glaring a different bit of sky or shack. It looked like a ship run aground in a dull field of snow. As I got closer, it showed me from angles I'd never considered myself before. I couldn't help but think how much Ivy would have appreciated the effect. I, on the other hand, looked like a rain-bruised crabapple and this conclusion shot dread straight through me.

Up the four wooden stairs onto the veranda, I walked in the one set of slushy prints. Someone had gone inside, but there was no separate set leaving. The room beyond was alive with ticking clocks—each out of step with the next. It

247

reminded me of spring peepers. A weak-chinned woman, small as a child despite wearing two wool sweaters, came out from a back room.

"You're supposed to ring the bell," she said.

"The what?" I asked over the ticking clocks.

"The. Bell." She pointed to a domed brass thing on the counter. She hit it twice and sent the air ringing. "That's how I know you want something."

"Okay," I said to be easy.

"And?"

"And what?"

"Do you want something?" She took in my ice-caked pant hems and soaking boots and then looked out the window. "How'd you get out here?"

"Walked."

"From Bracken?"

I shrugged and then, forgetting, took off my hat.

She backed up a bit, taking in my ratty hair and my greeny bear marks—scritch-scratch across my brow bones.

"Looks like you've been through the wars, kid."

"Most days I feel like it. I got to sell a necklace."

"Let's see it, then."

I pulled it out from my pocket where I'd wrapped it up in Amaël's hanky. I handed it across the counter, which I saw now was just an old door covered in a sheet of glass. The woman reached out one of her queer hands, like that of a raccoon or mink, and took up Mama's necklace. She screwed a little eyeglass into her right eye socket and peered at it.

"Pretty," she said. "Where'd someone like you get something like this?"

"Does it matter?"

"Might if I have to call our town cop to check on its provenance."

"Its what?"

The clocks struck the hour and the room filled with echoing bongs and cuckoos.

"Its where-you-got-it-from!"

"My mother. It belonged to my mother. Once. We don't need anyone to prove it."

The woman fussed around it some more, tapping it against the counter, resting it on a scale, listening to something inside it while she considered. "You going to the bootlegger's after this?"

"The what?"

"The bootlegger's!" Just then the clocks stopped their racket and she reddened with hearing her own voice hanging in the quieter room.

"No. Why?"

"Just, I got a deal with those who take their money to the bootlegger's after they leave here."

"No. I just want money."

She huffed on the pendant's spine and wiped it clean with a soft cloth. "Two dollars. Two twenty-five if you go to the bootlegger's. Two-fifty if you want to buy it back. And I don't dicker."

"Two dollars, then."

She creaked open a tin box and counted out some coins.

"I want paper money."

"Change is money."

"I don't want it rattling around in my pocket. More apt to lose it."

She nodded and pulled out two worn bills and handed them to me. "I'll get you a receipt. In case you change your mind."

On the veranda again, among the mirrors, I wiped at my stinging eyes and rolled my two bills and the receipt into my sock. Still January in my soul. All these months gone, my grief had not gotten smaller. But where our little lean-cabin had once been my whole life, so that Mama's and Ivy's deaths sat in the room with me, I now had other places. I had new rooms to stand in, if only temporarily: the Outside, the clinic, Broken Hill House, and Bruno's recovery. It was meager consolation for letting Mama's necklace go.

As I stepped off the veranda, I didn't take much notice of the fancy liver-colored car parked across the road under a black spruce sagging under its wet weight of snow. I didn't see the fancy woman from Stedmans get out and walk into Little Egypt. I didn't know that I was the source of some talk for those two women among all those ticking clocks. I walked down the gray road, back towards Bracken. I stopped to watch some kids of a hard nature roughhousing, burning things in a cut-down barrel while a red dog on a chain stood close to the withering flames. When they saw me, they made finger guns and shot me with quick spitty noises that riled up the dog and sent it pissing into an already deep-stained drift. Nearer to Bracken, I picked up a few windfall apples half-buried in snow for Bruno.

The clinic was just off the main road, two away from the Happy Birthday. With all the slush on the roads and my feet near frozen, I walked down the sidewalk slower than I should have. Two boys, twins, stood outside the pool hall's door. One lit a cigarette with a little gold lighter, the other cleaned beneath his nails with a jackknife.

"Wiggle wiggle!" he said. And me, not knowing any better, stopped to see who they were talking to. He flicked the knife blade back into its shaft. "You stupid or something?"

I stood there. Out of place. Ugly. One of them horked snot from his throat and nose, spat it up into the air, then caught it again in his mouth. He swallowed it, smiling meanly. I considered them dangerous, though it was difficult to name what the danger was.

"Get along, little doggie!" he wolf-howled. "A-roo-ooo-oo!"

They gave me one last back-look, then sauntered through the dark mouth of the pool hall like they owned it. As I watched them go, a man in a delivery truck shouted at me to get out of the goddamn road. I walked on to the clinic feeling about as small and shabby as I'd ever felt. Something inside me shot through with a new kind of sadness. Me and Bruno needed to go home.

mr. nine-dollar man

He woke in the morning with his face hard against a cold steering wheel. Someone was knocking on the driver's window. Roused, he struggled with something shawled across his shoulders and head. A black fur coat. The knocking stopped when he found the window crank.

"Son, you know you've just about stoved the front end of your truck into that snowbank?"

Inside Ansell's head was a prairie fire. "I, uh, I don't drive."

"I can see *that*," the man said. "But I'll be needing that fence beyond that bank come spring for my cows. You gotta move this thing."

Winter light caught at Ansell's eyes and teared up his vision. There were no houses anywhere around those white, raw fields. "Where am I?"

"Bad Luck Falls. Where'd you think you were? Good Luck Springs?" The man laughed, but it was lined with impatience. "Looks like you drink like you drive. None too good."

He eyed the fur coat. "And it looks like you missed the turn for the Hollywood route, eh?"

Ansell considered the place. He lifted up and set down various images from the night before, but each one stayed in shadow. Nothing stepped out to be seen. And then he remembered. Bad Luck Falls was, on Benight's map, about twenty miles south from where he'd been the night before. It was just about where they'd figured Pearly would have come out of the woods, out past the Junction. How the hell did he drive this truck twenty miles, in the middle of the night, on snow-thick roads, drunk?

"Hope you got some money for the tow truck," the man said now. "'Cause he's on his way."

Ansell paid the tow-truck driver—the farmer's brother-in-law—one dollar to haul the truck out of the bank and then paid the farmer fifty cents more to store the truck in his barn, along with a note that gave rough information concerning who the original owner might be. Money moved fast out of the woods. Ansell was used to not having any and then having some towards the end of the season, paying all his debts at once.

The tow-truck driver gave him a ride out to a road that would lead him to the highway. Still wearing the fur coat—beaver, not bear—he stood stupid beside the truck, thanking the man for the ride. "Hey, I'll give ya ten dollars for the coat," the man said through the wound-down window. "Wife could use a coat like that."

Ansell considered the offer. He couldn't walk around with the thing on, but he couldn't remember who it belonged to. Leave it with the truck? It'd be gone as soon as he was.

"Done." He shook free of its weight and the cold bit around him. Somewhere over the course of the night, he'd lost his scarf. "I'll keep this part," he said, snapping off the collar where it connected around the shoulders with small metal eyehooks.

The man shrugged. "Nine dollars, then." He pulled a few dirty bills from a box below his seat.

"You're all heart," Ansell said, handing over the coat. He started to walk up towards a main road.

"Hey, Mr. Nine-Dollar Man!"

"Yeah?"

"You watch yourself out there, okay?" The man threw the coat on the bench seat and waved goodbye. It looked to Ansell like he was driving away with a small bear at his side.

field edges, where light healed the grass

Amaël no longer held out much hope for the little bear. Bruno had been near motionless for four days, occasionally opening his unfocused eyes, taking a bit of water Amaël wrung from a terry cloth over his gums. His injured foreleg still had a lot of heat at the joint and he shifted in his sleep without lifting it. Amaël had given him a shot of sulfa the night before and one more that afternoon. Just to see. But Bruno had lost weight and was possibly still dehydrated, so that he looked like a smaller-boned creature lost inside an oversized bear suit. The quiet work of healing. Amaël was only a few weeks out from lambing season and thankful for the time indoors with the bear, away from freezing barns reeking with blood, shit, and afterbirth. Inside the clinic, he worked on little sketches while he kept him company. A small glass of something warm. And sometimes he spoke with Bruno, telling him things he could not say to others.

He did feel it, though, occasionally. It was something

he'd been able to do from a young age: to feel if an animal was willing to live or not. But that sense shifted with Bruno throughout the day. Last night, he'd slept in the clinic, in case he was readying to die. In those early hours, bears took possession of Amaël's dreams so that his sleeping world was both lit and lumbering. Bears were road openers—a way to reenter the woods and the world. Sometimes, they led him to the field edges, where light healed the grass and he could see their pelt-shimmer: blackish, bluish, brownish, reddish. A strange humanness in their gait. A lazy way with their turned-in feet as they disappeared, as they always did and always would, back into the trees. Taking with them their multiple belongings and meanings.

Amaël had put Bruno in one of the largest of the cages that lined one side of the clinic. There were two cats in smaller cages recovering from frostbite who made their unhappiness at sharing space with a bear known. Unlatching the door now, he crouched near his slow-rising chest. Could the bear feel him there, willing him to live? Horses, dogs, cats could all sense things unseen, feel something as it entered a room, kept to corners. A second sight. So why not bears? Until the past week, he'd never been this close to one before and so was uncertain if his sense was true. He slid his fingers through Bruno's shoulder ruff. He did not stir, but stayed what he was: something of shadow. He reached out and laid his hand on Bruno's big square head and waited to feel something more inside him. But no. Of course not.

==

On the fifth morning, Bruno's eyes began to twitch. Amaël pinched his upper lip and wiggled it. *Come on. Wake up, Bruno.* Low noises rattled in his throat, but he did not stir. Amaël checked on him every hour or so and he was the first thing he saw to after a house call. Later that afternoon, Bruno rolled over onto its back and considered his surroundings. He sneezed several times, shook his head, and stared hard at the cage around him and then at the ceiling light above. He stretched and flexed each leg, except the injured foreleg, though even that seemed to have more range of motion now.

"Well, hello, Bruno," Amaël said. He hadn't considered what might happen if the bear woke up with him there alone.

He walked over to the house phone. "Mrs. Po-kay, yes, could you make up some porridge with raw eggs . . . No, I know I just . . . it's for Bruno . . . the bear. He's awake, yes." Amaël watched him drag his long tongue over the stitches at the corner of his mouth. "Yes, just knock. I'll bring it in myself."

Amaël crouched over Bruno to get a better look at his wounds without touching them. Bruno half hid his face but settled his dark eyes on him a moment, before turning his face towards the wall. Amaël watched him for any sudden, unclear movements. Some kind of unlocking. Tiny signs. Bruno took measure of him again. A creature of myth, of dreams and nightmares, of steel traps and deep dens. Finally, he broke the trance, letting his goldy eyes gaze around the room. He dove his snout into the deep of a horse blanket and yawned. He offered Amaël no other clues to his nature. He had been judged and deemed unworthy of Bruno's attention.

257

Pearly came in soon after. "Hi," she whispered.

Amaël was swabbing Bruno's cuts with iodine. "Ah, you're here, Pearly."

She tiptoed across the room. "How's he doing?"

"Come see for yourself."

She hesitated, gauging the tone in his voice before coming closer. Bruno was lapping at a bowl of something.

"Bruno!" she squealed, rushing the cage.

"Gentle. He needs quiet."

She nodded then scooted closer. "Hi, Brunnie." He kept to the bowl, but watched her as he ate. "What's he eating?"

"Porridge."

"Just porridge?"

"And eggs. It takes a lot of energy to chew. He's worn down." He pointed at the bowl. "Tip that up for him. He's still too weak to hold his head up."

And there she was, a happy kid, less haunted, less troubled. She and the bear touched noses and then rubbed faces. Bruno set a paw on her lap. She held it. They sat that way for some time: the bear making small sounds and she answering with strange words. *Outside the lines*, Amaël thought. *Dark magic.*

"What does he like to eat at home?" Amaël asked to interrupt the moment.

"Deep-rooted things. Lupines, horsetail. Things with sun in them like dandelions."

"Guess I won't be finding much of that around here these days," Amaël said. "What else?"

"Jam, molasses, canned milk, trout. Mama helped him get fat each year so he'd go to sleep for a bit in his wintering box."

"We can get those," he said. "In a few days maybe."

Bruno shoved his face deep into the bowl, coughing and gasping for air when he came back up.

"Slow down," she scolded, petting the velvet of his ear. "He seems a lot better now. Yeah?"

Amaël didn't say anything. He'd seen it before. Sometimes, very sick animals regained some energy—an appetite, an interest in the world—for a day or two and then they'd die. There was no explanation for it, but he didn't want to tell this to a girl from such a pulled-apart world.

"In my dream, last night?" Pearly went on. "I grew bear teeth. Again." She pointed to an eyetooth. "I think that's a sign." She sat thinking a bit more. "I got bear paws too. I'm running, and then big bear feet!"

"What are you running from?"

She didn't answer for a long time. "I can't tell you. You'd have to see it for yourself."

singing of cold glass

Ansell walked for another week, stopping at each farm-house, Kiwanis club, and community hall asking after Pearly and Bruno. He got used to the looks strangers gave him, but he didn't get used to the weather—the being outside day after day, the cold and then the warmer days that filled the air with mud stink. A weary exhaustion was settling its anchor inside him. There were days when he moved much slower than he hoped and others where he found himself tramping at the edges of woods, thinking of turning back to camp. One afternoon, he picked up a road map at an Imperial gas station. He sat with it, over a coffee, beside the garage's woodstove with a couple of truck drivers and an old, arthritic teamster. Each gave him his own opinion on how best to find a girl and a bear traveling rough in early spring.

But deep in his heart, he'd already decided that today would be his last day searching. He had not heard anything about them anywhere. *Tomorrow, I'll head back. They might*

already be home. He'd thought he was made of better met-
tle, but every barn loft, church pew, or YMCA had dragged
him out of sleep with its drafts, strange noises, and midnight
reminders that he had, without a doubt, lost his focus. He
was tired of changing weather, loose dogs, and the men at
the YMCA snoring and shuffling beneath their rough wool
blankets—everyone reeking of old snow and feet. He missed
spending his days in the cookhouse's heat. He'd used a good
deal of time in the Outside thinking about Pearly and running over in his mind what he thought. And he'd come to a
sort of soft conclusion that his feelings for her were of a much
more complicated nature than he'd thought before he left
camp. She breathed life into things. And when he thought
of himself without her, something went off-kilter inside him,
leaving him a little bit sick without a real name for it. *We'll
give it one more try. Today's our one more try. But they're probably
already home.*

For the final time, Ansell asked after Pearly and Bruno at
a train station he stepped into to get out of the hellish weather
that was neither snow nor rain. The station master said no,
no, he hadn't heard anything that fantastical in a while. He
laughed some and sized Ansell up for a fool and told him if
he was looking for a quick way back out to the highway and
eventually to the lumber roads, he would find a shortcut up
past Asylum Road, through the back field.

Ansell paused at the steep hill in front of the red-brick
asylum to watch children sledding and arguing and playing

small games with complicated rules. The windows of the hospital were dark in the overcast gloom. The children's voices carried on long after he'd walked beyond the back field that edged the woods. Eventually, he came to a covered bridge, and crossed it, enjoying the meager shelter it offered. Only the old clay nests of swallows caught the pale light that hung from the edges of the bridge's mouths. Somewhere beyond where the trail bent, he could no longer hear the roads nearby, only the bare trees resisting the wind, creaking like grinding teeth. A thin path brought him out of the trees and into a clearing. Wrong way. As he was about to retrace his steps, he caught a glimpse of something between the trees. Horses. But they were far too big to be real horses. They looked to be made of bones. He walked towards them, thinking, *If nothing else, I can just sit down a minute, out of the wind.*

The horses were made from deadfall, driftwood, bentwood, stair spindles, and the turned legs of broken chairs. They stood some ten feet tall at the shoulder and each one had a particular mood about it: cantering, coltish, regal, free. They were of the type you found in mythology, owned by gods and stolen by those who envied gods. Their ribs and trussed openings held blue tonic bottles, wired up and hung so that the wind caught at their mouths and made sad music. They were shivered with frost and the sleet coming down.

He moved closer to see how the stark light slipped through their middles and left blue shadows in the snow. As he stepped down, something tightened around his ankle.

Coyote snare. *Shit*. At that same moment, a hackly German shepherd came out of the trees, barreling through the snow towards him. Low. All teeth and long jaw. Its ruff thick as a wolf's. As it came closer, Ansell grabbed his jackknife. "Git!" he said, still struggling to free himself from the snare. The dog reared up a few feet away, lunging back and forth but coming no closer. A deep scar traveled from its forehead back behind its ears. Ansell readied to make room for the pain the dog was about to give.

"Sheba!" a woman called. "Sheba!" She came out from around a dark wall of scrub pine, two dead hares hanging from her shoulder. She hopped over a few stumps to get a better look at the dog. She was light-footed but strong.

The dog's lips still flared in an angry snarl. Ansell thought he might be able to count all its teeth from where he stood. The woman grabbed a stick and beat it against a fallen pine's root plate. The dog stopped and turned. She motioned for it to come to her. It shied off a few feet, eyeing Ansell with its narrow gold eyes. Considering.

"She can't hear!" She struggled in the snow to catch up the dog before it lunged again, looping a handmade leash over its neck. "Farmer shot her for stealing chickens. Serves her right, I suppose," she said, "but she was only grazed, and this has left her one sorry deaf-as-a-doornail chicken thief."

"I think it's dead as a doornail."

"What?" she asked, fiddling with the dog's leash.

"Nothing. Never mind."

"Looks like I caught you good," she said, pointing at the snare. "If you lift up on it with your foot, straight up like, it should come away."

Ansell tried a few times. Off-balanced, he raised his caught leg up straight while the broken snow yanked him farther down. He felt foolish and wished she'd look away. Finally, the snare loosened enough to let him go. The dog returned, slinking crabwise now, snuffing around the snow he'd touched. Ansell ignored it as he figured it wished to be ignored.

"What are you doing way out here?"

"I saw the horses."

She glanced over at them. "Yes," she said. "I was called upon."

"You made them?"

"Over time, yes." A little wind kicked up and the bottles made sounds through the horses. "I wanted to paint them blue, but"—she shrugged—"never got around to getting the paint."

"Aren't you afraid of that dog getting hung up on snares?"

She shrugged. "They're not mine. I pull them out when I find them."

They stood a few awkward moments together, watching the dog sniff between them, listening to the singing of cold glass inside the horses. She threw the snare into some alders then collected the hares from where she'd dropped them in the snow when she'd leashed up the dog. "Suppose I could offer you something to eat at least?"

"I wouldn't say no."

The dog led them down a well-beaten trail until they

came upon a small blue house with gingerbread trim. Drifts had entombed its front, all the way up to the roof line. They entered at the side, past a half wall made of fieldstones that kept the slanting weather from the door.

"Your house is hidden," Ansell said, to say something.

"Yes," she said, "and sometimes I'm hidden from my house."

nothing with a shine on it

All the next day, I wanted to give Amaël our two dollars and leave Bracken. But by late afternoon, when I could get away from Broken Hill House, Bruno had taken another bad turn. He wouldn't eat or drink. He wouldn't leave his cage and kept his back to us. I felt like he'd lost his fight.

"I can still feel it," Amaël said. "This morning, when I took some porridge to him, he huffed at me to stay away from his food. There's fight in him."

I nodded, but felt like we'd never stop dragging ourselves out of our own grave. Amaël suggested we push him a bit, make him walk around, get his blood pumping. He had me massage his bad leg, ice-pack it, and rotate it gently. Some days earlier, Mrs. Pocket had sewn several flour bags together, attaching strong handles to each side. In this way, we slipped a sling behind Bruno's forelegs so that we could carry some of his weight. We were careful not to push him for too long. Just a few times around the room—a hobbling bear and two frog-walking hopefuls. Just one more time around.

266

At one point, Amaël asked, "Have you thought about what you're going to do if he can't walk on that leg again?"

"What do you mean?"

"An animal, especially a wild one, needs to walk, Pearly. And from what you say, there'll be a lot of walking."

"He'll walk or I'll piggyback him," I said through clenched teeth. "We got to get out of here."

Amaël, still holding the other side of the sling, nodded, but I could see soft pity in his eyes.

When Bruno would go no farther, we'd lead him back to his cage and I would sit with him a while longer. My head against his. I could hear his thorny breathing and smell his cuts healing and hear his fading thoughts. I laid beside him those afternoons, willing him back into our life, but his eyes, often now, kept little light. I didn't have the heart to think about the trouble I'd got us into. Instead, I wished Bruno one more day to stay because, if he might go and I should not, I would no longer love the world in the same way. And this knowing stained me with a new sort of loneliness. *Two-Eyes*, I prayed. *Two-Eyes, please stop sleeping.*

=

People on the roads. Horse clop. Tire swash. I skirted around it all, keeping to side streets and paths already beaten down through backyards and dog runs. I hated Bracken. I hated the open stares, the houses all eyes. And other things too. Lots of other things. On the way home, feeling bad about Bruno, I walked back to Broken Hill House beneath the gray sky a

different way, over to the church with the steeple like a jutting fang, just to see what was inside. I didn't know then there
were right and wrong places to be in Bracken. In the woods,
the wrong places were easy to know, but in the Outside, they
were less marked, less likely to reveal themselves for what
they were.

I walked over towards the church with no real plan. The
town felt, for a moment, quiet. Besides the croak of a crow
from time to time, the only other sound came from bedsheets,
flapping half-frozen on a line, stiff as butcher's wrap. Out in
the graveyard, some kids were playing where the drifts ran
high. I could hear their singsong voices, deep inside their
game: *What time is it, Mr. Wolf? What time is it, Mr. Wolf?*
They ran like harried deer, only to be chased back by a boy
in a hat with loose earflaps. Some of the children's faces were
still shapeless and others already suspicious and near to cruel.
A girl in an oversized plaid coat and worn boots turned to
watch me go. She was wearing a wolf mask. She alone was not
yelling across the fields.

The church was empty. Its stained glass many-colored
against the dreary daylight. I walked around a bit, fingering
the leather edges of hymn books, running my hand over the
waxy pew wood, before sitting down to think. I did not feel
any holiness of spirit. I did not feel a favored child of God.
Low-burning candles in red glasses flickered. A tall cross in
the middle. Jesus. A thin man, almost naked. Mary interrupted by an angel while reading. I knew the story, though
the part about interrupting Mary's reading seemed to be the

detail that stayed with me most. Books and angels with enormous wings. A forest and a snake that made a mistake. These were not the stories the Go-Preachers carried with them—stories crushed beneath the weight of their fiery endings.

"Tent of Meeting! Tabernacling!" I hooted into the cold air.

I unclipped my rabbit's foot from my overalls and pressed its claws into the pew's thick beeswax. BRUNO & PEARLY EVERLASTING. The church was just an empty thing. Empty of trees and all the sapping carnivores that ran their burrows into the underworld and popped up elsewhere inside spring's green wrestle. Just a bunch of boards, no different than camp. No better. I thought about Ivy. Thinking up new lives to live. Explorer. Lion tamer. Movie star. And me and Bruno? I thought about how shepherds in the Bible stories came back from their wanderings filled with news—what they'd learned and what they'd heard—from the scrabbly Outside. I saw me and Bruno a little like that too.

I slipped my two dollars from my sock and held them for a bit. Tomorrow I would give them to Amaël. I would smooth them out—their heads facing the same direction—and say, *These are for you, from me and Bruno.* I'd already practiced this a few times. And then I got up from the pew and shook off the cold. Still not filled with any sense of God, I closed the door behind me. I'd touched nothing with a shine on it.

some beast's far-off heartbeat

After the clinic, I walked back to Broken Hill House. Freezing rain glassed the roads—its sheen making the world look breakable. At the house, Loretta and Mr. Nevers were complaining about the cold. Mrs. Prue was resting upstairs with *one of her heads*, Loretta said, rolling her eyes. I'd noticed that these quick-coming headaches occurred with quiet regularity when the boarders accused Mrs. Prue of being miserly with the heat. Feeling lonely and shut out of too much, I thought Papa's spice cake might help mend feelings and give a good excuse to add some heat to the house.

In short time, my cake began to rise then come away from the edges of the pan. I opened the stove door with a creak and pressed my fingers onto the spongy surface. I turned to find Ruby Mae, Loretta, and Mr. Nevers in the doorway, watching. Ruby Mae, a scarf wrapped in a fortune teller's knot around her head, made the Persian dance on its hind legs like a string puppet and gave it Mr. Punch's voice, but it too had stopped its deep growling, as she seemed to give thought to how she handled the creature. For the first time, with her vague child's gaze, she looked less goblin than girl.

"What recipe's that?" Mr. Nevers asked. "It's like and not like—it's like—" but when he searched for the words, he was at a loss because Papa's cake was not a cake that wanted to be talked over.

"Can I have the recipe?" Loretta asked, her lips dark and polished as plums.

"I don't have one. It's different every time."

"And Chummy?" Ruby Mae asked. I scraped bits from the bottom of the pan and put these in her scratched-up palm. She closed her fist gently around them, then ran heavy-footed into the parlor to offer them to Chummy at his vigil.

While the weather sleeted against the windows, we stood, contented for a spell, around the small kitchen, drinking our tea and eating cake. Though I still shied around the boarders, I was just managing some talk about Bruno when someone banged on the back door. Everyone stopped—cake halfway to their mouths, teacups hovering mid-sip. It was as if we'd all started to play a game of statues and were waiting for the release word.

Mrs. Prue, who'd come back downstairs, lured by the smell of gingerbread, scuffed in her house slippers to the door. "Ethel? Why, you'll catch your death out there today," Mrs. Prue said to a woman we couldn't see from where we stood near the stove.

"What? My girl?" Mrs. Prue's voice prickly as she opened the door wider. "You'd better come in. Sort this out."

A woman stepped into the kitchen, stomping snow off her boots. She brought violet scent ahead of her. It stung the air, refusing to mix with the baking spices. Everything about her was moon-colored: grayish hair and filmy, nearsighted eyes. Except for her red coat of boiled wool, like something some-one might buy in the States, and her blood-red lipstick. The woman who'd stolen the barrette from Stedmans Variety. Her dead-eye fox scarf was gone now. In its stead was a scarf with a fin-like fringe, wrapped around her neck so that it looked as though her head sat on a frilly tray.

"Tea? Cake?" Mrs. Prue asked.

Ethel shook her head. Her small eyes mean on me. "There's the one," she said, her rings flashing as she pointed my way. "That's who I seen coming out of the church."

Mrs. Prue glanced between us. The other boarders set down their plates and mugs. I was thankful for them staying close.

"That's the one," Ethel said again, the frost on her words smoking through the kitchen's air. "Your girl. The one with the black eye. A common thief."

I hid in that word like a stair in a cellar. Still and stinging with private shame. My eyes on Ethel because I couldn't tell how deep her meanness went. And she, in turn, searched for the weak spots inside me. I'd met some who'd only had mean-ness on their surfaces, like a willful dog gentled with a bit of care. But some went marrow-wise, as I had witnessed with Swicker. I feared she might be of the second sort.

"Ethel's here on some foolishness, it seems. Says she saw

you selling jewelry, Pearly, and stealing around the church," Mrs. Prue said.

"I seen you," Ethel said, firmly.

I saw too many teeth—two rows smudged with scarlet lipstick.

"I seen you this morning over in Little Egypt selling gold things that don't belong to you and I seen you coming out of our tent and our church. I seen you and so did Arty Maillet." She pronounced Maillet in the English way.

"Arty Maillet?" Mr. Nevers snorted. "Hell, that one wouldn't give you the sleeves off his vest."

Something came loose inside me. "No, ma'am," I said. "I did no such thing."

"Preacher Ichabod told me—"

"Who's Preacher Ichabod?" Mrs. Prue asked. "Like that poor fella in the story? The headless cowboy?"

"Preacher Ichabod is at the Tent of David, of course," Ethel snapped, pointing towards the Blazing Fire Church Revival site, beyond the house.

"What were *you* doing running around up there with them holy rollers?" Mrs. Prue asked.

"Me? Well, I was volunteering, and this one, Preacher Ichabod told me in strict confidence, that this one, this one right here, marched into the tent and stole that necklace out from under his nose."

"Like a bank robber?" Mr. Nevers asked.

"No, not like a bank robber. Preacher Ichabod took the necklace off while preaching and set it by his Bible. Both from his dear, late mother. And this one skulked around while we was singing and stole it. Preacher Ichabod seen her. And then I seen her selling it and coming out of the church. Our church."

Mrs. Prue leaned against the counter. "Your church and your tent?"

Ethel waved this away with another flash of her rings. I thought about the church's cold quiet creeping out to sniff at my cuffs and edges. I thought about my two dollars. *Amaël, these are for you from me and Bruno.* Would she take them away now? I thought about Swicker—a crawling word, a prowling word, even in death. Police. Jail. Murder. All that blood. My heart behind my ears, the backs of my eyes. Could it beat itself dead?

"I'm not running no cave of thieves here, Ethel, so you'd best be having proof before accusing my boarders of stealing stuff from under our noses. Pearly's a hardworking kid." She peered at Ethel. "And what were you doing out at Little Egypt?"

"Me? Me? I was just going for a drive, no harm in that. But you know what some of them camp types're like," Ethel said, sweeping a glance around the room, sopping up any wandering attention. "Unchurched out there. Living with bears, no less. Imagine!"

"Now, you just hold on a sec. I worked some seasons in them camps before the war," Mr. Nevers said with some pride. "And I've seen nothing but hardworking people working in hard times. You accusing—"

"Unchurched," Ethel said again.

Mrs. Prue rolled her eyes. "Pearly, were you in Ethel's church and Ethel's tent today and did you sell a necklace belonging to Preacher Bob—"

"Ich-a-bod. Preacher Ichabod," Ethel squeaked.

"Yes, Mrs. Prue, but I didn't steal and he ain't no real preacher. He's an old Go-Preacher. I met him before, near a bonfire. He had holy dirt all over his face, and"—I looked everyone straight in the eye, knowing my story sounded strange—"and that necklace belonged to my mother, passed down all the way back to my eighth grandmother Slaywrock."

Mr. Nevers pondered this a moment. "Well, that's some story," he declared.

I left off explaining any further. All I saw in my mind was me being driven out of Bracken and Bruno, still at Amaël's clinic, healing and waiting for me to come back. I felt my face growing hot and, thankful for the kitchen's dimness, said quickly, "I didn't take nothing. I just, I just went to—"

"To pray or hear yourself think. Just like everyone has a God-given right to do," Mrs. Prue finished for me. "Now, Ethel, whyn't you come on in and have a slice of Pearly's cake and a cup of tea and we'll sort this out?"

Ethel stood her ground a few moments more before giving in, kicking off her boots and shuffling over to the little table Mr. Prue ate his breakfast at every morning. As if on cue, Mr. Prue came in knocking snow off his own boots, brushing it away from his pant cuffs.

"Village meeting, eh? Who we stoning today?" he asked, looking at each of us over his hazed lenses.

275

Everyone stayed quiet with their cold cups of tea. I was alone in my head. Untethered.

"Ethel here says Pearly's been thieving from the church and selling stolen necklaces," Mrs. Prue said.

"Ah, pillaging the locals? Wouldn't be the first," he said. He reached out like a blind man, touching each object on the counter until he found the sugar bowl and its little matching spoon. He stirred for a few seconds, then turned to Ethel. "I see you're not wearing them nice new glasses today."

She ran her fingers over her face. "No, Alwyn. Forgot them at the Hall yesterday when we was decorating for the Whitcome girl's wedding."

"Yep," he said, picking up a piece of cake in his dusty hand. "Might be hard to see a cat burglar twice in one day, eh?"

Ethel's attention prowled the room—her cheeks flamey as though she was catching fever. "I seen what I seen."

"Sure, sure," he said. "My god, this is some good. You make this, Pearly? Regular Fanny Farmer you are."

I nodded, not wanting to be seen.

"Some good," he said again. "Now, Pearly, since you've met the town's judge and jury, you got anything to say for yourself?"

"Now, Mr. Prue," Mrs. Prue whined. "This is no way—"

"It's Pearly Everlasting's turn, Mother Prue, only right that . . . Oh, but what was this cat burglar wearing while robbing the town blind, Ethel?" Mr. Prue asked, reaching for another piece of cake.

Ethel thought for a moment. "Red mackinaw, wool pants,

and black toque." She worked her jaw and hard-eyed me. Up and down. Up and down.

"Sounds like the whole damn village to me."

"I seen what I seen, Alwyn," Ethel said again.

"Thought I saw Harold or Gerald out and about today, highballing around in that new car of theirs," Mr. Prue continued. I wondered if he'd need a nap after spending so many words in such a short period of time. "Some swanky getup, that car of theirs."

"I seen one of 'em too," Loretta jumped in. "Can't tell 'em apart, but I caught sight of one of 'em shooting down from the factory, dressed just like that."

"And what of it? My boys are good boys. No law against them driving around. Boys will be boys. And we do own the factory."

It felt like the entire room smirked at this. Though I had no idea who Harold or Gerald were, I guessed they were Ethel's and they had their reputations too.

Ethel glanced around at the others—a cornered look in her face now—and the words that came out of her were half-hissed, half-whispered. "Dressing like some backwoods boy," she said, trying to regain some of her earlier ground. "Little miss does-as-she-pleases, I suppose. Up to their heathen throats in trees and not much more. Don't even want to think about what they get up to out there."

She made me see myself standing stupid—a fork, a plate, half-eaten cake gummed in my throat. The same look Swicker used to give me and Bruno. The air closed around us. "I saw you, you old bat. I saw you stealing a barrette in Stedmans!" I waited for the black stars to clear from my eyes, my heart beating time with my fist to quiet. She fidgeted something in her pocket and I wondered if the little barrette might still be there.

"The mouth on her," Ethel said. "And I was only buying something pretty for Lucille's little girl. She's been bedridden for weeks now. Got the lung trouble. I was buying her something pretty." That terrible smile again.

"No law against that, Ethel," Mrs. Prue said. She began stacking plates and forks, making a show of something ending. I helped her bring everything over to the sink.

"You get going on these and I'll finish the laundry, Pearly," she said as she picked the iron off the stove, heavy as an anvil. I heard her leave the room, her slippers scuffing over the cracked linoleum. I heard Loretta leave and Mr. Nevers leave and Mr. Prue take out his pipe and tamp the old tobacco from the fire bowl. I kept my back to Ethel, though I could feel her hateful energy and the burn of her stare on the small bones in my neck.

Finally, she stood up. "This ain't over, missy. The minister's going to hear about this. And then the police." She said some other words, a garble of French and English that sounded like spell-speak to me, but they were only for Mr. Prue, still sucking deep into his pipe.

"Thanks for stopping in, Ethel," he said as the back door slammed shut, hard enough to knock snow off the veranda's roof.

"Piece of work, that one, Pearly," Mr. Prue said, stepping into the quiet left in Ethel's wake. "Always up on her high horse. She's been a member of the Lutherans, the Uniteds, the Latter-day Saints over in Joli-Rocher, think the Presbyterians were saddled with her for a while and then a few others, including them holy rollers. All to say, her church isn't her church."

I nodded and turned back to the dishes. Tears in my throat like hot grit. Behind me, the door closed and opened a second time.

Mrs. Prue came bustling back into the kitchen. "Lord only knows how that woman gets under everyone's skin," she mumbled, watching Ethel's wiry figure march down the walkway and fade off, reclaimed by the blowing snow. "And I should know." She busied herself, collecting the bits and pieces from our little party. "Now, where'd that sugar spoon get to?"

Mr. Prue laughed. "That Ethel. You got to weigh her coming and going." He winked at me as he wrapped another piece of cake in wax paper, slipping it into his work coat pocket. "Reminds me of this little brindle she-goat we had. The one that ate the upholstery from the neighbor's old Ford, remember her, Minnie?"

Mrs. Prue bit back her smile. "Enough, Alwyn," she warned.

Once he'd gone back out to the shop, Mrs. Prue stopped her puttering and turned to me. "I'm proud of you, missy. Standing up to Ethel," she said, not without a little softness in her voice. "She's a hateful one. But if you say that necklace was yours, then it was yours to sell. It's nothing to her."

"I saw her steal at Stedmans."

"Well, her stealing's old news, but you watch yourself. She turns ugly when cornered."

"What will she do?"

"Oh, run you down all over town. She's as two-faced as they come."

"How do you know?"

She paused for a few seconds then sighed. "She's my sister."

"But you never—you don't."

And that's when she told me about Ethel Broade. She told me that Ethel's husband's family owned the axe factory—its turbine wheel picking up and dumping water into Frederick Stream's tailrace thundering loud like some beast's far-off heartbeat. The Broades had owned the business since 1905, when they'd bought the building from the defunct Bug Death Chemical Company. In a certain light, you could still see the word Death from the old sign burning through the new—sharp-cornered and edged in gold—that often caught the afternoon light and glowed biblically across the front of the factory.

"I have no use for the works of them nor they for me," Mrs. Prue said as she shook crumbs from her cloth into the sink. "She married into 'em, she's stuck with 'em. Besides, we're Scottish, Pearly, which means a bit clannish. Something to be said about who holds a grudge longest. If I die last, I'll have won." She handed me another plate. "Now, tell me about how that old bear of yours is doing."

And just like that, me and Mrs. Prue became friends of

a sort. I told her then about selling Mama's necklace to pay for Bruno's care, though I did not tell her how I'd come to have it in the first place. I told her about Bruno's good days and some about his bad. I showed her the two dollar bills and hoped it'd be enough for her to reconsider the police, if she was thinking that way. And then I asked her how I might get some molasses and jam and apples.

"Where do you get those things?"

"A&P, like everything else. Why?"

"Where I bought the beans?"

"Yep."

"Can I get all that for forty cents?"

"Why forty cents?" She handed me the final plate.

"That's what I got from working here. Bruno's still off his food, so I thought I could buy his favorites."

"But isn't that your savings for your mail-order boots?"

"I can save again."

She sighed. "Oh lordy, now I'm feeding a bear." Limping over to the pantry, she brought out some molasses and a jar of strawberry jam.

"You keep your money," she said, handing me the jars. "You're going to need it."

a stranger was on their way

The day after Ethel came tattling, a Mr. River-end Michaels decided to visit Broken Hill House to talk to me, the girl from away. He claimed as he came through the door—all bustle and sharp-soled shoes—that his visit was simply an offer of quiet counsel, which would have little to do with silver plate and lesser to do with God or the Tent of David. He said his intentions were but to see for himself how one girl could stir up so much anger in a woman made up of so many hateful, moving parts.

"Might close the curtains," he suggested as he came to stand in the dim kitchen, throwing awkward smiles my way.

"Pearly, pull 'em tight so no looky-loos can see us in here," Mrs. Prue said, taking soft control.

"Well, Pearly," he said when we'd settled around the table. "I'm Reverend Michaels. I hear you're from a mountain some ways away from here."

"Yes, River-end. Greenlaw Mountain," I said in my nice voice. "We're mountain royalty."

"It's Reverend," Mrs. Prue corrected.

"That's what I just said," I whispered.

"Why, that must be some three, four days' walk in good weather," he went on. "Those are some pretty lonesome miles."

"Bruno's with me," I said. "And I've got good snowshoes. Made by the Paul boys."

River-end Michaels nodded and bobbed his head around some more, reminding me of a Jack pine with the wind inside it. "The Prues have been very kind, giving you a job and a room. And I hear the animal doctor's also been good to your pet, your bear?"

"Yes, sir. But his name's Bruno, River-end. He's my *brother* and we plan to get back to the woods as soon's we can."

"Can I ask why you think of him that way? Bruno?"

"Me and him grew up together and he keeps all my secrets and I keep all his," I said, though I was getting tired of having to explain this to people from the Outside and this River-end seemed to want to hear more, more, and more.

He waited for me to say something else, but I didn't want to share much else about me and Bruno. "If you're here about the church stuff, I didn't steal—"

"I know that, Pearly. I saw you leaving the church yesterday. You didn't look loaded down with loot. I didn't really come here to talk about any of that, but—" He smiled slightly. "I'd like to help if I can. If you're in trouble, say, or if, if you're worried about Mrs. Broade and that wheeler-dealer preacher and their accusations."

"Ethel Broade refuses to be seen in any light but her own,"

Mrs. Prue said as she set a mug of tea and a slice of my gingerbread before the River-end.

Still, he tried to draw out my story. How did I find myself
in Bracken? How could a bear be kin? How could a girl
survive the winter woods? How could she fight wild bears?
How? How? How? How? He went on. He studied me and
said something that sounded like bring us bale and bitter sor-
rowings.

Not knowing what to say to that, I sat quiet for some time,
working my jaw and cracking my knuckles the way Ansell
did, before saying, "Some men just didn't take to Bruno overhome."

"And the necklace?"

I cracked another knuckle. "It's mine. Always has been."

The two long, steam-bent rockers on Mrs. Prue's chair
creaked as she went back and forth, back and forth, matching
the kitchen clock's heavy tick. "You sure you're not in trouble?"
she asked, looking hard at me. "You can tell us."

She'd put on her pearl necklace, which she called her
Mississippi River Pearls, sent up from the Boston States by
an aunt, though they were just glass beads painted with fish
scales and oil. She'd ran upstairs as soon as she heard the
River-end's car cough up the drive. The pearls were itching
in the coal stove's heat now, which was only alive because he
was visiting. She pulled at the beads when she thought no one
was watching.

I queered my eye at the River-end. "Can your god get
Bruno better, River-end?"

I could tell this question rattled him more than he let on. "Well," he said, "we could pray and—"

"Pray!" I said, mad because I already knew that answer. "If that's all God can do, then I don't got no use for him."

Rather than argue, as I suspected he should, he fell quiet beside the little stove, picking small morsels off his cake crumb, bit by bit. The Persian sat on the floor beside the fire. He'd given her a small crumb of her own and she'd laid before the coal fire on the braided rug, kneading at the stitches and running her little motor. Her back to the fire, meaning a great snow was coming. And then she turned her paws towards the fire, meaning a stranger was on their way.

meager anything, but still

I'm going to clean these up first," she said, setting the hares on the counter. She hung her wool coat on a peg behind the door then did the same for Ansell's mackinaw. She slipped off her boots and put on a pair of deerskin larrigans. Ansell sat down in a musty, overstuffed chair in the afternoon's dim blue light. He watched her mend the flames in the old stove with its red-brick hearth and arrange the hares on the counter with a delicate touch. She was tall and moved like she was made of water. What was the word? *Willowy.* He liked that word and he liked watching her, lost in her task, despite his being there. The dog lay down on a blanket near the stove but did not take its eyes off Ansell. Ansell watched it watching him.

He glanced around the small one-room cabin for signs that someone else might live there with her. But the place felt singular. Stroking her hand down each pink-stained pelt, she flensed the fur from their slinky bodies. With a filleting knife, she slit their bellies then reached inside them like a pocket and rummaged out the deep-purplish mass. She slopped this into a bowl before breaking down their walls of meat and bones.

The sound turned Ansell's empty stomach. She set the bowl down on the floor and the dog came over and began to eat the offal. "If I cook the bones first, they're apt to break one of her teeth. Except the weight-bearing ones. Then they're too brittle for her."

"Uh-huh. I'm Ansell, by the way."

"Anastasia."

"Anastasia? That your real name?" He regretted the tone in his voice, but the day, the damp, the decision to go back to camp empty-handed was bringing out some uncharted mood in him. He needed to keep talking so that his thoughts didn't bump up against the dog swallowing the guts whole beside him.

"No, but it's the one I like and these are changeable times. We're all in the business of after these days, aren't we?"

She cut a nob of salt pork and browned it. She put the butchered hare morsels and some chopped onions and water into a pot and covered it. "I'll make a gravy in a bit." She looked inside a crock. "I've got some *soupe à n'importe quoi*, if you want, for now," she said. "Anything soup. Meager any-thing, but still . . ." She warmed up the crock and soon the room smelled of onions and root vegetables. She gave him a bowl with a thick slab of oatmeal bread, slicked with molasses. She gave the dog a smaller piece with a smear as well.

On the windowsill above the sink, an assortment of carved horses sat. On a low table, another whittled shape. Ignoring the dog's glower, Ansell picked it up: a bear with a little cro-cheted red scarf around its neck.

"Made that one just a few days ago. Saw one out here in the strangest way," she said, wiping her piece of bread through the molasses on her plate. "Wish we had pie," she sighed.

"So the bear you saw?" Blood thrummed his ears.

"Oh, yeah. I was checking my traps and, it was the damned-est thing, I look up—well, Sheba did first—low growling and hackling. I look up and there, back in the woods some ways—where the snow's thicker between the trees?—I see a boy in a red coat and then I see a bear walking beside him, wearing a bright-red scarf." She nodded at the carved bear in Ansell's hands. "Something from a fairy-tale book. I called to them, but they didn't hear. Just kept walking—no—snowshoeing through all that deep snow. And the boy—" She paused to lick molasses from her thumb. The nail bed dark with the hares' blood. "The boy, I kid you not, was in deep discussion with that bear."

Ansell exhaled. "Which way were they going?"

When she'd answered all his questions, he was startled to realize it was almost dark. Ice hissed against the window-panes. He said yes when she invited him to stay.

that kind of anger towards the world

They weren't identical, but close enough. The boys from the Happy Birthday. One wore steel-rimmed glasses. One carried a jackknife in a deerskin sheath attached to his belt, though he had little cause to use it. They dressed like men in faraway cities—men much older than their late-teen years. Something cinematic about the way they wore their homburg hats slanted over one eye, where most men in Bracken wore flat caps or the kind with earflaps. Everyone in town called them the Musketeers of Pig Alley behind their backs, or, less descriptively, the Twins.

And it was hard to miss them in that roaring Nash Special Six—a boxy coupe the color of raw liver. The first time I saw it, it reminded me of some creature belonging in a field or swamp. It prowled the few streets of Bracken, gunning, rattling, and roaring up the hill towards their house or across the other way, to the axe factory.

The first time, I stopped, thinking they needed directions. Both had clearly readied for this encounter and had screwed their faces up into something they thought menacing, something seen in a movie, no doubt. They were not handsome, and their gangster touch only showed up their homeliness. And while one was long and lanky, the other bull-necked, both were wide-nosed, weak-chinned, pale-faced with dark circles beneath their eyes, their upper lips too short and their teeth too square and horsey. They both breathed through their mouths. A touch of the goat about them. Something weighty and unintelligent that made them want to talk too much. Prove themselves smart.

I would come to learn that their being from the only moneyed family in town also set them apart from the other boys in Bracken, and their unspoken fates as heirs to the axe factory had left them, over the years, relying heavily on their own company. They were known in town to bad-mouth each other to no end, and often added other family members to their grievances. But if anyone should say something wrong-sided about Harold to Gerald or Gerald to Harold, they would draw their circle in tight. If a boy wanted to fight one of them, he'd have to fight them both. They held grudges long, and for this reason they'd decided that their mother—a woman they held with particular despisal—deserved their loyalty against the strange girl from the woods. Some would say later it was this very meanness that was the Twins' undoing, why things happened as they did.

Because sound carried different out there in the open, away from the woods' dark geometry, I mistook distance when their car pulled up beside me that first day as I was headed to the clinic. It slowed until I could hear small gravel pipping beneath its tires. Pulling up just a little ahead of me, the Nash waited. While it was the only new car in town, I could see where the right bumper and grille had already been stoved in and two of the wheel spokes gouged. I'd heard Mr. Prue complain about the boys a few days earlier, how they'd tried to overtake a horse and cart. They'd passed too close, and the horse had cow-kicked the car and broken from its traces.

"Them two of Ethel's in their toad-skin hats out high-balling around them horses. The pair of 'em oughta be taken out back and shot," he'd said over his steeping tea.

"Need a ride?" the one with glasses asked, his arm hanging out the window, a cigarette smoldering between his fingers despite the cold.

The driver drummed his thumbs over the walnut steering wheel, staring at the empty road ahead.

"Couldn't tell what you was from back-to," the one in the passenger seat continued. "Boy girl boy girl. Hell, you got us all confused."

I walked beneath the slung telephone wires, hearing the wind come off them. I walked on, holding myself carefully at the edge of the road, in case I fell to pieces. I knew in the Outside my clothes were something to be ashamed of. I knew what I looked like, I'd seen others look at me since I arrived: up and down up and down up and down. *Dirty little wood rat.* But it didn't give them reason to be mean.

"We hear you've been telling stories about mother dearest," the one in the passenger seat continued, yelling over the engine. "Saying she's nothing but a thief. That's some rich coming from you!"

The wet seeped through my two pairs of wool socks as I walked on through the slush puddles. I dug my rabbit's foot into the meat of my palm. In my mind, I grew thick underfur and guard hairs—an oiled layer against the damp around me.

"Maybe someone needs to put a bullet through that bear of yours, eh? Teach you a lesson."

I bit down so hard on my bottom lip, I swore the blood meant I was cutting new teeth.

"There a problem?" Amaël called from in front of the feed store. He carried a teddy bear and a new pair of leather gloves. "Something happening here that ought not to be?"

Why was he holding that stupid bear? I looked down at my bootlaces and shook my head. No. No trouble.

"No? Then you two better just hightail it home."

The Twin in the passenger seat hooted at Amaël. "That your new boyfriend?" He goat-squealed with laughter.

The Twin at the wheel gunned the car, spraying slush along my pant legs. They yelled a word I didn't know as they went. When I turned to Amaël, his face was heated. He shrugged and gave me a lonely laugh. "You all right, Pearly?"

"Yeah," I said, not wanting to talk about it.

He studied me for a few minutes. "They do that before?"

I felt stupid talking to him with that toy in his arms. I waited until the car's drone faded away. "What are those for?"

"Bruno."

"Bruno?"

"Yep, I thought this teddy bear might be nice company in his cage, and these"—he waved the leather gloves—"are for me, when Bruno decides to really wake up."

I thought it all a waste of money, but I liked to think of Bruno sleeping on something soft. Amaël handed me the bear to carry back to the clinic. "I've never held one of these before."

"You never had a teddy bear?"

"Not fancy like this. I had a sock bear and a real bear."

He laughed. "Yes, you have a real bear!"

"We won't be able to take it when we go," I said, hoping not to hurt his feelings.

He nodded and smiled. "That's okay, Pearly. It's just for now."

"Okay," I said. "Just for now."

=

"I have a surprise for you," he said, inside the clinic's quieter light, handing me something snaky.

"What is it?"

He put the thing into my ears then led me over to where Bruno slept. I knelt down and he placed the flat part against Bruno's chest. I'd seen Amaël do this before, but it hadn't occurred to me to ask if I might hear too.

"I'll be out with the Fire Horse," he said, squeezing my shoulder as he left.

And then. Tall noises. Only a skin away. I listened to the strings inside Bruno stretch and cross. His pathways sounding, leading us back into the woods and smells: a suspicion of mice in the corner of a shed yawning then turning over in damp straw. Hand oil on a doorknob. Dead wood lice wedged between floorboards. Night air churning and rising. Vinegar seeping into cucumber skin. Menthol over tongue-bite. *I am in you*, I said to Bruno's sleeping form. The expression on his face always the same now, if bears could say goodbye.

=

After that afternoon, the Twins treated me like a project, a way to fill up their days. They made it their work to stand outside the Happy Birthday and say mean things to me over the clacking balls and jukebox. To drive past Broken Hill House five, six times a day. To follow me in that roaring Nash when I walked into Bracken. I knew Ethel was spreading rumors about me. I saw how people's eyes glanced off me. And each time I heard a loud engine coming up behind me, I felt faint-legged. The Twins flicked lit cigarettes from the passenger window and once left a pink mark on my cheek where the cherry had singed. Doubting I would ever feel of a piece again, I walked now with my hands deep in my pockets: one holding my little Green River knife, the other my rabbit's foot. I grew to hate them. I'd never known I was capable of such hate. Despite Miles and Swicker before them. And sometimes, I stood at the clinic's window at night, while Amaël and Bruno slept, my knife ready. I watched the sky blue and haze—the curve of the April moon hanging above—and when the Fire Horse kicked at the sides of its stall, I knew I was not alone with that kind of anger towards the world.

bone and sky and woods and weather

Storm-stayed. Ansell slept in the blue house two more nights, and then two more as he waited for the ice storms to pass. Anastasia, or Anna, as was her real name, told him lonely stories those long hours of tall horses, an aging tiger, a train leaving a station, and sometimes she returned to the bear in the scarf and the boy who sang to it, but she did not pry him for details or how he might have found himself searching for them or what they might mean to him. She did not ask about his scars or what he felt in his heart. They talked about other things and ate bowls and bowls of hare stew. And sometimes the tree branches, sleeved in thick ice, snapped like gunshot outside the windows and they would pause to listen to the silence that carried after, before they spoke again.

She told him she'd come up from the Boston States after recovering from a long sickness that had made her stay too long in the night-part of life. And when she'd recovered, she gave herself a new name and left her family because she no

295

longer believed they afforded grace and forgiveness to the ones who needed it most. So, she came *north of* and found her little house and created her horses and worked three days a week up on Asylum Road, cleaning rooms at the hospital, and on other days she drove the library van, when there was enough gas. She was content in this world now: her world of bone and sky and woods and weather, she said. It all, she said, opening a bottle of strawberry wine she'd put up against winter, suited her just fine.

Ansell could not always follow her turns in thought and sometimes she talked on for so long he felt lost somewhere in an in-between—her voice matching that of the wind. When she grew tired of talking, she had him describe Bruno in detail—his antics and trespasses—and she sketched him in various poses in Ansell's little notebook. He described Bruno's eyes, which held a certain light, and were not the eyes of a full wild thing. But he wouldn't describe Pearly Everlasting. He didn't want Anna to bring her into the room with them. Anna thought they must be in Bracken, the last town before the long walk back into the woods, and she felt—as she made a point to say many times over those few days as a way to comfort Ansell—that they must be near there. Waiting out the storm. Waiting for him.

Over those nights, he dreamed of Pearly. Pearly with a rock in her fist. Pearly with that determined look that could be mistook for anger. He listened to his night heart flicker, counting the time until he'd be able to track her again.

When he woke that fourth morning, everything was glazed in ice. The horses shone in the dim light like metallic filigree. The birches' crowns locked into the ice so that they created a tunnel.

"You could stay. If you wanted to," Anna said, placing a palm against his chest. "You'd be happy."

The first comfort he'd had in a while. It would be easy to say yes. It was easy to say no too.

The next morning dawned gray with no real horizon and then the sun came out—spring's fugitive colors lit from within—and snow began to drip off the house eaves and slide off the roof.

"Soon afternoons will return," Anna said, standing in the early light. She watched him struggling to tie up his sorry, busted boots, worn down from all the winter walking he'd done the past month. She walked over to a wooden chest in the corner of the room and pulled out a pair of almost-new boots. "Size elevens?" She handed them to him, holding them at their tops and soles like something precious.

"Who do those belong to?"

"Does it matter?" she asked, and went back into the kitchen to brew some tea.

After breakfast, he followed her out, past the horse sculptures, piebald now in the damp and melt. Sheba trailed them, down through the path, deep with puddles. They went on, not talking, until they reached a small building: *Reading Room.* She went around back. After a few moments, an engine coughed to life and a van came around the corner. He and Sheba got in—the space heavy with the fume of paper and things that have sat some time in the cold. She drove him up to the highway and apologized that she didn't have enough gas to take him farther. She stayed at the shoulder, watching him, and he saw her there still when a truck finally pulled over and offered him a ride.

and there in the middle of it all

Now that the Twins were hunting me, it took me longer to get to the clinic. I had to skirt backyards and the narrow places between houses and barns to avoid them. Sometimes, I stirred up dogs on and off chains, chickens, sheep, a red cow dozing in the sun. Each bawled at me as I tried to make myself unseen along those roads. And then Mr. Prue found a faster way for me to get between Bruno and Broken Hill House. I'd just come back from another visit with Bruno when he called me from the backyard one afternoon.

"Pearly, com'ere a sec." He stood near his work shed with an old, wide-framed contraption balanced against his leg. "Found this in the shed. Thought it might be handy for getting to Bruno."

"What is it?"

"Well, it's a bicycle. You never seen one before, I guess." He eyed it now, frowning, reconsidering its worth. "This one's in poor shape, but I've been oiling it up."

It was something to wonder at, its blue frame sheening in the afternoon light.

"If you've got some time now, I'll teach you to ride it," he said.

"Okay," I said, unsure what was going to be required of me.

He measured me up. "You're a bit smallish for it, but should be fine." He pushed it over to the back doorstep. "Okay, now step up there and swing your leg over."

I did what he said.

"Now, why you doing that?"

"What?"

"Walking around the front of it like that and getting on the left side? I've got it lined up here for the right side, so you'll head straight down the driveway."

"Because that's what you do with a horse. Don't walk around the back. Get up on the left."

"It's not a horse. It's not going to kick you."

I shrugged. "Still."

Mumbling something to himself, he shifted the bicycle around so I could get up on the steps and climb onto it left-wise. One foot touched the doorstep, the other touched nothing. "It's taller than me!"

"That's okay. Now I'm going to hold on to the back of the seat here and you get to pedaling."

But lifting my feet from the doorstep and putting them both on the pedals felt like I was suspended where I didn't belong. I fell straight over into Mrs. Prue's Dorothy Perkins ramblers.

"Those my roses?" Mrs. Prue yelled from the kitchen window.

"It's all right, Mother Prue!"

"You best be staying away from—"

He yanked me and the bike out of the thorny bushes. "Let's give 'er another whirl," he said, winking. "Somewheres away from here."

I spent another hour leaning and falling, scrambling to get my feet back onto the ground, and snagging my pant leg in the chain until I could have just about hurled that bike back into the roses. Ruby Mae had a Sky King tricycle, a faded red thing with brassy head badges. She called it her velocipede, which made me think of many-legged creatures that lived deep in dirt. She dragged it from the barn and rode along beside me, wobbling down the drive, warbling, "It's real easy, Pearly!"

As I concentrated on Mr. Prue's muzzy instructions— *keep your head up, pedal, brake, don't lean, pedal, don't brake, look ahead, no, ahead*—I'd hear Ruby Mae's hard tires coming up behind me and her off-tone singing, "Broc-o-lee! Broc-o-lee! Broc-o-lee-hee!" She had an old leather shoulder bag with a too-long strap that she wore diagonally across herself. The Persian, cinched inside, wore a fuchsia scarf. It scowled each time Ruby Mae overtook me.

After a couple of hours, I could ride the bike in right-handed circles, moving tighter and tighter into the middle until I simply fell over for lack of ground. Soon after, I could go in an almost-straight line. Mr. Prue stood close by, watching my progress. He no longer called out directions, so I knew I was doing things right. Besides the time in Ebony's backwards car, I'd not considered there were other ways to move through the world without touching the ground that did not involve sleds and horses. It felt good to travel in a way that made the world run blue and green and strange with a kind of animal flight. And though I thought Bruno would hate the bicycle, I came to love the sound of the chain spinning on its gear and the soft ticking when I coasted down Broken Hill. It carried me into a kind of peace with the world, which always ended when my feet returned to the ground. Already, I knew I would miss that feeling and that bicycle something awful when it came time to leave Bracken.

=

Over the next few days, Mr. Prue asked me if I'd seen Ethel Broade around in my travels about town. She was the last thing I wanted to run into, I said. Still, he said, if I should run into her, I should tell her to come find him. He wanted to speak to her. I said I would, but hoped I wouldn't have to.

When I parked my bike at Amaël's that Friday, Mrs. Pocket and several other neighbor ladies were gathered in a tight knot outside the clinic, while Bracken's harness-maker and a couple of other men held small children up to the window. "Can ya see it? Can ya see it moving?" they kept asking.

Mrs. Pocket, her face like a dead clock, stepped out from the protective ring of clucking women, their breath smoking above them, when she saw me. "Well, it's about time!" she said, loud enough for the sizable crowd to turn and stare. "You know what's going on in there?"

I pressed my rabbit's foot claw beneath my thumbnail and pushed past those damming up the window. *Well, excuse you.* At first, I could see only my own face in the dim glass, but then dark movement, low to the floor. Stopping. Moving again. And then the fragments of the breakfast plate I'd left on the desk earlier that morning skiffed across the room, alongside casting pliers, tooth rasps, and there in the middle of it all sat Bruno, lazily licking butter off a piece of toast.

"Bruno!" I knocked on the glass. He turned at my voice, but I was already letting myself in.

Amaël stood on his desk, whispering, "Good bear, good bear." He swatted a broom at Bruno, who was now monstering around the desk's legs.

"Ah, Pearly!" he said. "Finally! I opened the cage to check on our friend and for the first time, he broke out, and now you see." He shrugged. "I am a quick prisoner."

"Brunnie! How the hell are ya?" Weak-legged, he still had a shipwrecked look about him. He shoved his head under my arm, knocking me off balance. He snuffled around me—his bandaged leg knocking into things, his feet slipping on the linoleum, taking in my skin, clean with strange soap.

"I tried to give him some food and he became so angry!" Amaël said, climbing off the desk, the broom still held in front of him.

"He wanted his bowl," I said, pointing to his wooden trough I'd brought down that first night. "He'll snack without it, but he'll eat his dinner no other way." I poured everything in it, and he came gamboling over, sniffing at its edges before shoving his face in. He hacked into the porridge and then took a big breath before diving in again. "Slow down."

I handed him a piece of toast I found on the floor. He sat down on his rump and placed it on the back of his paw like a little plate and took small bites around its corners. He licked the butter from his fur, sniffing each hair for greasy leftovers. His shaven patches and puckered stitches made him look like a tossed-away child's toy. Amaël pulled down the blinds so that the neighbors would go home. He stood some distance away now, eyeing Bruno.

"Bruno, come meet your healer," I said.

Bruno followed along, nearly on top of my heels. He had an uncanny knack for knowing when he was the center of attention, a pure animal vanity that kept him underfoot. Amaël handed him an apple on the flat of the broom to keep some distance between them. Bruno took it then sat back to eat it with his good foreleg, studying Amaël all the while. Amaël told me he'd have to give Bruno a small dip of tranquilizer each day, until his stitches healed completely and the swelling went down on his leg.

"It won't hurt him and he'll still be awake. Just not so awake. The stitches in his mouth are hard ones to keep from splitting. But they're close now to being healed."

He sent me out to the snow to wet down a cloth and I brought it back and we unwrapped the swollen shoulder joint. I pressed the cold cloth to it. All I wanted was to stay with Bruno all day. I never wanted to leave him again.

"Now, if that's not the most pathetic thing you ever seen,"

Mrs. Pocket tutted when she brought down Amaël's tea, watching Bruno, from the safety of the house door, knock into chairs with his crooked leg. Since Bruno had come to the clinic, she'd refused to come past the door for fear she might be mauled. "He's a devil on four legs," she'd said more than once.

I wanted to stay that night with Bruno, but Amaël said no, he still needed his rest. So I biked back to Broken Hill House feeling fifty pounds lighter than I had in months. I'd almost forgotten about the Twins and their hate. I'd almost forgotten that this town saw us as ugly and strange.

in the roar and the setting light

Some miles outside Bracken, at Canaan River, was a booming ground—its logs now off the winter dumps, high-gated and bottlenecked. Its lower waters shadowed deep with salmon. The truck driver who'd taken Ansell thirty miles that day slowed to watch the head-works kedge and warp the logs across the lake. The winch so loud and creaking, it spooked the men after long, wet hours on the mean water. Back in camp, Ansell had been called out more than once from the cook tent—dark but for the beacon fires burning on the shores—to bring out a five-pound chunk of pork fat to rub into the spindle hole to cut the screeching of the tensed, soaked wood.

"You watch out for that ol' Dungarvon Whooper, eh?" the truck driver said, smiling wide enough to show his tobacco-stained back teeth. With a three-finger wave, he turned his truck around and headed back the way he'd come. The Whooper, splinter cat, shagamaw, wampus, hidebehind. The creature the men claimed sat on stumps and watched them work and made them feel judged and hunted. Pearly called it Jack in the Dark. Other men laughed uneasily when the creature's names were spoken aloud, because woodsmen were a superstitious lot, even the shithouse crazy ones, which were always the river drivers—the bubble jumpers—who weren't afraid of swindling death.

Though the sun was sinking, the river drive went on. The camp lights broke on the water's chop. Fast water fed fury into the river that carried the butt-stamped logs down to the mouth of the mill. The truck driver had told Ansell the road beyond went up some miles before you could cross the river. He'd suggested crossing below the sluice instead, meeting the road on the other side to save time so late in the day. As Ansell stood at the river's edge, he could see where the boom had gotten hung up and where the men were herding the loose logs and pulling at the jam with their cant dogs. Men in calk boots upriver traded directions with each other: "*Allez, les gars!*" "Try that bastard there!" as they set up to break the jam.

The river-work was dark as rust from the slurry of bark stripped from logs. Whenever Ansell crossed water like this, he felt the dead just below the surface, deep in the murderous currents. The logs had a way of colliding and severing water from air. And Ansell knew, in many cases, nothing surfaced again. When a river driver died, the crew buried him beneath a tree and nailed his boots to the trunk. Ansell had come across these sad memorials over the years: strips of rotting leather and rusting calks still clinging to a black spruce trunk.

"You looking for a place to cross?" a kid in a drive boat down-country of the boom called over to Ansell. He'd been sacking the shore and shallows for stranded logs, but had to wait now for the jam up-country to break.

"That side take me into Bracken?" Ansell asked over the driving racket.

The kid poled the boat closer.

"Will that thing hold the two of us?"

"She could float on heavy dew!" the kid said, keeping one eye on the jam above. "But if you're crossing, you'd best be crossing now! They'll move up there like scalded cats if they find that key log."

Ansell lowered himself down the greasy bank and jumped the few feet onto the boat, and the kid, a few years younger than himself, poled back across the river. "You must be in some kind of hurry," he said, still watching the men upriver.

Ansell nodded. "I'm looking for a girl and a bear."

"They yours?" The kid laughed. "Damnedest thing. My sister told me she heard about them over in Bracken, from her hairdresser's brother's cousin. Some mechanic who won't work on blue cars." He paused, thinking. "A bear and a girl. Walking around all night. She swears they cut through her backyard."

"I plan to bring 'em home," Ansell said, his heart flickering with being so close to finding them.

"Where's home?"

"Was Camp 33. Not sure where it'll be next year."

"The promised land all but promised." The kid smiled. "But nothing beats being out here." He waved at the river with his pole. "She's one of the roughest goddamn streams that ever laid outdoors."

They were halfway across when a stillness overcame the men working the jam, and then they could hear, downwind, whistling.

"Oh, Jesus," the kid said. "Barnwall Jackson's up there!" He paused in his poling, and they both squinted up to the jam where all the men had parted to let one man walk before them, whistling. He took off his coat and walked out to where the thickest snarl lay. He bent down and knocked on each log and then bent down farther to listen as though the logs might speak with him and then he began to whistle again.

"We better get over there!" The kid pointed with his chin towards the shore. "Barnwall always finds the key log, come hell or high water. He'll get 'er done. He'll run them logs down!" Admiration and a little fear in his voice now. He dug into the river like he was stabbing into a great curling beast. Ansell's head was full of the roaring current and the whistling and his own icy fear of slipping inside the water. "You can't shoot that man off a log for nothing!"

He stabbed into the river again and again until the bow slipped into narrow water. He held the boat steady, watching upriver. "Best to wait here," he said. "Could all be lashing to foam in a sec. Bet she's gonna be a deafener!"

Sure enough, the man upriver whistled across the jam again, then pulled at a middling log with his cant dog.

Another roar like a beast prodded awake. The logs creaked then exploded down towards where Ansell and the kid stood in the shallows.

"*Ça vâ le djâble!* Break and go, boys! Break and go!" the kid hooted, waving his felt hat at the oncoming logs and the haloed form of Barnwall Jackson, standing up there in the roar and the setting light. He stood in the jam's shifting center, cat-footing logs, still whistling to that wild tumble of wood and ice and dark water.

As the logs came down like thunder or random rifle shot or a cattle stampede, one canted. Before the kid could get clear, it hit the drive boat. The kid kept his balance, but Ansell was pitched into the water backwards. He dwindled and glanced the surface, once, twice, and then felt his shadow cut away from his spine.

For a few seconds, his ducking coat held him afloat, belled beneath the surface, but then the water seeped in, pulling him downwards with its expanding weight. His windmilling limbs stiffened. The heavy water's heartbeat pushed against his ears, his searing lungs. Pain radiated whitely into his limbs, which, even in their numbness, were being struck with things unseen moving below the surface.

I have seen the best and the worst of this river.

And then it was over. The kid hauled him up into the gray air and he came back into the world anew. The river water, oily with slush, froze on him like fish scaling. The boy was saying something, but Ansell's teeth were chattering, his heart ba-booming in his ears. He felt too light to stay sitting in the bottom of the boat. He felt an unexplainable sadness.

"She's a mean piece of water! But I got ya, by the jeeze, I got ya!" The kid rowed him back to the side of the river while the logs came down in a rutting fury behind them. He shouted at the tent and some day men came running. They brought Ansell into the tent, which kept fires going twenty-four hours a day to dry and warm the men. Someone stripped his clothes from his inflexible limbs, but it was only another sort of lightness. And then he was weighted down with thick wool blankets and brought closer to the heat. He felt bloodless. In time, he could feel his hair, roached up with ice, start to soften in the heat. The cookee gave him a pannikin of tea and made him hold it tight between his hands.

Okay, he thought. *Okay.*

"These goddamn woods will be the death of us all yet," someone said from the far side of the tent where he was washing up dishes in a basin.

Ansell stayed with the men that night, his body sore where things unseen had struck him and from so many peavey and pike men coming in for a change of clothes, taking the time to slap him on the shoulder and tell him what a lucky son of a bitch he was. Even Barnwall Jackson, the listener of logs, came in at one point to shake his hand in his own bearlike paw. When it was too dark for the drive boat, the kid came in and sat beside Ansell, still near manic with his retelling of the story. *I reached down into the dark and re-born a man.*

slow singing that brought down the rain

Spring wind. A ravel of geese split their arrowy routes and other birds returned to the trees' greening crowns, half-filled with crows living thick with their reasons. There was always trouble at the clinic now. One day, when I came to check on Bruno, I found him following along behind Rankin, the groundskeeper who helped muck out the barns and recovery rooms. Rankin would often let Bruno play with a shovel or rake if he wasn't using it. Bruno liked to trail along behind him, thinking his own thoughts, so that from the courtyard, the two of them looked like salt-witches coming home from a hard night's work. But people wouldn't leave Bruno alone. Kids, standing up on the fence, taunted him. One day, he got out of the barn and shinned into an oak tree to sleep, all his legs dangling down. I caught boys throwing rocks at him, trying to wake him.

Though Bruno still resented his collar and leash, I couldn't risk getting caught with a bear in town. So, we walked through Bracken only at night. Shut out from the daylight world, we tramped through the last fields and woods fringing town and wandered like wind, so that Bruno would sleep more during the day. Some nights, spring swung its temperatures so the snowbanks smoked and the trees' new leaves whished in the wind. I felt him there still: Jack in the Dark, hunched on his sit-bones, running the smallest shadows down. Sometimes, he was a slow singing that brought down the rain. Other times, he was just that rotting smell of spring coughing up through ground hollows. Still, I forced the bad thoughts, the hidden half of things, away. Bruno was near healed now. We were ready to get overhome.

=

I still took side roads and backyards to avoid the Twins on my way to the clinic. Still, they found me. One day, they drove up beside me, so close one of them grabbed on to my handlebars and wouldn't let go. And then the one driving sped up. For some seconds, I could do nothing but try to stay on the thing, the Twin holding on to me shaking the handlebars, leaning me hard to the side.

"Look out, little doggy! Oh! Oh! Almost fell over there!"

A man in a truck heard me screaming. He cut off the roaring Nash, left his truck in the middle of the road, and marched over to the Twins. He was bull-necked and anyone could tell he was strong.

"Get out of that goddamn car!" he said to the Twin driving.

The boy didn't move. The man stalked over to the driver's side and pried the door open, despite the kid holding on to the inside handle. He dragged the boy out by his coat collar and shook him. Hard. "You looking to kill someone, you pissant?" he shouted. "And you!" He pointed at the other Twin, still holding my bike. "You let her go."

The boy held up his hands in surrender. I crashed to the road.

"You okay?" the man asked.

I nodded, wiping the mud off my face and hands.

"You two oughta be shot," the man said, shoving the boy into the side of his car again. I could see scratch marks on his neck where the man's nails or the boy's rough collar had raked against his skin. The Twin staggered to get his footing in the mud. "I see you pulling a trick like that again, I don't care who your daddy is. You hear me? She coulda been killed!"

The Twins, pale like they'd been bled out, concentrated on the toes of their shoes.

"I asked if you heard me, you little suckholes."

"We said yes!" the Twin driving said, his chin quivery.

The man glanced at me. "You get on home, okay?"

I nodded, but knew I wouldn't be able to climb back on my bike. Not yet. Not with them there still. I pushed it instead and felt the weight of my Green River knife in my coat pocket as the bike rattled and wheezed through thick tire ruts. When I got around the corner, I leaned hard against the side of a barn, waiting for the trembling to get out of my body. I heard the man drive away and I thought the Twins would start at me again, but the Nash roared up through town, spitting gravel at the corners, and then went on towards the big stone house on the hill beyond the axe factory. I stood there a few minutes more, until my palms stopped bleeding and my legs stopped shaking.

=

The clinic was in chaos when I got there. Bruno had managed to flip the latch and escape his cage and then the clinic. He'd been caught stealing from the milkman and upsetting the delivery horses while he sat on his big rump and drank three bottles of milk. The milkman was telling anyone in Bracken who'd listen about it, which meant only a matter of time before the police came by to see what was what.

"You need to make some fast plans," Amaël said, brooming up shards of window glass.

"Did Bruno do that?"

Amaël kept sweeping.

"Amaël?"

He stood up, the fine blades of glass balanced on a rim of newspaper. "No, Pearly," he said. "Someone shot out the window early this morning. I just didn't have time . . . with the milkman—" He pulled a couple of shotgun shells from his pocket.

"That was meant for Bruno," I said.

"We don't—"

"Hell we don't."

He paused, picking his words. "I think you and Bruno need to go now, Pearly." He touched my shoulder. "Hey," he said, waiting for me to look at him. "Hey, something bad might happen. Okay? Even at night?"

"Okay," I said, feeling drawn down, wondering if our lives might ever settle. "I'll get us ready today."

=

When I got back to Broken Hill House, Ethel and the River-end were there. I came into the kitchen to find them standing with Mrs. Prue.

"—it's not just the thieving, she's been chasing after my boys, and—"

"What's happened?" I asked.

"Pearly, good you're back. Come on in here," Mrs. Prue said, her voice hiding something.

"You need to just tell her. Tell her what's coming for her!" Ethel said, pointing one of her shiny ringed hands at me. "Go on, then."

"Pearly," the River-end began, "it seems Ethel has taken it upon herself to report you to the police for theft. That preacher what's-his-name—"

"Preacher Ichabod. Ich-a-bod," Ethel said.

"Yes, well, she says she has a letter from that preacher claiming you took the necklace. I've already told them you didn't take anything from the church, and they believe me, but it's going to be difficult to prove the necklace, since you sold it here."

"It's mine. Why won't they believe that?"

"Not about your word, Pearly," Mrs. Prue said, narrowing her eyes at Ethel. "It's about who's got the money around here."

"Now, the police asked if I might come over here first and talk with you," the River-end said. "Ethel happened to see me turn into the drive. They plan to head over to the animal doctor's tomorrow to see about your bear, and—"

"No!" I said. "No! We'll go tonight. We'll go right now, just don't let them near Bruno. None of that stuff about the camp is true. I'll go to jail to keep him safe!" I said.

"I told you, eh?" Ethel said. "Thing's ready to go to jail. To think of it. Oh, she'll get what's coming to h—"

"That's enough, Ethel," the River-end said. "She's only a child."

He looked at me, his face shadowy in that light, and I knew then he had no idea how to fix this.

"Ethel, you better think about leaving about now," Mrs. Prue said. "I've had just about enough of your foolishness."

Ethel queered her eyes at me and took her time leaving. "Never should've been here in the first place," she said. "Trash. Simple as that. Trash."

"Ethel, you're one nasty piece of work! Go on home!" Mrs. Prue said, warning in her voice.

"I'm going to do whatever I can, okay, Pearly? This isn't over yet," the River-end said after she'd left.

I nodded, but I could barely breathe. Jail. Prison. A hang-man who might know my future. As the River-end walked to his car—Ethel waiting beside it, jittery and tight-jawed with bad reasoning—Mr. Prue came back from delivering some of his signs where spring flooding had washed the old ones away. Before he'd parked his truck, he was explaining something through his open window.

"I've been over hell's half acre looking for you."

"Me?" the River-end asked.

"No, Ethel there. Got something I've been trying to show her for days now."

"What is it, Alwyn?" she asked. "I've got things to do."

Mr. Prue jumped out of his truck like someone much younger than his years and hopped up the steps. "Well, come get a load of this."

"My shoes are a bit wet," the River-end said as Ethel marched into the kitchen.

"Oh, leave them on," Mrs. Prue said.

At the kitchen table, Mr. Prue pulled out a magazine he'd tucked into his vest. "Now, I found this at a Texaco, up near Kings County." He smoothed out the pages. "Pearly, seems you're in a magazine."

"In the funny pages?"

"No, Pearly. A real magazine."

He flipped the slick pages until he came to the middle, where the staples showed. And there we were: Mama and me and Bruno. All of us together. Me and Bruno on her chest, beneath her double-horn necklace. I on her right breast grasping her floral dress and Bruno, who was just a dark, fuzzy mound, latched closest to her heart. She was looking down at both of us with what I believe was whole contentment. It was a quiet moment. It was rare. Beside the photo was a copy of Mama's handwritten note, a permission slip of sorts, which she gave to Song-catcher, who'd taken the photo all those years ago. Mama had signed it Bruno's foster mother.

I was far away from myself and the air trapped in my lungs hurt.

"Well, I'll be," Mrs. Prue squeaked, tapping her finger on the grainy photo. "That little necklace belongs with Pearly."

The River-end reached for the page. His hand shook a little. "Is that the necklace?" he asked. "Is that it?"

I nodded.

"But how'd you get in the magazine?" Mrs. Prue asked.

"Song-catcher, just like I told you from the start. She does talks and writes articles about the old ways, murder ballads and sung-of people and me and Bruno."

"Not sure this constitutes the old ways," Mr. Prue said, chuckling, until Mrs. Prue slapped his arm.

"That's not proof," Ethel snapped. "Nothing but an old, blurry picture." But no one was listening to her now. And the lack of attention soon sent her out the door. "This isn't over," she called from the yard, her tires chewing into the drive as she pulled away.

The River-end promised to take the magazine to the police the next morning and clear up Ethel's accusations. I knew he couldn't help but turn his thoughts towards our photo and a world he had no imagination for, a world that had not been there before that night: the dark, cavelike closeness of our lean-cabin and the thin woman—our mama—feeding us at her breast. And I knew he could not say if it was wrong or unholy or of a nature he had no means of knowing. He could not say if what he'd seen was good or of a terrible conjointness, but it didn't matter now. We'd be absolved. And we were more than ready to leave such low places as Bracken had proven itself to be.

old timber tells and wind-leveled stands

Everyone asleep except for us. Bruno had woken up dark-tempered and mad at the world. So I thought a longer walk that night would help. We tramped out past the train station and followed the creosoted ties until we found a thicket of woods. We'd been walking about an hour parallel to town. We'd played hide-and-seek—me hiding behind some of the bigger trunks, jumping out at Bruno when he got near. We'd wrestled until Bruno started to take it too seriously—his nips getting sharper, his bite adjusting.

"That's enough," I said, knocking him on the snout with my knuckle.

We sat some time on two fallen trees, listening. Strange cracks and rubbings. The thump-thump-thump of the Hercules turbine that ran the axe factory farther off like a heartbeat. Patches of snow and water around peat moss sinks.

"It feels like we've walked through . . . we've walked into a room and interrupted something," I said to Bruno, who was grubbing around a stump too far off for me to see. I called out to him. It took two tries before he came back, toothy with the packed-in green smell of spring.

Up ahead, something flashed between the trees. Long and dark and low. My put-away thoughts came back. I stopped up, listening for a wail or howl or a heavy tread over deadfall to follow the shape. "Are you my death?" I whispered, testing the air. Nothing. I studied the spot thirty, forty paces away and I watched Bruno to see if he might catch a scent. But no, he was still winkling for ants—his long tongue flipping over punky slabs of bark.

"Nothing," I said, though I didn't recognize my voice. It was hard, really. To stop looking for Jack in the Dark.

To get out of the wind, I walked over to the axe factory and waited for Bruno. We'd come here a few times before, just to get into the warm, through a side door closed off with some baling wire. And then up the back stairs where the fifth step creaked on its right rise, past the machines that looked like a deconstructed freight train. Bruno didn't like stairs much, so I had to let him go first, giving him rump shoves with my shoulder whenever he stopped too long to grub at the dark corners and skirtings.

That night, I waited on the lee of the building. In the daylight, I would have been able to see Broken Hill House, the town's two chains of street lights, and the tips of the roofs that made up the rest of Bracken, and beyond that I could imagine our woods: the edges of old timber tells and wind-leveled stands, balsam overtopping the canopy and the cold air making everything sound closer. Spring supping on its budding brags.

Eventually, my shivering got the better of me. And that's when I did it. Without thinking, I stepped out from behind the factory, put my hands around my mouth, and sang out Bruno's song. My call set the gun dogs barking, down at the other end of town, the ones that lived in the big open kennel. I waited for the familiar twig snaps, for Bruno to make his way back to me. Instead, I heard muffled footsteps coming from the other side of the factory, the stream side. Human steps. Two sets. And that's when I realized my mistake.

==

They'd been quarreling over a bottle of rum. The shorter one trying to snatch the bottle from his brother's fist as they came around the corner. They weren't dressed in their town clothes, which was why it took me a minute to place them. Instead, they both wore wool hats with earflaps. They also seemed starved for a fight.

Later, years later, I heard they told the story differently: a panther, they said. A panther had broken away from the dark. A pack of wild dogs had given tongue. Howling and then— Jack in the Dark coming home through his woods. His ratted back. His grinding sit-bones. His gamy breath. His toothsuck and—

"What the hell's she doing here?" the one without glasses asked.

"Spying," the other said, batting my hat off into the snow. "Seeing how else she can badmouth our family."

As I reached down to pick up Papa's cap, a kick to my stomach knocked me off my feet. The night felt darker down there in the snow slush. Trying to get up and being kicked down again, I felt that everything up to that point in my life had been one mistake after another. *I could die out here*, I thought. *I might never get back overhome*. I was afraid they'd hurt Bruno.

They let me get to my feet. As I was wiping the snow and slush from my face, trying to remember not to turn my back on them, the one with glasses caught sight of my rabbit's foot hooked onto my belt loop.

"Well, lookee here. Early birthday present for our dear ma, I think. Don't you, Harold?"

I clasped it hard. Harold squinted. He was having a hard time standing still, focusing. He looked glassy, keyed up. Down near my knee, an axe helve was half-frozen in a puddle. I tried to get to my Green River knife tucked into my boot. I tried to get to the helve. Gerald grabbed my free wrist, wrenching me backwards until my spine seized. "Please," I said. "Please don't hurt me."

his heart beating, and then, soon after

Ansell cursed the Outside. He cursed the damp, the mud, the mud, the mud, the all-day chill he couldn't shake. He cursed the long days and longer nights that had, over the past weeks, reordered and diminished his thoughts. How had the woodsmen come back to camp night after night after wrangling with so much weather every day? He'd heard them curse at the wind, damn its shoving presence when it kicked up and pushed them too far—spooking the horses, howling through the trees, making their own thoughts strange. He'd seen an even-tempered man rage at the weather like it was hunting him.

He walked on until he met a sound: gusty and called out. A following sound. A sound turned out, not unlike Pearly's bear song. It cracked high over the frozen air, calling and weaving, back and forth—unsettled, searching. And then everything stilled. And waited.

He walked in the direction where it had begun. A few feet away, like a scorch against the dim moonlight, something moved across the snow. It came closer, head low, lips smacking, teeth clacking. In the moon's milk glaze, it reared up, tall as a man. It raised its blocky head to gauge the air above it, then bluff-charged, snorting, kicking up snow duff.

"Git!" he yelled, stomping towards it, making himself bolder. "Git!"

The bear rocked its head side to side, considering him. And then Ansell saw it: the leather collar with the oxen hearts. "Jesus Christ. Bruno?"

The bear stood down, still lipping the wind, then ran full force into Ansell's chest, knocking the air out of him, shoving him back a good six feet before he could gain purchase in the slushy mud.

"You don't fool me, you sneaky son of a bitch!" he said, laughing between the throbs in his ribs. "What happened to your face, old bud? And where the hell's Pearly?"

The one with the glasses grabbed my wrists and sank his thumb into the soft underparts, between my smaller bones, so that I could neither bend nor splay my fingers. My rabbit's foot fell somewhere nearby. The boy, his eyes magnified and babyish now, whipped my hands hard against my face.

"Why ya hitting yourself?" he barked, before swinging my hands at my face again. His rage, a rage I could almost under-stand—was intended for something or someone not me—knocked through my bones.

He hit me again and the bottle of rum fell from his coat pocket

326

and smashed on the ground. He watched the slush turn dark then spun back to me. "Now look what you made me do!"

I couldn't tell if I was crying from the pain or from the sheer indignity of my own hands slapping my half-frozen face. The strangeness cut channels into my sense of reality.

All this time, Harold leaned against the factory wall, his face into the wind, his color waxy. No courage. No opinion to call his own. I saw his entire life then, living under his brother's leathery wing.

Blood slicked my teeth where my hands caught my mouth again. I heard the small bones in my right wrist break. Pain sparked behind my eyes. My bottom lip split. I started to crumple to the ground, still trying, with my free hand, to reach the axe handle, my knife, my rabbit's foot, anything. In my mind, I asked one final time, Are you my death?

Gerald stumbled again and we both tripped to the ground. I grabbed my rabbit's foot. I saw Jack in the Dark incarnate in that boy's rage. I fisted my rabbit's foot and my body gave over to something else. From somewhere outside myself, I felt my haunch bones grow long and bend like a rabbit's might. Heat filled the violet-shot meat of me. A reek of musk and gland. I raked the boy's face with my rabbit foot's hard claws.

An animal scream shrilled again. Bruno, up on his hind legs, huffed the air, trying to locate its source.

"Just some fox getting a rabbit," Ansell said. "They sound like that. Human."

327

Bruno woofed several more times then took off at a sprint. Ansell followed as best he could. He could just keep up because Bruno was thin beneath his raggedy coat and carried a limp in his foreleg. His own range of calls was almost human now as he charged up the hill and around the back of the factory.

I raked my rabbit's foot over Gerald's face again. He released his grip giving me a chance to get some light between us. Enough so I could pull my Green River knife out of my boot. The next thing I knew, I fell backwards onto Harold, who still could not stand up straight. I heard him yelp before he tumbled down the rough hill and into Frederick Stream. And then I slipped my pain.

When I came to, Bruno stood above me, so that I could not follow the boy into the water. I collapsed into the snow and wrapped an arm around Bruno's neck. My knife dull in the slush. He curled up behind me, his snout tucked under my chin, a long-clawed paw across my chest. I imagined us both safe, deep inside the King's Tree. Eventually, the dark took everything away. All I could hear: his heart beating and then, soon after, I could hear my own. No longer a rabbit's heart, but my own once more.

our shared darkness, our sense of world

For many days afterwards, we stayed down inside the King's Tree. Me and Bruno conjoined in sleep. And still, Jack in the Dark squatted nearby, clothed in smoke and the black from old fires. Sometimes, I woke and there was no breath left inside me. Sometimes, I woke to find his leathery touch just inches from my face.

In other dreams, Ansell was there, holding my hand, tracing my lip with his thumb. Or I met with a strange face, toothed and jowled—a mask made up of soot and red Avon lipstick on creased butcher's wrap. Ruby Mae. She tip-toed into my room with her sweep of death cards before her. *Pick a card, Pearly. Just pick one.*

Then one morning, the room cooled, and I climbed out of the King's Tree and found myself at Broken Hill House once again. An eddy of an early spring breeze pushed the net curtains against the screened windows like some creature slow breathing. The chair was once again only a chair piled high with my tattered clothes—its shadow by its side—so that I felt a childish shame in thinking it had ever been otherwise.

The rest of the truth came slow and in pieces between spills of sleep. Mrs. Prue visited when I could finally stay awake. The littlest bones and some of the biggest in my hands were broken, she said, and so my hands were knotted in thick windings of cotton gauze so that they felt to belong to someone else. I shook them from time to time to bring blood back into them, to stop the fizzing that spilled over the ache. My loosened teeth. My swollen face. My split lip, stitched up blackly like an old boot. I felt like I was sitting inside someone else's sore-begotten body, while my tree-climbing, bear-wrestling, kindling-chopping, singing-through-the-felling-grounds one had been lost for good.

I listened and sometimes asked questions. Mrs. Prue told me Ansell and Bruno had gone away from Bracken.

"Ansell was here?"

"He came out to find you and Bruno. And from what I hear, it took some doing."

"But now they're gone?" I blinked back tears and tried to find a path through my thoughts. "But I only make sense in the woods with them."

"I had a feeling. I had a feeling something bad was going to happen, practically saw it in my dreams." She shook her head, disappointed maybe that the signs had not been clear. "You could have been killed." She toyed with the bedspread for a few moments before going on. "Amaël and his friend Raymond took them. Bruno and Ansell. In his truck." She patted my arm. "Pearly, it wasn't safe for Bruno here, with everyone all nerved up." She straightened the hem on my bedsheet again. "Some said boys will be boys and they were just joking. Things just got out of hand with you. And some are wondering why you were out there anyways. At that time of night. Alone. A girl. But that's all a bunch of foolishness."

"So no one's mad?"

"No, not like that. Amaël was worried about Bruno. Some loony hunters around here, you know, and—" She smiled, sadly. "It's fixed now. You'll see them all soon enough."

=

Later, I'd learn that not everyone felt that way about Bruno—him being a no-count bear. Many called him a hero and some said he had more sense than those two Twins put together. I'd learn that the Twins' father, Bad Check Charlie, had demanded the police shoot Bruno, and some of the men at the axe factory had threatened to leave if anything untoward befell my brother.

"When?"

"When what?"

"When'd they go?"

"Last Friday."

"When was that?"

"Two days ago."

"So, they're there, then."

"Amaël should be back any time now."

All the men gone to their own villages and towns for haying and herding and foddering or following behind a bull-tongue plow in places I only knew by name. And the others, with no connections, wandering where they might to pick up work or drink in lonely taverns until the following fall when the Walking Bosses would lead them back through the woods to the camps again. I saw our camp in my mind's eye. Dismantled. Bruno's den box and our tree fort. Built again elsewhere. All the fir boughs piled up like some animal's abandoned nest.

"I didn't hurt Bruno, did I?"

"Of course not."

"I was . . . I had my knife and—"

I could not tell her how I momentarily became rabbit. How my vision rounded that night, giving back Jack in the Dark's own ruinous reflection. Something old or of other origin had sunk itself inside me, something that had settled into the keep of my long, felty ears. How do you speak about that sort of crossing and then the coming back?

"I don't climb up these stairs every day, with the cold in my hip, to bask in your gloomy face. Now, why don't you see what you got over on that stand?" Mrs. Prue said.

My little Green River knife, my two dollars for Amaël, and the magazine with me and Bruno and Mama in it. My lucky rabbit's foot was gone. I leaned a bit farther from the bed, and there, beneath one of my dollar bills: a glint of gold. Mama's double-horn necklace. "But how?"

"Oh, I think I'll let Mr. Prue explain that one," Mrs. Prue said, taking up the necklace and clasping it around my neck. "No real need to doll yourself up just now, but suppose it can't hurt." She called into the hallway, "Father Prue! Get on in here."

A shy shuffling and then Mr. Prue peeked his smudgy face through the gap in the door. "Ah, Pearly. You awake, then?"

"Well, get in here," Mrs. Prue said. "He's been outside your door for days now, hovering around. Bad as the Persian. Worried sick about you, he was."

"Thank you for my necklace," I said.

He stared at something beyond the scrim curtains. "Girl deserves her mother's things. Special necklace given from the king and all. Stitched him up after he fell off his battle horse, she did, Mother Prue."

"So I hear. Some fancy history she's got."

He patted my shoulder and set his wet eyes on me a few seconds more before turning to go. "Well, I'll pop back in when you don't have so much company."

"Some nights he came in here and just sat in that chair over there in the corner, just watching you sleep, making sure you were safe," Mrs. Prue said after he'd left. She tucked me in again. "You just give a shout if you need something, okay? Ruby Mae's bat-eared enough for all of us. She'll hear you bellering."

"Thank you, Mrs. Prue."

But she was already out the door, pretending she hadn't heard.

———

When I was awake more than asleep, she read me newspaper pages. One day, she told me a hangman had been hired for a double execution. She flipped a few more pages, and there, in

333

a small square of news was a brief report of what had happened to me and the Twins. Three teenagers, it said, had been injured behind Broade's axe factory over the weekend. One boy was still in the hospital with a fractured skull. It went on to say things about safety standards and security. It had nothing to say about me and Bruno.

She made a sharp hiss between her small teeth. "A slew of locals came forward to say how ugly the pair of them boys had been with you. Ansell also brought with him some newspaper clipping about your camp boss dying and said you and Bruno had found him and that all this time you'd been scared them Mounties were going to take you away? For murder? Lord have mercy, you should have said something, Pearly." She narrowed her eyes at me, looking for the heat in a lie. "You don't know anything else about it, do ya? That scaler's the only one to blame?"

"What took Swicker never showed itself to me." And this was, I thought, truth enough.

In the morning, there was a milk jar on my little table filled up with roadside flowers. Mothy-green stems, white blossoms. Dried Pearly Everlasting. Mama always used it in her sore throat tea. But I could not fix in my head who sat beside me. He leaned in close while my eyes cleared of sleep.

"Pearly," he said. "Boy, you're a hard one to find."

"Ansell?" Sitting there, he was just as beautiful as the first time I saw him.

"Well, good morning, sunshine," he said. "I took Bruno back to camp with Amaël, but I wanted to be here when you finally got around to waking up."

He looked just about as out of place as you could imagine, sitting there in his overalls and plaid shirt in Mrs. Prue's rose-sprigged room. "Is that pearly from Mama's herbs?" I asked.

"Sure is," he said. "I put a little bunch in a jar and brought it along. A little piece of home." He touched the dried tufts, thinking. "You think you and Bruno might be ready to quit your gallivanting?"

"I was, I was down inside the King's Tree for a while with Bruno. Like when he's well-larded in the fall."

"He's working on getting that way now, Pearly." He reached out to touch the stitches along my lips, but then changed his mind.

"They don't hurt much now," I lied.

"*Hovela, hovela*," he said, waving his hand over my face. Smiling a little.

Of course, he remembered me telling him Mama's healing words for me and Bruno. I let the tears roll down my bruised-up cheeks. There was no help for it. "I think maybe I've had my fill of town life now, Ansell."

He laughed a little in a guarded way then reached for my hand. "It's some hard being a city slicker, eh?"

We stayed quiet for a bit like that—hand in hand—and then I asked, "Bruno okay?"

"Right as rain." He patted my shoulder. "You done a good job looking out for him, you know?"

Thinking about how far away Bruno was sent an aching straight through me. "Is Papa real mad?"

Ansell got up from the chair and came to sit beside me

on the bed. He put his arm around me and let me lean into his chest. He smelled like home. "No one's mad, Pearly. We're just glad to find you in one piece." He patted my hand. "Sort of one piece, eh?"

"I want to go home, Ansell."

"Well," he said, "I've just been sittin' around here, waiting for you to give me the say-so, little lady."

=

The next day, as we were readying to go, Song-catcher and Ebony came over from Smoke River. They'd seen the newspapers. My name had not been printed, but one Twin's insistence he'd been attacked by a grizzly bear had got them thinking. I wanted them to meet Amaël, but he'd been called away for a ceremony of sorts as Bracken was finally retiring the now-healed Fire Horse.

"Much is changed," Song-catcher said when she sat down beside Ansell, giving him a quick hug.

I knew what she meant: I was to go home and Bracken would, in time, close up around this unrest and in weeks or months to come, no one would remember that Bruno and I once walked through these streets and yards at night. We saw into windows when no one thought us there. We glimpsed into private spaces and for that we were punished and nearly killed. "I'm ready," I said to her.

"I bet," Ebony said. "You're your own adventure book, wild one."

We talked for some time about the woods and Bruno and

recollected for Ansell Bruno's rescue from the animal trader's shed. And when there was nothing else to say about my hands or face or Bruno, Ansell reminded us that Amaël would, in short time, be pulling up outside.

And in my mind's eye, I could finally see all the way home. I say to Amaël, *Here's two dollars from me and Bruno.* And he accepts. And then we drive away from Bracken—its shopfronts and streets, its farmsteads and stone walls—to where the highway splits with a road that leads into the woods. In short time, we pass again through the twitching trails, the birches with their following eyes, the camps being built and the camps being torn down for salvage—their forgotten tools growing into the meat of the trees. And though my eyes want to close, I stay awake.

Through the trees, I glimpse some of the men and the younger boys Mama tried to heal over the years. The ones caught in quick accidents and soon after death. I see the overgrown sinks where the old camps once stood and the draft horses lay, long dead though I can still call up some by name. I see Ivy in her Hollywood scarves—gaudy stars and things that might hold a shine—down at the river's sticky lip where she catches her reflection and sparks the air with a bit of mirror. I see Mama sitting where the Crooked Deadwater's dark iris rickles over mossed-up rocks, and its quiet click of water passes on to elsewhere. And I see Mama just sitting a spell on a stump, listening to her thoughts, singing her song about the poor monk dancing, dancing, always dancing.

And as we go up and on, these touched worlds step farther

apart like spalls of granite—toothy and split along a glittering seam. In my mind's eye, Amaël pushes the truck hard, whispering *merde* when the soft tires don't catch in the gravel or the truck bucks the rougher patches, but *bon, bon* when they do. I lean into Ansell and pray the truck up the steep dirt S-bends. And when we reach the last kink in the high ditched switchback before the cabin, where the sun sets best, I see them, down in the creek rill's shallow. First, Papa, standing tall when he hears the truck's engine, waving his hat at us. Though he seems much aged, his face is bright like those of the just-saved. Ansell opens the door and I step down from the truck and sing out my song. Once. Once more. That's when Bruno, my brother, my bear, his snout stained with kinnikinnick juice, will hind up on his back legs and taste the air.

He shakes the creek wet from his fur as he starts off towards me, and water glisters about him, catching on the summer light like spangles of fire. He is skeltering now through sunlight and then through shade, full speed, towards me. In my mind's eye. Through sunlight and then through shade. Only a minute more. A half second—the wrong and the right—before I am curled again around our shared darkness, our sense of world. And we know, in another forest, somewhere not so far away, snow is already beginning to fall.

Last

All my memories bound up in trees. Living trees and imagined woods and woods now gone—the ones I still dream I walk through like others must dream of houses they once knew.

And Bruno and me? We don't get away from Greenlaw Mountain much anymore. My hands pain me something awful when the weather turns and my nails never grew back straight. And Bruno, he's an old bear now and gets tired with just his basic getting on from day to day.

Ansell lives with me and Bruno now and we love each other the best we can. He still tells the old stories in the village when he goes down for supplies, though I'm not sure who'd really be interested anymore. To this day, he swears finding us some fifty miles out of the woods was no feat. He also swears strange things are living out in our woods, just out of sight.

Just as Papa had warned, the old ways are going. Companies bring in machines now to tear up the land and strip it of trees. The air down there often smells unhealed and scorched. But the old yarding trails, thicketed with raspberry canes, are still tramped by deer, bear, partridge, and hare—travel where the machines don't go.

The new lumbermen are living among our ghosts and graves down there now. The same ones me and Bruno pass on our walks through the overgrown tote roads. And sometimes I write to the Prues and Amaël, to Song-catcher and Ebony. I write them slow, carefully spelled letters and I take them down to the camps for the mail. I like to tell them about Papa still cooking the best camp grub around. I tell them how the trees have grown so big up here on Greenlaw Mountain the spring light lives inside their boughs and rarely comes out to warm our yard. But by summer, the light climbs down and spills itself wide—a carpet Bruno naps in longer each day. This is how we take our days. This is how we make them stay.

Acknowledgments

In the winter of 1903, William Lyman Underwood, a wild-life photographer, made his way to a lumber camp deep in the woods of Maine to photograph a woman nursing her newborn daughter alongside an orphan bear cub. This encounter inspired his memoir, *Wild Brother: Strangest of True Stories from the North Woods.* And while *Pearly Everlasting* is a work of fiction, it was initially inspired by Underwood's encounter and lengthy friendship with Bruno after the bear was sent, at two years old, to live out his days in an animal sanctuary in New England. Though my story takes place in New Brunswick, I'd like to apologize for the great geograph-ical liberties I've taken. In the end, it is Pearly Everlasting's and Bruno's New Brunswick.

The following books also helped me in my research: Donald MacKay's *The Lumberjacks*; Mike Parker's *Woodchips & Beans: Life in the Early Lumber Woods of Nova Scotia*; and Michel Pastoureau's *The Bear: History of a Fallen King.* "Clip clop, clip clop, where will the bone horse stop?" is a traditional "Hookland" rhyme transcribed by David Southwell.

For the kindest welcome: all those involved with the UBC/HarperCollins Prize for Best New Fiction. For care and consideration: the HarperCollins team, especially my editor, Janice Zawerbny, whose thoughtful suggestions guided this story's direction. For saying yes, and for believing in the story I wanted to tell: my agent, Rachel Letofsky. For financially supporting this book: the Canada Council for the Arts and Arts Nova Scotia. For always being up for a chat about bears, despite time differences: Jeff Melland. For their inexhaustible support and optimism: my Moore family, especially Laurie Moore, who read an earlier draft with so much enthusiasm. For these years by the ocean and a quiet room of my own: George Moore. For my family who worked in those Depression-era New Brunswick woods—the teamsters and blacksmiths and axemen: I've carried your kitchen stories and tried to tell them tall. For first saying some years ago, "I found a little story about a bear you might like," which was an excerpt from Underwood's memoir in *Down East Magazine*: my mother and longtime visitor to my world of make-believe, Carol Seger. For always knowing just what to say: Dawn Lyons. For his friendship and love of words: Joe Nelson. I wish you'd had the chance to read all the way to the last page, Goodly Joe.